"Poetic. Profound. Painful at times. *Saving Grayson*... story not just read but experienced, immersing me in Gray's turmoil of trying to grasp life, only to find it slipping through a sieve of unforeseen circumstances. Chris Fabry is a masterful storyteller, capturing my attention from the first page to the very last. His thought-provoking message is clear: Even in the cruelest situations, even when we are not all that deserving, grace and mercy can be granted."

T. I. LOWE, bestselling author of *Under the Magnolias*

"*Saving Grayson* has more spellbinding twists and turns than the scenic mountain roads of Chris Fabry's native West Virginia. It's a story of betrayal and love, sacrifice and selfishness, anger and release. It's a portrait of the transforming power and very essence of forgiveness. I wept as I neared the conclusion of this novel, one I will remember for the remainder of my days."

JEFF CROSBY, author of *The Language of the Soul*

"Our friend Chris Fabry does a remarkable job of blending fiction, mystery, well-developed characters, and the message of God's love into an enjoyable, poignant novel. *Saving Grayson* has humor, heart, and a large dose of reality as the characters unpack the truth that God's love isn't earned—it's a gift we receive. Thanks for taking us on this engaging journey with Grayson, Chris!"

ALEX AND STEPHEN KENDRICK, writers and directors of *War Room* and *Courageous*

"Chris has penned a tender and moving story about a man's struggle to mend a broken heart. Told through the cracked lens of a failing memory, Gray finds an unexpected remedy through the healing of selfless love and the transformational power of forgiveness."

CHARLES MARTIN, *New York Times* and *USA TODAY* bestselling author

"From the first haunting line of *Saving Grayson,* master storyteller Chris Fabry mesmerizes with the tale of a man at war with the ticking clock of his own fragile mind. Employing the epitome of his prodigious evocative skills, the Christy Hall of Fame novelist takes us on a heartrending journey of pain and ultimately hope, redemption, and forgiveness."

JERRY B. JENKINS, *New York Times* bestselling author

"Chris Fabry's *Saving Grayson* is a heartbreakingly honest tale of life with Alzheimer's disease. With masterful storytelling, Fabry takes readers on an emotion-filled journey, navigating marriage and family, love and sacrifice, forgiveness and acceptance. One can't help but cheer for the protagonist while at the same time identify with those who love him. Despite a topic that often brings fear and uncertainty, the pages of *Saving Grayson* are filled with brilliant nuggets of warmth, humor, and hope."

MICHELLE SHOCKLEE, award-winning author of *Count the Nights by Stars*

"Fabry's signature style shines as he draws readers into the story of Grayson Hayes's last-ditch effort to unravel his tangled memories and make peace with his past. *Saving Grayson* is a stunning testament to the power of love and how a shift in perspective can monumentally alter the human capacity for compassion and forgiveness. This redemptive tale reminds us that the most beautiful stories we have to offer are the ones we write with our lives."

AMANDA COX, award-winning author of *The Edge of Belonging* and *The Secret Keepers of Old Depot Grocery*

"This poignant and imaginative story lets the reader peek inside the mind and musings of Grayson Hayes as Alzheimer's disease slowly erases a lifetime of memories. *Saving Grayson* is an intriguing, bittersweet story, made all the more memorable by Chris Fabry's masterful use of language. I truly loved this book!"

DEBORAH BARR, author of *Grace for the Unexpected Journey: A 60-Day Devotional for Alzheimer's and Other Dementia Caregivers* and coauthor of *Keeping Love Alive as Memories Fade: The 5 Love Languages and the Alzheimer's Journey*

"The world of an aging writer comes full circle, from haunting guilt to the freedom of forgiveness, from lost loves to found family, from mystery to discovery, in this tender story of a man at once losing his memory and finding himself. Readers seeking a story alive with faith and hope will relish journeying along with Grayson Hayes."

LISA WINGATE, #1 *New York Times* bestselling author of *Before We Were Yours*

"Chris Fabry is one of my favorite novelists (and people). What makes a great story isn't just the plot, it's the characters who linger with you, like real people you know, or wish you knew, or are glad you don't. Two weeks after finishing *Saving Grayson*, I'm still thinking about the characters. Chris tells an engaging and important story with a powerful ending. I'm delighted to recommend this book!"

RANDY ALCORN, bestselling author of *Courageous* and *Heaven*

Saving Grayson

a novel

Chris Fabry

FOCUS
ON THE
FAMILY.

A Focus on the Family resource
published by Tyndale House Publishers

Editors: Jerry B. Jenkins, Larry Weeden

Cover design: Ron Kaufmann

Cover photograph of silhouette of man copyright © Tara Moore/Getty Images. All rights reserved.

Cover photograph of bridge copyright © Zoonar/Depositphotos. All rights reserved.

For information about special discounts for bulk purchases, please contact Tyndale House Publishers at csresponse@tyndale.com or call 1-855-277-9400.

Library of Congress Cataloging-in-Publication data can be found at www.loc.gov.

ISBN 978-1-64607-148-7 Hardcover
ISBN 978-1-64607-056-5 Softcover

Printed in the United States of America

29 28 27 26 25 24 23
7   6   5   4   3   2   1

We are all under the same mental calamity;

we have all forgotten our names.

We have all forgotten what we really are.

G. K. CHESTERTON

PART 1

Page 1, Yellow Legal Pad

I keep telling them I'm fine. I keep saying there's nothing wrong. But by the way they look at me and the stirring I feel, I believe we're both right. There's nothing wrong and everything wrong at the same time.

My life is a muddy river, and the river is a story, and the water is the words inside. All we are is rivers and creeks and streams, and where we meet is the confluence of our stories, the way we intersect with one another and flow toward something bigger to find meaning and purpose and, above all, love.

I'm trying to get this out. I don't know if it's right.

Think about your life as a river. And you are being carried toward the rocks and white water.

I have to focus on what I know and what I can do with what I know. That's why I write it down. So here's what I know.

She died at the river. Someone killed her.

CHAPTER 1

GRAYSON EVERETT HAYES sat in a lawn chair in his garage, bathed in flickering fluorescence, slathered in sweat, wearing nothing but his boxers—a yellow legal pad in one hand and a nail gun in the other. He couldn't remember why.

The sweat was not just the result of the oppressive desert heat. Gray had awakened with the recurring fear that he was not the man he wanted to be and had failed at the most important things in life. And the fear compounded because he could not remember what the important things were. That had awakened him and opened his pores.

Gray's gray-speckled, sandy brown hair stuck up in the back, like the comb of a chicken. His piercing blue eyes and weathered face made strangers stop, thinking they might have just seen someone from the movies. Innocent eyes and a boyish look often belied the confusion inside, making many judge him as someone who seemed to know the answers to life's questions. Just over six feet tall, with broad shoulders, his belly slightly spilling over the elastic in his shorts, he sat staring at his hands.

Grayson was in the deepest kind of trouble, with a heart that could not rest. His was an isolated heart, not simply from those around him, but from himself as well. And he hated the distance.

The dream that woke him felt like a sign, something real that life, or God, was speaking to him. His subconscious was working on it, and he tried every day to pull the words from inside and get them onto the legal pad so he could know the truth from one day to the next and remember.

Her screams and the jumbled mess of his life had made him sit up in bed, grab the pad, and wander toward the door in the dark. He cracked his toe on a box that shouldn't have been there, and he cursed and hopped.

Stay quiet. In the dim light of the clock on the nightstand, Lotty lay with her eyes closed, chest rising and falling. She seemed so exhausted these days.

A whimper from the corner. Rustling. Paws on metal.

Dubose scratched at the kennel, and Gray reached to still him. Could dogs see in the dark? The animal settled, and Gray went to the garage.

In the harsh light he opened a leather binder, flipped to the last page he had written on in the legal pad, and willed the story to return. Dreams and reality merged, and he used them each day to decipher his life.

He studied the words, and it came to him that the dream was not the only reason he was awake. He stood and patted the vintage VW bus as he would an old friend. From a large toolbox, he retrieved a DeWalt nailer, turned out the lights, and felt his way back to the lawn chair.

Gray awoke to Lotty's frantic voice. His neck hurt, and he slowly straightened to discover where he was. Strange. He wiped his brow with the back of his hand and stared at the power tool.

His dream felt more real than not at times, but the sweat running down the back of his leg and the fear in Lotty's voice convinced him he was awake.

Light leaked around the garage door and through a side window. A yellow glow surrounded an overgrown agave.

She was asleep when I came here.

Thoughts were like birds on a fence. Try to recall something, and they flew. He sat still.

"Gray?"

He almost answered. Lotty was inside. She didn't call for him often. She always seemed to know exactly where he was. Was it the connection the two had?

The patio door opened with a *kathunk*. She called again from the backyard, her voice leaking through the window's cracked weatherstripping.

She's rattled. Afraid. Angry?

He closed his eyes and saw her long black hair. Milky white skin. Her smile. When she gave him that flash of white, the whole world seemed to come alive. Green eyes that seemed to look through him. They said he had a disease and that it had already taken so much. But it couldn't take her. It would never take Lotty.

She called again, and he took a breath to answer but noticed the nail gun. He set it on the floor and opened the legal pad, but it was still too dark to read. Light through the window. Behind him, boxes were stacked to the ceiling. Lotty's handwriting. Kitchen. Living Room. Dining Room. Beside the old van, tools hung on a pegboard, and a red tool chest stood in the corner next to fishing rods and a tackle box.

A diesel engine rumbled to a stop outside. Brakes squealed, and there came a release of air. And like a bird returning to its nest, Gray remembered. He picked up the nail gun and sat straight.

A dog barked. Dubose. Inside. He sniffed at the garage door and scratched.

Why was Lotty calling for him? Her knowledge of him was uncanny. He would take Dubose for a walk through the neighborhood, where all the houses seemed exactly alike, and just when he felt the fear encroaching, she would appear next to him, just drive up and he would get in the car.

He opened the pad to a fresh page and jotted a note about it. Had she called out for him? Was he forgetting? That bothered him most—not that others mistrusted his recall, but that he had begun to.

Distant memories returned with frightening specificity. Images from childhood. Batting averages. Even phone numbers returned without effort, like a flashing dashboard light. The past felt closer than the present, at least some of it. The rearview mirror was gigantic, and the windshield so small. Remembering something from the present, a name, the

6 II SAVING GRAYSON

reason he opened the refrigerator, or even why he was in the garage, was like picking up a toothpick with mittens.

Dubose barked.

He heard the front door open, metal on metal of the screen hitting the jamb.

"Hello," Lotty said.

Who is she talking to?

He imagined her younger, her face bronzed by the sun. A smile so bright it could blind. The years had been kind to her, but there was something cruel about aging and all it did to the eyes and the smile.

He wiped his forehead again and stared at his bare legs.

Deep breath.

Lotty spoke again. "Thank you for being on time. I'm a little scattered—I can't find my husband. Let me show you what we have. I hope you can fit it all."

"I have plenty of room, ma'am."

The garage door strained, the chain clacking. Gray shielded his eyes from the sunlight.

"Gray," Lotty said, "I've been looking for you. What are you doing?"

He studied the stranger in jeans and T-shirt. A pack of Pall Malls in his pocket. Dirty baseball cap. Stained hands. A diesel truck idled at the end of the driveway in front of the realty sign that said *SALE PENDING*. A long trailer was hitched behind the truck. Was it big enough to hold the tools, the boxes, and the van?

T-Shirt Guy pulled leather gloves from his back pocket. "Good morning, sir." An easy tone. Nonthreatening.

"What's good about it?" Gray said.

The man glanced at Lotty. "Gray, give me that," she said, her voice soft, like a mother to a fussy infant.

"No."

"Gray, listen to—"

"Sometimes you have to take a stand." He pointed the nail gun at T-Shirt Guy.

"Whoa, hang on," the man said, stepping back, hands raised. "Come on, man."

"Keep backing up," Gray said.

"Hey, I'm only here because you hired me."

"I didn't hire you."

"It's okay," Lotty said. "He's just confused."

"Not true. You are the confused ones."

"Gray, please. Listen to me."

T-Shirt Guy stopped in the driveway and shoved his thumbs in his pockets, as if he considered himself out of range. Gray stood and moved into the sunlight, still inside the garage. "Look at me," he said. "I'm glistening. That's a good word, isn't it? *Glisten.*"

The man said, "I didn't sign up for this, ma'am."

"You got tools at home, pal?" Gray said.

Eyes darting. "Yes, sir."

"Tools you've gathered throughout your life, right? Some you bought. Some were given to you. Some you borrowed and forgot to return?"

"Yeah, sure."

"What if somebody backed up a truck to your house? Loaded up your tools and the van you've restored? Worked so hard you could taste it? Poured your heart and soul into? How would you feel?"

The man pulled off his cap and scratched his head.

"You wouldn't like it at all, would you?"

"Unless I hired somebody to come get the tools."

"I told you, I didn't hire you."

Gray pointed the nail gun at the garage wall. Air hissed from the compressor, and the nail shot into the drywall.

Lotty jumped back and put her hands to her mouth. T-Shirt Guy retreated farther. "Whoa, settle down, man!"

"Don't tell me what to do," Gray said. "I got people telling me what to do all day long. It makes me nervous. And you don't want me nervous."

Dubose barked at the door.

"I'm not telling you what to do, sir. Please, put that down."

"There you go again." Gray pointed at the side wall again, the nail pinging as it punctured metal.

"This is getting out of hand, ma'am. I ought to call the cops."

Lotty said, "Give us a minute."

"Go ahead and call them," Gray said. "They'll be on my side."

She held out a hand to Gray, her eyes pleading.

"I'm protecting what's mine, Lotty."

"You don't want to hurt anybody. I know you."

Gray clenched his teeth. "You don't know what I want. You're against me like the rest of them."

He saw the pain on her face, but he couldn't spike the feeling of betrayal. "This is not right, and you know it."

"Give it to me," she said.

Gray pointed the nail gun at the man. "This is not happening today. You can leave."

The man pulled out his phone.

"Who are you calling?"

The man moved behind his truck. "Just checking where I'm supposed to be next."

"Good. You'll be early."

Across the street, a man retrieved a newspaper from his driveway. Gray couldn't remember his name.

"Nothing to see here!" Gray yelled, waving the gun. "Move along!"

The neighbor hurried to his house.

"Gray, we've talked about this," Lotty said. "Remember? We're moving. We can't take everything with us."

"Where are we moving?"

Lotty sighed as if the weight of the world had shifted onto her back. "You need to trust me. I'm not against you; I'm for you. You have to believe me."

Lotty walked toward the truck and spoke to the man, her voice too low for Gray to hear. Dubose barked and scratched at the door, and Gray clenched his teeth again. He aimed at the mailbox.

T-Shirt Guy ducked behind his truck at the ping.

"You can't take a man's tools!" Gray yelled. "You can't take what means the most! Get out of here!"

At more barking and scratching, Gray retreated into the garage and opened the door. Dubose bounced out, tail wagging, hair bristling as he ran to Lotty. He walked beside her as she returned to the garage.

Gray moved toward her. "You don't understand. I don't just see wrenches and hammers and saws. And that van is more than four wheels and a transmission."

"You told me you trusted me." Lotty was inches from his face, eyes searching his. "We agreed," she said, pleading.

"No, we didn't. And you saying that doesn't make it so. The van stays. I'm almost finished with it. It almost started the other day. And the tools stay. My fishing gear. For crying out loud, Lotty, you'd sell my fishing gear?"

"Of course not. You can use your fishing gear when we move, remember? There's a lake near . . ." She turned from him as if trying to muster the strength to lift something too unwieldy for one person. "We can go through the tools now and keep what you want."

"I want it all. That ball-peen hammer was given to me by my father— the only thing I've got left that he touched. When I hold it, I feel his hands. Why would you want to take that from me?"

Lotty stared at the wall, her face twisted. "Gray, you hated your father."

"I did not. Who told you that?"

"You did. You've told me the things he did to you."

Gray grabbed his ear. He had clear memories of the past, but others were fuzzy, like a photo taken from a car at a high rate of speed. "Okay, he was a terrible father. But I love that hammer. And you don't have a right to take it."

"Who gave you the nail gun?" Lotty said.

He stared at it. "I think I bought it at Home Depot."

"Give it to me. Do you want that man to call the police?"

"They'd be on my side."

"Gray, *I'm* on your side. Why can't you see that?"

"Because you hired some ne'er-do-well to take this and sell it to God knows who."

"Do you want to give it to someone? Is that what you're saying?"

His body tightened. "I can't make you understand, and I don't know why."

"I'm trying, Gray."

She put her hands over her face and dropped to her knees on the dirty concrete, shoulders shaking. Shame rose in him like a high tide. When any woman cried, he felt responsible, as if he had somehow contributed to her grief.

But maybe she was trying to get him to do something he didn't want to do. She was . . . what was the word? Manipulating him?

"Get up," he said. "The neighbors will see you."

She sobbed now, falling apart in front of God and everybody. He scratched the back of his head with the nail gun and saw her tears were real.

"Get him to leave and I'll give it to you."

Lotty approached the truck and leaned in. The man pulled the phone from his ear, shook his head, and waved her off. Gray aimed the nail gun at a back tire. He lowered the tool and, like an old dog looking for comfort, found the lawn chair and sat. Dubose settled and laid his head on Gray's leg. The truck pulled away.

When Lotty returned to the shadows of the garage, Gray surrendered the nail gun. She held it like it was a venomous snake. "How do you turn it off?"

Gray hit the power button on the compressor.

"I couldn't find you when I got up. You had me worried. Come inside. Get dressed and we'll have breakfast."

"Don't treat me like a child. I can wear what I want."

Someone shouted from the end of the driveway, and Gray could tell from the man's red face and the veins in his neck how he felt. Lotty went to talk with him, and Gray stared at his legal pad until she returned. She sat and faced him, her eyes rimmed with water.

"What was that about?" Gray said.

She appeared to force a smile. "He wanted to make sure we were okay."

"It's none of his business! You want me to go over there?"

She shook her head and touched his leg. "I know this is hard for you. It's hard for me. So let me explain it. We've sold the house. We need to move. And we don't have room for everything. The boxes are going into storage."

"What about my books? And my desk? You can't take my desk."

She swallowed hard. "I'm doing it so we can be together. Do you understand that?"

"You're saying the truck is coming back."

She started to answer, but he held up a hand. He looked into her eyes, trying for a connection he felt he had lost. "I love you more than life itself. I know that sounds like something I made up, but it's true. And I know you're trying the best you know how. But there's something . . . If I let go of these things, it's all going to leave. And it's not fair of you to ask that of me."

"I do understand," she whispered.

"No, you're just thinking I'm not going to remember any of this. But I will, in my own way. And there are things I have to do."

"I know all this scares you."

"I'm not scared. Well, maybe a little. But I'm going to prove how much I love you."

"You don't have to prove anything."

"Yes, I do. And I have to prove it to her. I'm going to figure out a way."

He saw something in her eyes, as if she were holding something back, like a reservoir ready to spill over and flood whatever lay below.

"Why can't you just let me love you, Gray?" Lotty smiled sadly and patted his leg. "I'll put on some coffee and get breakfast. Come in when you're ready."

When she was gone, Gray flipped to the last page of his legal pad, where he had jotted a few notes. When he entered the house, he heard Lotty talking in the kitchen and lingered at the door.

"I know; it was my fault. I'm so sorry. I'll pay the extra fee."

CHAPTER 2

GRAY SAT FLIPPING THROUGH HIS LEGAL PAD and glanced up when a man in a white coat entered and sat behind a maple desk. Medical books lined the shelf behind him, and diplomas and licenses on the wall bore the name Dr. Edward Barshaw. Gray had been here before. How many times?

The doctor gave a slight smile. "Charlotte tells me you're a crack shot with a nail gun."

Gray looked at the chair next to him, then at the door behind him.

"It's okay, Grayson. She's just down the hall."

"Everything else had been boxed up. It did the trick, though. Shoots straight and true."

"From what your neighbor says, it has pretty good range."

"What does that mean?"

"The man across the street found a nail in a picture on his wall. An anniversary photo." He pointed to the middle of his forehead. "Hit his wife right here."

Gray's eyes darted. "I didn't do that. Must have been somebody else."

The doctor raised his eyebrows.

"I'll admit, my aim's not what it used to be." The man appeared to stifle a yawn, but Gray sensed a smile.

Dr. Barshaw sat forward, elbows on the desk. "How are you feeling, Grayson?"

"You tell me. Or get Lotty in here. If she told you about the DeWalt, she can tell you everything else. You don't need me."

"I don't want you to lean on her. I want to hear from you. That's why I asked her to wait."

"Fine. Ask away."

The doctor twirled a yellow pencil like a majorette, then tapped it against his palm. "I'm going to say three words, and I want you—"

"No," Gray said. "I'm not playing that game. If you can't remember your three words, I'm not going to help you."

"So you remember we've done that before."

Gray glanced down. "You think? Of course I remember. When I walk in here, my chest gets tight because I know you're going to try and stump me."

"Fair enough. Forget the words, let's talk about your move. Do you know where you and Charlotte are going?"

Gray clenched his fists. "No. She's not telling me."

"Are you sure she hasn't?"

Gray leaned close and lowered his voice. "You know what I think? She's rented an apartment, and she's putting me in a facility. That's why she's giving everything away."

"Do you really believe that?"

"She's got boxes stacked on boxes. And there's some outfit that sells your stuff to God knows who. The van I've been working on. And my desk—how am I supposed to get anything done if she takes my desk? Answer that one."

The doctor's voice was calm and measured. "It's a big adjustment, isn't it?"

"Is that what you call it? This isn't like a chiropractor popping my neck. Adjustment, my foot. This is wholesale change. And I have no say."

"So that's why you camped out with your nail gun."

"A man's got a right to defend what's his."

The doctor nodded and seemed to study his pencil. "You realize Charlotte is trying to care for you, right?"

"That's not her job. It's my job to take care of her."

"Must be frustrating. All that responsibility."

"Frustrating as all get-out."

"What does that mean? *As all get-out?*"

"It's something we said where I'm from."

"The hills."

"Right. Means *extremely.*"

"Thanks for telling me that. I want your perspective, because I know what she's going through. I sympathize with both of you. She's carrying a lot right now."

"She's not having all her stuff taken away."

"Well, she's under tremendous stress. She's making decisions about the sale of the house, the move, and in all of that she wants you to be happy. She doesn't want to agitate you."

"Well, she's not doing a very good job. How would you like it if somebody came and packed up all your books and plopped them in boxes where you couldn't get to them? And took your desk to boot."

"I wouldn't like it at all."

"See? Now you know what I'm feeling. My whole life is a box. And somebody keeps taping it shut so I can't get to what's inside."

"Grayson, the stress, the agitation you feel, is at least partly due to your condition. And the decisions Charlotte—"

"I'm not stressed, okay? I'm just tight." Gray shook his arms. "Like you wind up one of those toy airplane propellers. We had them when I was a kid. Thin wood that broke real easy . . ."

"Balsa?"

"Yeah, balsa wood. That's it."

"I remember those. Put the wings through the body. Wind up the propeller."

"Right. But if you wound it too tight, the rubber band would get stuck."

"As all get-out."

Gray gave the man a sideways look. "You catch on quick."

"So that's how you feel—twisted and tight like a rubber band? Sounds like stress."

Gray pressed his palm to his forehead. "You got a pill for it? Just add it to the pile Lotty gives me every day."

The doctor leaned back, and his chair squeaked. "Charlotte says nothing makes you happier than writing. To be in the flow of a story. How's that going?"

Gray ran a hand over the page on his pad. "Why do you want to know that?"

"I'm interested."

Gray sat straight, his body rigid. "You want to see it, don't you? Make a copy of it."

"Grayson, I don't want to steal your words. I asked because I'm interested in how your condition is affecting your output, your creativity."

"You keep bringing that up. My *condition*."

"I mean the disease. Your diagnosis. You remember that—"

"I know you think I'm sick, but I'm not. I feel fine. There's nothing wrong except for all the boxes and giving my stuff away. You need to talk to Lotty about that."

"Charlotte says you still write a lot. Do you mind telling me what you're working on?"

"I never tell people what I'm working on. Not the specifics. It takes all the energy out of it. If I talk about it, I don't write it." Gray turned his head. "But Lotty's right. When I put words down, I feel like I'm alive. I write to remember. I write to explain my life to myself."

"I like that. We all handle the hard things differently. So writing helps you."

"Words are flashlights. They help me take another step in the dark."

The doctor smiled. "That's a beautiful way to put it, Grayson. You ought to write that down."

Gray pointed to his chest. "That one's in here. Some things you can't take away no matter what *condition* you have."

"Charlotte said you're researching another story."

"She said that?" Gray's eyes darted. "How did she find out?"

"Maybe you told her."

An empty feeling. Had he told her? Had she read his legal pad?

"Is it fiction or nonfiction?" the doctor asked. "I know you've written both."

Gray ran a finger along the edge of one ear. "You and Lotty have spent a lot of time talking, haven't you?"

"A fair amount."

"Has she told you about the dream?"

The doctor nodded. "She mentioned she's heard you in the night. That you wake up frightened."

"It's as real as real can be, Doc. The whole thing is like walking around in a movie. I'm in the river, and I can see the bridge, and the water is dark and cold." Gray looked up. "Do you believe in God, Doc?"

"I do."

"I've been thinking. What if he's giving me this? What if he's leading me to something bigger than I can comprehend? When I write, I have to look close at the broken places. And it's counterintuitive. Moving toward pain actually gives hope."

"I agree with you."

Gray glanced at the door, then back. "I have to go back to where it happened. I have to stand in the river and look up at that bridge. If I can go there, I think I can figure it out."

"And that's what the van is for?"

"I would have left six months ago if I could have started it. I think the problem's electrical. It won't fire."

"Why do you need the van? You could fly, take a train. Drive Charlotte's car."

He held up both hands. "Why do I need to explain this? It's something I know in my bones. You don't have to believe me if you don't want to."

"I believe you, Grayson. But if you're trying to solve a real crime, don't you think you might be in danger?"

"Life is dangerous, Doc. Walking across the street is dangerous. Ask Martha Mitchell."

A quizzical look.

"Wrote *Gone with the Wind*."

"Aah. *Margaret* Mitchell."

"Taxi hit her. My point is, I want the truth. And you believe my *condition* is closing the window on my abilities. If that's true, which I doubt, I need to do this now."

"So, the trip would take some stress from you."

"As all get-out."

The doctor smiled and doodled on a pad. Gray glanced at the back of a picture on the desk. The doc's family? Him holding up a fish?

"What are you thinking, Grayson?"

"I'm thinking life is cruel. It kills us slow and targets the softest hearts. Then it goes for the throat. Why, what are *you* thinking?"

"Nothing that deep. But you've given me an idea." He took off his glasses. "I see how much this trip means to you. What if I talk with Charlotte—"

"She won't go. She won't set foot in that town." He held up the pad. "I wrote it down."

"Why won't she go?"

Gray flipped a few pages, finding the handwriting difficult to decipher. "The memories, maybe?"

The man's face brightened. "What if someone else went with you?"

"You got that kind of time?"

The doctor laughed and pulled out his phone. "No, not me. I think you'd like this fellow. Smart. Good sense of humor. You could pay him something. I bet he'd go with you."

"He out of work?"

"Something like that."

Gray squinted. "What sort of fellow is he? I don't get along with just anybody."

"He's a deep thinker, like you."

Gray's eyes wandered. "You think you could convince Lotty?"

"If it gets you on the road, it's worth a try, don't you think?"

"I'd need to get the van started. What's this fellow's name?"

"Josh Chambers," the doctor said slowly and seemed to study Gray. "I bet he could help you."

Gray wrote down the name. A good, strong name. The doctor had listened. And in the hearing, Gray felt a little hope.

CHAPTER 3

GRAY HOVERED over the rear-mounted Microbus engine, tugging on belts and wires. Dubose sat in the passenger seat with his head out the window, tongue lolling. When Lotty brought a cool drink to the garage, Gray motioned for her to put it on the toolbox. She made a face, so he took it, and the drink sloshed on the concrete.

"Can't you see I'm trying to figure this out before he gets here?"

"You don't have to be mean about it," she said.

A heavy sigh. "Just let me do my work."

"Gray, are you sure you're up for this? Leaving with someone you've never met? That's not like you."

He reached deep into the engine compartment. "That doctor of yours suggested it." He wiped his hands on a rag and took a long drink. Then he smiled at her and looked into those green eyes, and his heart melted. "This is good lemonade. Thank you."

Her look was priceless. Gentle words always made her back rise, like petting a friendly cat. Why didn't he do that more often?

"Good news." He grabbed his legal pad from the front seat. "Found this last night in my notes. There's an old boy I grew up with, Howard. His father owned an auto shop, and I think he took it over. So I'm going to put most of my tools in the van and take them to him. What do you think of that?"

A bigger smile, then a hug. "Great idea."

"Instead of their going to somebody I don't know . . . There's something about grooves in wooden handles, a connection. To one person it's just a file or a hammer. To the man who uses them, they take on a life of their own."

She smiled again, and he could tell the words connected.

"She came to me last night," he said.

Lotty cocked her head.

"The girl in my dream. But it wasn't a nightmare like usual. I didn't wake you up, did I?"

"No."

"She reached out a hand. She asked me to come find her. And I said I was on my way. She was on the bridge, but Lotty, this time she was wearing a wedding dress."

Lotty put a hand to her mouth.

"Does that upset you?"

She shook her head. "I want to hear your dreams, to hear what's going on inside."

He took her by the shoulders, leaving a mark on her white blouse. "Lotty, I can feel it. The old steam is rising. I sat at my desk this morning. The words came so fast I couldn't stop. It's taking on a life of its own."

"I'm glad, Gray."

"Promise me you won't get rid of my desk."

"I'd never do that. You can trust me." She ran her hand across his unshaven face. "But when you go, you have to promise to be careful."

"Careful about what?"

A car pulled into the driveway, and a man approached. He looked to be in his early thirties. Hair short. Chocolate skin. Sunglasses. Jeans and a short-sleeved shirt and white tennis shoes. Like some advertisement from a men's magazine.

"I'll handle this," Gray said.

Lotty touched his arm. "Gray, wait."

"Whatever you're selling, we don't want any," Gray said, raising his voice. He stepped out into the sunlight.

The man flashed a smile, but there was something tentative about him. "Are you Grayson?" the man said. "I'm Josh. Dr. Barshaw said he talked to you about me. I'm here to talk about your trip."

He reached out a hand, and Gray stared at it. "He didn't say you . . ."

"You thought I might be taller?" His eyes were wide, and he still smiled.

Gray limply shook his hand.

"I'm Charlotte, Gray's wife. Thank you for coming, Josh."

Gray looked away and pulled at his ear. "I can't believe this."

"So this is the infamous van," Josh said. "How long have you been trying to start it?"

"Stay away from that," Gray said.

"Sure is a beauty. You've done good work."

"Listen, I've changed my mind," Gray said. "I don't need anybody to go with me."

"The engine looks fantastic." The man moved past the passenger side. "And who do we have here?"

The dog sat up, tail wagging. Josh stroked his head, and the dog licked at his hand.

"And stay away from Dubose. He'll take your leg off. And then there'll be a lawsuit. Just what I need."

"Dubose? I've never heard of a dog named Dubose. How are you, boy?"

Gray patted his pockets. "Look, I can pay you for your trouble to come here. I just need my wallet."

"Gray, can I see you inside for a minute?" Lotty said.

Gray lowered his voice and spoke through clenched teeth. "I don't want him with me."

"Inside," she said. "Now." She added, "Josh, could I get you something to drink?"

"No," Gray said. "He's not staying."

"That would be real nice, ma'am."

Gray followed her to the door, glancing back. He hurried to the kitchen as Lotty poured lemonade.

"I don't want to leave him alone with my tools."

"You think he came here to steal something?"

"I don't know why he came."

"You invited him. Dr. Barshaw set it up. Remember?"

"Why in the world would he do this to me? I'm calling it off."

"Gray, stop. You're better than this."

"I don't know him. I had no idea he would be . . . the way he is."

"What difference does it make what color he is?"

"You know I don't have a racist bone in my body. I just like to be prepared."

"Okay, so now you know. Josh is Black. Big deal. If he were white, you'd be packing for the trip, right?"

"I'm not comfortable traveling all that way with somebody so different."

"Maybe he's not that different. And if there's not a racist bone in your body, it shouldn't matter. I don't understand."

"Exactly. And I don't have the energy to make you." He rubbed the back of his neck. "I don't want to be thinking about it all the time. I can't do what I need to do if I'm constantly worried I might say something that offends him. One wrong word with these people and you're in trouble."

"These people?"

"You know what I mean."

"Dubose seemed okay with him. He's usually a good judge of character."

"Dubose is a dog." He shook his head. "I should never have trusted that doctor. Did you know this? You did, didn't you? And you didn't say boo about it."

"What happened to your excitement, Gray? The momentum and the energy? The dream?"

"Don't do that, Lotty. Don't bring up—"

"You know what? I don't care. Do whatever you want." She pushed past him. "I didn't want you to go in the first place. Stay here and help me move."

"Now, don't get mad just because I'm having a hard time."

She opened the door and turned, sadness in her eyes. "I'm not mad, Gray. I'm just tired. Tired of your being suspicious of me and Dr. Barshaw and everybody who's trying to help you. It's exhausting. All of this would be hard enough, but your pushing everybody away makes it twice as hard."

She stepped through the door and stopped, turning again. Her face became softer. "I know this is not your fault. I know you can't help it. But I'm still exhausted."

As she turned back to the garage, Gray couldn't believe what he was hearing. From the whistle and chug, he knew it was the van. He hurried to catch the door before it closed. Dubose stood on the seat and barked. A plume of blue smoke hung in the air.

Josh tinkered with something on the engine.

"What did you do? How did you get it started?"

"A little ether. Just needed priming. Sounds good, doesn't it?"

Gray had heard this sound in his dreams. "But I did that. I sprayed so much ether in there, I nearly fell asleep."

"Purring like a German kitten now," Josh said. "Hop in and we'll go fill it up."

Lotty shrugged and smirked. "Get your wallet."

"Who taught you to drive a stick?" Gray said as he swiped his lone credit card at the gas station and Josh cleaned the windshield.

"An uncle managed a grocery store, and he let me drive the empty parking lot after hours. I figured it out."

"Why didn't your father teach you?"

Josh hesitated. "That's a complicated question."

Gray finished pumping but spilled a few drops on his leg. He tried to dry it with a towel, but that only made his hands smell.

Josh came back to replace the gas cap.

"No," Gray said. "I can do that. Get back in."

Josh held up both hands as Gray struggled to screw the cap on.

Back on the road, Gray said, "Looks like it's been a while since you drove a manual. You're not engaging the clutch far enough. You want it smooth and not so herky-jerky. Yeah, that's better."

Back home, Gray told Josh to back into the garage.

"Want to put the tools in tonight?" Josh said.

Gray didn't answer.

Josh used the side mirrors to ease into the bay. The neighbor across the street stood watching, hands on hips.

When Josh turned off the ignition, Gray spoke, facing the windshield. "Look, I appreciate your starting the van. I can tell you're a good person. So this is not personal. But I've decided to take the trip by myself."

"May I ask why? You don't trust me?"

"There's not a lot of people I trust these days. But it's not that. I don't travel well with people I know, let alone strangers."

"Maybe if we got to know each other?"

"I got a gut feeling about this. I've learned to listen to those. It's a mistake to push it down."

"I understand," Josh said, his voice soft. "It's funny, though."

"What's funny?"

"I had the exact opposite feeling. I think we're more alike than you know."

"How's that?"

Josh rotated his wedding band. "I've been trying to give something to my family. Provide. Talking with Dr. Barshaw made me feel a little hope. And when your engine fired, I thought I was on my way. Helping you and helping myself."

"Why don't you find a real job instead of playing chauffeur?"

"I thought I was helping. And that both of us were getting something out of the trip."

"I can't live with another obligation. I've got a lot on my mind, so I have to focus to keep things settled and—"

"No conflict."

"Exactly."

"And I would be a conflict."

"It's not your fault. That's just the way it is."

Josh leaned back. "I thought they took your license. You can't drive alone, can you?"

"I'll figure it out. Maybe convince Lotty to go."

"She sure loves you. I can tell."

"The feeling's mutual most of the time."

"From what Doc told me, she's busy. And does she drive a stick?"

"She catches on fast. On the open road, you get it into fifth and let it go." He shook Josh's hand, strength to the grip this time. "Sorry it didn't work out."

Gray sat on the bed, jotting notes, when Lotty collapsed on her side as if carrying cinder blocks. His pen jumped, and he made a mark the length of the page. "Hey, watch it!"

"Sorry." Her voice carried a familiar resignation. She put a hand on his back. "You decided against Josh?"

"He knew it wasn't going to work."

"He said that?"

"I don't recall the exact words. Didn't write them down."

She scooted closer. "Anything interesting in there?"

He angled the page away. "I've never run out of ideas."

"When can I see?"

"One of these days." He closed the pad and stared at the closet. "I always thought I'd come up with a story that made you laugh and cry and felt so true you would ache inside. And that would be the one that would really sell and set us up."

"A lot of people have read your stories."

"I never found the one I was looking for."

"Your words have never been good enough for you, Gray. You could have had fifty bestsellers."

"You have to push yourself," he said. "Go deeper. If you're satisfied with what you've done, you don't . . ." He waved. "I can't make you understand."

She propped herself up on an elbow. "Maybe this story, what you're writing now, will be what you're looking for."

The cover of the legal pad, its design and ridges, felt like tracks of some forgotten railroad. "One good story. I thought if I worked long enough I would stumble onto it. Like a blind hog finding an acorn."

"You're not a blind hog, Gray."

"You don't understand."

She lay back on the pillow and whispered, as if ready to fall asleep. "This is the one. They'll make a movie out of it."

"Over my dead body. A movie spoils a good story. It does all the work for you. Tells you what to look at and think about. There's no room in them, no white space. I have to paint it on the page for people to see. Books reach into your soul and make you stop and underline. You can't dog-ear a movie."

"Have you ever thought . . ."

She sounded too tired to finish her sentence. He shifted and looked at her face, the milky, smooth skin that bore the weight of time and worry. She'd developed wrinkles like any mature woman, but somehow she seemed to carry them differently. Was that just in his head? Did his love make him see her differently from other women her age? And did her love for him do the same?

"Have I ever thought what?" he said.

She rolled onto her back. "Maybe instead of writing one good story, you're living it."

He laughed. "I don't think anybody would say what we're living is a good story, Lotty. But we might be able to change that."

"How?"

He leaned down. "Come with me. Let's just go. It'll be an adventure."

She turned away, but he could tell she was awake.

"I can't write this one in the West. Everything's dried up like the desert. Back home, though, where the trees change color and the hills rise and the river runs over the rocks, something good will happen."

"You mean you'll find her."

Gray opened the legal pad, searching.

"Not just her, Lotty. Both of them."

"Both?"

In the dim light of the lamp on the nightstand, he saw the truth about the scene that haunted him. She was calling out to him from the grave. Asking for justice. But there was another desire, and he could tell no one, trust no one with the truth. Only the page.

"Come with me, Lotty."

"There's so much to do here, Gray. And you know I can't go back."

"You say that every time, and I have no earthly idea why."

She sat up and dangled her legs over the edge of the bed. Dubose moved in his kennel, as if sensing her unease. She stood and walked out, closing the door.

She had been so tired, but now she was fully awake? And instead of talking, she moved away?

Gray plopped the pad on the nightstand and marched out, the door banging. He found her in the dining room, sitting in the corner, hugging her knees to her chest. And there came the soft sobbing he hated.

"Why'd you leave? Why don't you stay and talk it out?" His voice echoed off the walls and the stacked boxes.

"Dr. Barshaw gave you a way back, and you refused it."

"You mean . . ." Gray tried to pull up the name. "The Black guy?"

"Yeah, the Black guy."

"You don't understand."

"Gray, the moving truck is coming. I have to get everything out. You opened boxes I had packed in your office and put books back on the shelf."

"I need those to do my work!" He stalked back to the bedroom.

Dubose whined.

"Shut up!" Gray threw a pillow at the kennel, and the dog quieted.

Gray found an empty page in his pad.

Lotty says they're coming for all the stuff. That means they'll take the van and the tools. I can't let that happen. Tonight is the night.

When she returned, he was careful not to move and breathed heavily. The clock read 2:15 when he pulled back the covers and, fully dressed, grabbed his pad and stole through the door and found his shoes. To be able to think all that through made him smile. He'd show old Dr. whatever his name was.

He manually opened the garage bay's overhead door, fearing Lotty might burst in at any moment.

He shifted the van into neutral and got out, holding the steering wheel and rocking the vehicle until it rolled and the back wheels fell off the lip of the concrete. Gravity on his side now, he jumped in as the van rolled down toward the street. Gray heard a thump. He ran to quietly lower the garage door, returned to the van, and buckled in.

CHAPTER 4

AS FIRST LIGHT SHONE ON THE HORIZON, Gray nearly passed out from the ether. He slammed the back door and got in the front one more time to try the ignition. Not even a sputter. He cursed his luck and tried to think of the Black guy's name. He could remember batting averages from his childhood, but not the name of the man he'd met the day before.

The van sat at an angle, back tires on Gray's driveway and the front two on the street. The mailbox lay on the ground. How had that happened? And how long had he been out here? How far down the road would he be if the thing had started? He walked to the rear of the van and noticed movement around the curve. The community consisted of a series of horseshoe-shaped streets of identical homes and lots measured to the millimeter.

A thin dog loped toward him. It was two mailboxes away when Gray realized it was a coyote. Something black dangled from its jaws. He picked up a smooth river rock from the landscaping and ran toward the animal.

The coyote cocked its head and darted into a yard, and Gray threw the rock, leading it and judging the distance like a skeet shooter.

The rock passed through the sparse limbs of a mesquite, and Gray heard a sickening crash of glass. The coyote disappeared past the house that now had a broken window.

Gray moved back to his garage but found the side door locked. How had he gotten outside? A door slammed somewhere down the street. Dogs barked. He retreated to the side of the garage and stood in the shade like a guilty child.

What had that coyote carried in its mouth? And what was his van doing at the end of the driveway? Gray had always been sure of what to do and how to do it, unafraid to risk, to launch, to paddle faster toward the white water. Some saw this as a gift, a confidence that sprang from some belief that he could achieve whatever goal he set.

So why was he cowering? What had he done wrong? What had happened to his confidence? How could he calm a scattered mind that felt only fear?

A figure moved near his van. Gray stepped into the half light and raised his voice. "Can I help you?"

"Grayson, what's going on out here? What are you doing?"

It was his neighbor from across the street.

"I don't answer to you."

"Where's Charlotte?"

"She doesn't answer to you either. Mind your own business."

An older woman in a robe and fuzzy slippers approached. "Somebody broke my window," she said.

"Know anything about that, Grayson?" the man said. "And your mailbox is broken."

"Must have happened last night," Gray said.

The man turned to the woman. "He shot into my house with a nail gun the other day. Could have killed us."

"Grayson," the woman said, "did you throw a rock through my window? I might have to call the sheriff."

"You people don't understand the threat, do you? You're oblivious."

Gray walked into the street, and the man muttered, "Something needs to be done."

Gray made it around the curve of the horseshoe where, between houses, he could see stately saguaros that had grown for a hundred years or more in the desert beyond, stretched as if they were praying to the light on the horizon.

He picked up his pace, feeling his head would clear the farther he got from his house. Gray tapped mailboxes as he passed. People moved behind windows, the scurry of morning routines, hurrying to meet the day. How many days had he spent doing the same, and what had the hurry brought him? What was the point?

A car approached slowly, both windows down, a man behind the wheel and a young girl in the passenger seat, her eyes red.

"Excuse me," the man said. "Have you seen a black cat?"

"No, but I'll keep an eye out. Where do you live?"

The man told him, but the numbers went by so fast he couldn't hold on to them.

"It was my fault," the girl said, choking. The man put an arm around her.

"Don't you worry, sweetheart," Gray said as gently as he could. "He'll come back. He's probably out hunting something for breakfast."

The emotion of the girl and the gentleness of the father touched a nerve like a distant whisper he couldn't make out but knew was real.

"We need to go," the man said. Gray wanted to say something else to make everything better, but the words wouldn't come.

As they drove away, he whispered, "I hate coyotes."

He reached another horseshoe, and the sun was up over the mountains now, not a cloud in sight. The air crisp, he could feel the fall heat approaching—no matter how cool the nights.

A man in work clothes hurried out to a pickup that seemed out of place in the neighborhood. In the back lay tools and sheets of drywall. The man drove off, and smoke plumed behind the truck, making Gray cough.

He had no idea where he was. He tried to swallow, his tongue thick. His heart rate climbed as he walked faster, his head pounding. Gray wiped his forehead and caught a whiff of ether. Where did that come from? Maybe that's what made his head pound.

He spoke aloud. "I need water. And I need coffee."

He retraced his steps, jogging toward the middle of the empty street, the sun on his back, sweat dripping. He patted his back, feeling for his legal pad. He always tucked it there when he went for a walk.

Gray stopped.

Had he dropped it?

He turned around, head down, scanning the street.

Stop it. Just stop it. I'll find it.

Two blocks farther, a car approached. It was Lotty, her window down. She slammed on the brakes.

Gray didn't move. "What are you looking at?"

"Get in the car, Gray." She was still in her pajamas. When he slid in, she said, "Seat belt."

"My legal pad. I can't find it."

"Is that why you're out here?"

"Just get me back to the house." He banged on the dash. "Come on, move it!"

"Seat belt."

He fumbled with it till she reached over and pushed it into the lock. He waved her forward and leaned to read the speedometer, because it felt as if she were crawling.

"How long have you been up?" she said.

"I don't know. I couldn't sleep."

"The neighbors woke me."

"Busybodies. Why doesn't anybody mind their own business anymore?"

"Did you throw a rock through Irene's window?"

Something darted into the street, and Gray threw up his hands. "Look out!"

A black cat raced into a yard and up a tree.

"Look at him go!" He felt elated but couldn't figure out why. He opened his door, but the seat belt held him. "I have to get him."

"Close the door, Gray."

"I don't remember why, but I need to get that cat."

"Gray, we need to get home. We need to find your legal pad. The cat will be fine."

When Lotty pulled up, the mailbox was still on the ground, but the van was in the garage, a scent of ether in the air.

"I could've sworn . . ."

"Sworn what?"

"I thought the van was outside."

"It was. At the end of the driveway. I couldn't get out."

"Then how did—"

"The neighbors helped. Where were you going with it?"

"What do you mean they helped?"

"Where were you going?"

"I wasn't going anywhere."

"Gray."

"I was just seeing if it would start."

She turned off the ignition. "Gray. Look at me. Tell me the truth. Where were you going?"

He unbuckled and opened the door. "They might have taken my legal pad. I have to check."

He found it in the van's passenger seat. There was no key in the ignition. When he closed the door, Lotty was there.

"We need to talk."

"I'm dry as the Sahara. And my head is pounding. Did you make coffee?"

"I've been out looking for you, Gray."

"Charlotte!" someone called.

The nosy neighbor from across the street had something silver dangling from his hand. The keys.

"Go inside," Lotty said to Gray. "I'll be right there."

He heard scratching at the door, opened it, and patted Dubose on the head.

Inside, Gray went to the sink, turned on the water, and put his mouth down to the stream. He remembered his childhood, drinking from a garden hose, water that smelled of warm rubber. He tried to wash the ether off his hands.

Dubose whined.

"You want to go out?"

Dubose didn't budge. Gray filled the dog's water dish, and Dubose lapped as though he had been outside in the sun all morning.

Gray went to his office and sat at the desk surrounded by boxes. He untaped a box and then another. He was on his fourth when Lotty arrived.

"Do you know which box has my poetry books in it?"

"Gray, each is labeled. It says *Poetry* right here."

"Oh. You don't have to be mean about it. I was just asking."

"I'm not being mean. I'm . . ." She sighed.

"I'm looking for James Dickey. Poems from '57–'67. It's green."

"Gray, we need to talk."

"I feel the sap rising, Lotty. It's finally back. It's going to be a good day. I can tell already—hey, here it is!"

He flipped the book open to a dog-eared page.

Lotty leaned to push the book down. "Gray, I need you to look at me."

He saw a glint in her eyes, water welling, but he had to go back to the page. "You don't know how hard it is to get the words to come. I used to walk into a field of wildflowers every day and find them everywhere, just waiting for me to pick them. Now, I walk into nothing but dust. Tumbleweeds instead of words."

"I know it's been hard for you."

"Hard?" He tilted his head like a dog with water in its ear. "God is punishing me, Lotty. He knows how much it means to find the words, and he's gathered them in his hand and closed it into a fist. Do you think God is punishing me for things I can't even remember?"

"Oh, Gray, that's not it."

"It's like he made me to do something, like run a marathon, and then he paralyzed me. So when I feel it coming back, I have hope. I'm happy again. But I'm scared it'll leave just like it came. Or it'll come so fast I won't be able to get it down. The words are birds that'll fly away if I get too close."

"Tell them to me, Gray. Don't worry about writing."

"I can't dictate."

"Not dictate. Tell me what's going on inside."

He looked at the legal pad. "I think through my fingers. You know that."

She handed him the pen, and he felt someone turn on a hose that led to his thoughts. He closed his eyes.

"Frustrated. Deep down. Like I'm drowning. Like there's something

CHRIS FABRY || 33

just out of reach, and the more I try to grab it, the farther away it moves. Everything's stirred up. I can't see."

She whispered, "What overwhelms you?"

"Knowing what I want to do and not being able. Terrified of failing you. I can see the sand slipping through the glass. Scared I won't find the man who killed her. And if I do find him, I won't remember what he's done, and she'll never get justice."

"You don't have to do that, Gray."

"Yes, I do. You don't understand. There are things a man has to do." He opened his eyes. "When I thought the van would start, I felt free again, Lotty, like I didn't have to depend on you or some doctor. It felt like an empty page."

"But the van wouldn't start."

"God closed his fist again."

"I want this for you," she said. "I want to see you do this."

"Then come with me."

A sad look. "You know I can't. And you know you can't go alone."

"I had to try." He faced the nearly-empty bookshelves. "I've never told a story to the depth I wanted. I always get off track, and what I put down is different from what was in my head."

Dubose sat by his chair and licked Gray's hand, then sniffed at his knuckles.

"But not this time. Even through the haze, I see it. I see her. I hear her."

Lotty put her head on his shoulder and gave a soft moan.

"*Please help me*," Gray said. "That's what she said to me. *Save me.* She was standing so close I could touch her hair."

Gray's voice softened. "I know you think I don't see how hard this is on you. I know I can be obnoxious. I don't want to be. That's the truth."

"You don't have to take care of me," she said.

"Yes, I do. And I'm going to figure out a way."

Gray found an underlined section in the book of poems and smiled.

"The fellow who was here. The Black guy."

"Josh?"

"Yeah. Why don't you call him? If he can start the van again, I'll let him go with me."

CHAPTER 5

FOUR DAYS EARLIER

Charlotte sat alone in Dr. Barshaw's office. It felt like the end of one thing and the beginning of another, and she wasn't ready. She checked the app on her phone that showed Gray in an exam room, the locator she had inserted in his belt giving her peace of mind.

Dr. Barshaw entered and angled the chair next to her so he could speak face-to-face. The uncomfortable silence made her put her face in her hands.

"It's time, Charlotte," he said finally. "I know that's hard to hear."

"I took the nail gun away. . . ." The look on his face made her stop.

"I'm not just concerned about Grayson; I'm concerned about you. When it was time for him to stop driving, you were on board."

"Because he could hurt someone on the road. But he's harmless now."

"Except for your neighbor. If someone had been in that room . . ."

"I have it under control." She stared at the floor.

"He thinks you're having an affair."

"What?"

"With me."

"I'm sorry."

"You have nothing to be sorry about. This is Gray's mind we're dealing with."

"What did you tell him?"

"I asked what he would do if he discovered he was right. He said he wouldn't pay his bill. And I laughed, and that eased things."

"I won't lock him away."

"I'm not suggesting that. At least, not yet. But understand, I'm not just his doctor. This is about everyone connected to him. You're the one feeling this the most."

"Other than a neighbor with a nail in his living room wall," she deadpanned. "Life is changing, and I have to change with it," she parroted the doctor. "Put on my oxygen mask first and all that."

"Your husband is not the only stubborn one in the family."

"He's losing himself, and he knows it. At the same time, he's obsessed with writing his last story. And it seems to make him come alive. I don't want to thwart that."

"You have to admire that. The writing and everything that goes with it seems to bring him great joy."

"Except when it doesn't."

"Has he gotten physical with you? Hurt you?"

"He would never do that."

"And he would never shoot a nail at someone."

"He gets something in his head and becomes this other person."

Dr. Barshaw paused. "That's what concerns me. We talked before about what we call the *fiblet*—calming him with an answer that doesn't upset him further."

"Lying, you mean."

"Patients who have lost a spouse become agitated. Where did he go? Instead of telling a woman over and over that her husband has been dead five years, the caregiver says he's at the store."

"How can that help?" Charlotte said.

"Within a few minutes, she forgets even that. The point is to love them well. The truth can put them in a state of constant grief."

"Wouldn't I be just sparing myself the grief? I don't want to lie to Gray."

"I understand. But with new situations, especially the move, he's likely to become even more confused. And more aggressive physically."

"So what do I do?"

"Consider letting him go on this trip. It might provide some closure. And help you transition to this new season."

CHAPTER 6

GRAY LOVED MAKING LOTTY SMILE. She didn't smile much anymore. She filled a cooler with ice and packed gluten-free snacks and turkey sandwiches made with antibiotic-free meat and millet and chia seed bread. "Hope those were cage-free, hormone-free turkeys sung to sleep each night by vegetarian, grass-fed farmers," he said. That made her smile.

Gray arranged the tools in the van in such a way that he could get to the cooler or to the mattress on the back bench for a nap, but things were tight. He brought a few books "to prime the pump," he told Lotty, and she hadn't argued when he opened additional boxes to find them.

Lotty had called the Black guy—Gray couldn't recall his name—and he would arrive early the next morning. Gray insisted Lotty take him to the auto parts store to stock up on cans of ether.

"Think the van will make it all that way?"

"That engine will be running long after I'm in the ground."

Gray woke at sunup and stowed a stack of legal pads and an extra pen. He told Lotty he was too nervous to eat but accepted a cup of coffee.

"Where is he?" Gray said, looking out the front window.

"He'll be here. Just be patient. You're really excited, aren't you?"

"I feel like a kid again. Wrinkled on the outside, twenty-five on the inside."

His traveling companion showed up in khaki cargo shorts and a new Arizona Wildcats T-shirt, blue with a red *A* on the front.

Lotty brought him a cup of coffee and thanked him for coming so early. "You have one excited passenger, Josh."

Gray stiffened. "Passenger my foot."

Josh. That's his name. Gray opened the van door and wrote it on the first page of his legal pad. He rearranged a few items while Josh followed Lotty into the house. He found them at the kitchen table in a muted conversation.

"Time to get this show on the road," Gray said.

Lotty handed him a plate of food. "Take it. You don't want to stop for breakfast."

He nibbled at the food.

"Josh has your medication and dietary rules."

"Dietary rules?" Gray said, bits of food flying from his mouth. "When you're on the road, you make do. You eat what you need. Food is fuel."

Josh had the plastic pillbox under his arm.

Gray growled. "I'll grab a can of ether; you open the engine."

"Hang on," Josh said. "I want to try something. It may start without the ether this time."

Gray squinted. "It won't even turn over for me."

"Just let him try, Gray," Lotty said.

He threw up his hands as Josh climbed in and started it with one turn of the key. "How did you . . . ?"

"I think it flooded the other day. But it's good you got extra ether. We'll keep an eye on it."

"Isn't that great?" Lotty said. "You're as good as there."

Gray shook his head and opened the passenger door. Lotty turned him around and pulled him close, eyes glistening. "Listen. I want this to be the best trip ever. Unforgettable."

"With me, everything is forgettable." He had made her smile again. He ran his tongue over his bottom lip and moved her hair back from her face. "I wish you'd come with us."

"I wish I could."

Gray kissed her on the cheek and clapped. "All right. Come on, Dubose, hop in."

The dog jumped in and sniffed his way toward the back.

"Gray, you can't take Dubose. It's going to be hard enough—"

"Of course I'm taking him. He's my writing buddy."

"You don't have his food or his dish. His leash. You don't need the added complication."

"Why are you making a big deal out of it?"

"Because you're not thinking."

"It's okay," Josh said. He came around the van. "I think it's a good idea."

"See," Gray said.

Lotty stared at Josh, shook her head, and stalked into the house. Josh followed, and they returned with dog food, two dishes, a bed, a leash, and a jug of water.

Gray got in, and Lotty said, "Be nice to Josh, okay? You know how you can be."

"Me?" Gray said, mugging.

Lotty looked past him to Josh. "Call me. Let me know your progress."

"We'll be fine."

"Finer than frog hair." Gray said, slapping the dashboard. "Let's go." As they chugged away, Gray waved at Lotty and she smiled, but it looked as if it took effort.

They headed toward the interstate, and Josh slowed as they crossed two sets of railroad tracks. A few minutes later, Gray pointed and told Josh to pull over.

"What for?"

"Just do it."

Josh stopped, and dust plumed around them. Gray opened his pad and flipped to a dog-eared page. "Where do you live?"

"Excuse me?"

"Which way do we go on the interstate to get to your house?"

"I don't understand."

"I'm dropping you at your house and going alone."

"Mr. Hayes, that's not going to happen. We had a deal."

Gray looked at the pad and pulled out his wallet. "How much? You need money, right?"

"That's not why I'm going with you."

"How much?"

"Mr. Hayes, I'm not letting you go alone. I promised your wife. I don't go back on a promise."

"Every man has his price." Gray jotted a note. "Would a thousand make you change your mind? That's pretty good for a day's work, isn't it?"

"It doesn't matter how much you offer."

A semi passed, and the wind shook them. "That's what I was afraid you'd say." Gray flipped the page. "If you're intent on going with me, we need to set the ground rules."

"Ground rules?"

"First, don't repeat everything I say. It bugs me." Josh's eyes widened. "It's not personal. I don't want you here. But it looks like the only way I'll get to go is to take you with me, even if I don't get along with your kind."

Gray stepped out.

"Wait," Josh said. "My kind?"

"Don't interrupt. Now trade seats. I'm behind the wheel."

Josh reluctantly exited the van, and when Gray was behind the wheel, he opened the legal pad again.

"I'm not supposed to let you drive."

"You're not letting me do anything. I'm doing it." Gray tried to get the seat belt to click. "Do you let women rule your life?"

"You don't have a driver's license."

"I was driving before you were a gleam in your daddy's eye. I acknowledge you're a necessity, but I call the shots. We stop when I say so."

"Fine, you're in charge, Gray."

"Watch your tone. And don't call me that. It's Mr. Hayes. Show some respect." The belt finally clicked.

"If I were your *kind*, would you let me call you by your first name?"

"Get that chip off your shoulder, son. That's part of the problem with you people. Every little thing sets you off. Develop a thicker skin. Not everything people say to you is personal."

Josh stared at the windshield, and Gray tracked his list with an index finger.

"All right. We're going to drive straight through."

"How is that going to work? It's more than a twenty-four-hour drive."

"I'll drive the first leg and go back and sack out. You'll drive the second. We tag team it." He handed Josh three sheets of paper. "This is the route."

"We could just use my phone. It would tell us every turn."

Gray closed his eyes and shook his head. "Your generation is so tied to a phone."

"How were you going to do this alone?"

"Same way, except I'd just pull over and get some shut-eye at a rest area or gas station."

"No hotel?"

"Waste of time and money. I got places to go and people to track down. You need to know there's danger ahead. You okay with that?"

"I think so."

"There's no *think so* about it. You either know or you don't."

"Is that all that's on your list?"

Gray squinted at Josh, as if sizing him up. "You and my wife were talking before we left. What about?"

A pause. "Both of you have lists. She was going over hers."

"What was on it?"

"Lots of things. Your medication. She said you'll probably fight me about taking it. She said when you get upset, you pull your ear. And that I need to be prepared for you to get mean when you're agitated."

"She said that?"

"It's why I suggested we bring your dog. He seems to calm you."

Gray looked out toward the interstate. "Noticed that, did you?"

"Why did you name him Dubose?"

Gray shifted into first gear. "We've talked enough."

Josh grabbed his arm. "Hold up. One more thing. What did you mean when you said you don't get along with *my kind*?"

Gray yanked the van back into neutral. "For crying out loud, is this what it's going to be like for two thousand miles? You and I are different, that's all. I'm pointing out the obvious."

"You don't even know me."

"And if this is how you're going to act, I don't think I want to."

Gray turned the wheel and accelerated, but the engine only raced. He jammed the van into first and pulled onto the road.

CHAPTER 7

❧

GRAY HEADED INTO THE RISING SUN, clouds stretching like a canopy. Yellow and salmon pink spread out like a welcome, and Gray stared.

Josh reached over and jerked the steering wheel to the right. "Keep it between the lines, Mr. Hayes. Big truck's coming."

Gray saw he was going forty-five, and a truck passed, horn blaring, like they were sitting still. Gray sped up but again gaped at the sky. "Would you look at that?"

"Pretty."

"Pretty doesn't begin to capture it. Be more descriptive. Try and describe that to somebody who can't see it."

"I'm not a writer."

"Don't give me that. If you can see, you have an obligation to tell others. You don't have to be a writer to do that. You have to be breathing. Describe it."

Josh sighed.

"Here, I'll close my eyes and you—" Gray said.

"No, don't do that. All right, I'll try."

Gray smirked. Josh stared at the sky. "Looks like a skeleton's rib cage."

"Hey, that's not bad. I can see that. But throw in some colors."

"A yellow and white skeleton's rib cage."

"Now you're not even trying."

"How would you describe it?"

"I see ripples in a stream. Like God skipped a rock against the sky and it landed right on the horizon. And I'm seeing all the waves the rock made with the colors in his palette. White and pink and red along the edges. Like window shades on eternity."

Thirty minutes later they came over a ridge, and the land stretched so far Gray thought he could see a hundred miles. With the window down and the wind in his hair and a steering wheel in his hands, he couldn't stop smiling. He felt something he hadn't felt in a long time and wasn't sure he ever would again.

"Wish I could bottle this feeling," Gray said, finding Dubose's head and scratching it.

"Where did he get his name?" Josh said.

"Character in a book I read when I was a kid."

"Book must have made an impression."

"Sure did. Made me want to do for somebody else what Harper Lee did for me."

"I read that book. But I don't remember a Dubose."

"The old lady down the street. The one with the flowers in front of her house."

"Oh, yeah. She had a Confederate pistol under her blanket."

"There you go."

"Why her name, though? Why not Atticus? Or the little girl's name?"

"Scout."

"Or the kid who comes to visit."

"Who would name their dog Dill?"

"Who would name their dog Dubose?"

Gray gave a long sigh. "You can't understand the story without that old woman. She's central to the whole thing." Gray put a hand on the dog's head. "Dubose here, somebody else owned him, and he had a heart problem or some such. Lotty piped up and said she would take him."

"And you were okay with that?"

"I doubt I did cartwheels. The point is, there was every reason in the world to give up on this dog. Just like Mrs. Dubose."

"I don't understand."

"She was hooked on a drug to get her through her pain. And she decided she wouldn't leave beholden. So she kicked the habit before she died."

"The boy read a story to her, didn't he?"

"Good memory. That story was about finding the courage to live even though you know you're going to lose. Atticus knew what that jury would decide. But he fought. Same thing happened in the Garden."

"What garden is that?"

"First one. God knew what was going to happen. He created anyway. Same with Jesus' prayer in another garden. 'Take this cup from me.' It was sincere. Human. But he knew he had to drink it. And drink it he did. Down to the dregs."

As the sun rose higher, the van warmed and they rolled all their windows down. The wind whipped Gray's hair and made his shirt billow. Dubose put his head out the window and closed his eyes, and his ears blew like flags.

The desert road wound into a land that looked like moonscape. Miles of barrenness and rock formations that made Gray think of dinosaurs. The only movement was cars and trucks and the occasional buzzard or hawk. The van bogged and slowed as they chugged up an incline. A pickup passed with its tailgate down, an ornate casket strapped in tightly with nylon rope.

"Death is everyone's destiny," Gray said. "The living should take this to heart. Ecclesiastes. Ever heard of it?"

Josh nodded.

"That's where we're all headed," Gray added. "Strapped down in the back of a pickup."

"I didn't know you were religious."

"The light comes on later for some than others."

Gray fiddled with the radio but couldn't pull in a signal. When they crossed into New Mexico, trucks boxed them in and Gray slowed, nervous. When they neared Deming, he exited and pulled into a gas station. Gray stretched, and Dubose found some weeds and relieved himself.

"Mind if I take over for a stretch?" Josh said as he filled the tank. "I feel like I'm ready."

"I suppose you'll hound me until I say yes."

They ate sandwiches from the cooler, and Josh found a Walmart. He stopped in the shade of a mesquite and removed the keys. "I'll only be a minute."

"There's nothing we need in there. Let's get back on the road."

"Need something for the trip," Josh said. "You'll like it."

"I say when we stop and go. That's one of my rules."

Josh's face contorted. He shoved the key in the ignition and continued east.

They wound through Las Cruces and down to El Paso, following the border. Gray made notes on his legal pad, but the motion of the van made him woozy. He put his head back.

"What do you write in that?"

"Things that come to me. For my eyes only. Don't go nosing around in it."

"I don't plan to. You can lie down in the back if you want."

Gray kept his eyes closed. "You don't think I know that?"

"I just meant I'm fine."

"I know what you meant. I can understand English."

They were passing Sierra Blanca when something dinged. Josh picked up his phone. "Your wife texted to know how we're doing."

"She's a worrywart."

"She cares."

"She's paranoid. Maybe she thinks you're going to dump me across the border and take off with all my worldly treasure."

"You think that's what I want to do?"

"I'm not sure what you want to do."

"She trusts me," Josh said.

Another ding and Josh dictated a message, telling Lotty where they were and that things were going well.

"You didn't tell her I drove the first leg."

"She doesn't need to know everything," Josh said. "She's a worrywart, remember?"

In another mile Josh spoke tentatively, as if nudging a rattlesnake with his bare toe to see if it was dead. "May I ask you something?"

"Depends."

"Tell me about the girl."

"What girl?"

"The dream."

Gray stared at the passing wasteland. Tumbleweeds. Rock outcroppings. A dust devil in the distance. *Barren as a childless woman*, he thought.

"How do you know about that? Wait, don't tell me. Lotty?"

Josh nodded. "She said the dream is the reason you're taking this trip."

Gray's mind flooded. "She's not a girl; she's a grown woman. And I don't want to talk about her." He moved his hand in a circle beside his head, meaning that the stirring inside was too much for him.

Another ding. "She wants to know how far we're going before we stop," Josh said.

"Tell her I have promises to keep and miles to go before I sleep."

Josh put the phone down. "Resting overnight *would* give us a fresh start."

"If you're tired, I'll drive."

"I'm just saying, by the time we hit Fort Worth, it'll be more than twelve hours on the road."

Gray was wide awake now. "You going to take her side the whole way?"

"I'm here to help, Mr. Hayes. To get you to your destination in one piece. And to calm your wife's fears at the same time."

"Sounds like you're caught in the middle of something bigger than you are."

"I'm trying to make both of you happy."

Gray growled and fiddled with his ear. "Tell you what, if you can find a place that allows Dubose in the room, we'll stop."

"Deal," Josh said.

Gray chuckled. "Good luck with that."

They stopped for gas in Abilene, and Gray went inside to use the restroom. On his way out he passed a rack of pastries and paused, his mouth watering. When he returned to the van, Josh looked sideways at the pastries.

"What? Did she tell you to keep me away from sugar? You going to rat me out?"

Josh smiled. "No, sir. But you've got enough Hostess cupcakes in there to feed an army."

"Well, maybe we'll come across one between here and wherever we're staying."

Josh held up his phone. "Your wife found a place that accepts pets."

The room was stuffy, and the first thing Gray did was turn on the air-conditioning. Josh handed him the remote and said he'd be back with dinner.

"See if you can find the fish place with the yellow sign and get me a feast. I could eat a whale."

Josh lingered until Gray began channel surfing. He was frustrated to find only a news channel. Demonstrations and people blocking traffic. Police accused of something terrible again.

Josh returned with a bag and two Styrofoam containers full of breaded fish and shrimp, hush puppies, French fries, and coleslaw. He poured a mountain of packets of ketchup, tartar sauce, and cocktail sauce onto the table.

"You got the whole shootin' match," Gray said, turning down the TV. "Feast fit for a king." He rubbed his hands together. "Don't you dare let Lotty know. She'll make us turn around and go home."

Josh turned up the TV. Someone was interviewing a man about the demonstration.

"Shut that off; it's giving me a headache."

"This is important," Josh said, sitting on the edge of one of the beds. "You see what happened the other day?"

"I don't watch much anymore. Lotty says it gets me agitated. Those people have no right to shut down that road, I can tell you that. I don't care what happened. There could be an ambulance trying to get through. Or a fire truck."

"They're just angry, Mr. Hayes. Upset at what's going on."

"Well, I get angry every day, but you don't see me shutting down the interstate. Ought to arrest every last one of them and haul them to jail."

Josh hit the mute button and fell silent himself.

"So you're for blocking roads?" Gray said, his mouth full. "Against law and order?"

"No," Josh said. "I just understand why they're mad. But I also understand where you're coming from."

"And where am I coming from?"

"You don't think this is the way to handle it. But a lot of us, *my kind*, are tired. There's a soul-weary feeling when we see another Black man die and police are involved."

"And the circumstances don't matter? I sure misjudged you. I thought you had a good head on your shoulders."

Josh opened his Styrofoam box. "Maybe if you had seen what I've seen, you would think differently."

"I've seen plenty, young man. And this is still the best country on God's green earth. And there's nobody, I don't care what color you are, who can't succeed here in the good old U.S. of A."

Josh wiped his fingers on a napkin. "What about that book that made a big impression on you? Doesn't it talk about walking around in somebody else's shoes?"

"That was a long time ago. Things have changed. Are we perfect? No. But the worst is behind us. We need to move on, not wallow in it."

Josh turned off the TV, and they ate in silence until Dubose belched. Gray rose. "I'll take him for a walk."

"No, let me do that."

"He's my dog, okay?"

The sun was down, and the fluorescent lights buzzed as Gray led Dubose across the parking lot. When he looked back at the room, Josh was watching him through the curtains, a phone to his ear.

CHAPTER 8

IN HIP WADERS AND A FLOPPY HAT that held his flies, Gray stepped into the stream with a heavy crunch in the gravel. As he moved toward deeper water, a leaf swirled on the surface as if suspended by time. He cast toward the mountains in the distance, his line arcing over and behind him, and focused on a spot by the leaf. Movement felt effortless, and he sensed something good ahead, a calm spreading through him. He felt rocks on the riverbed as the current enveloped him. With each step smooth, he felt he had been made to do this one thing well.

The river licked at rocks upstream and trickled over logs, and he slipped on something slick but caught himself, regaining control. The ripples, white and fresh, sounded like strings in a symphony, and his rod was a conductor's baton, beads of water dripping from his line like melted wax. When it unfurled, the fly landed gently in the shade of quiet water near the leaf, and it all felt like perfection.

Insects sang, creation coming alive as he waded deeper, to his waist. A gentle swirl appeared near the fly—a hungry fish. The strike would come at any moment.

To his left, a narrow bridge spanned the river, and two figures in shadows struggled, a man pushing a young woman. His hand was over her mouth. The bridge swayed, but the current and insects drowned the noise, and Gray felt the water at his chest. "Hey!" he yelled. "Stop it!"

The man wrapped both arms around the woman and lifted, her bare feet in the air. She kicked and grabbed the rickety railing, but he was too strong.

The water lifted Gray from the riverbed, and he drifted, the rod in one hand, trying to paddle with the other. A flash of white—the girl's dress billowed, and he let go of the rod and swam. The current also carried him toward the bridge. The man violently shook the girl, and Gray thrashed, water in his mouth, trying to yell but struggling to breathe.

Under the bridge now, through the space between the boards, he saw the girl go limp and the man reach for some kind of sack. He threw it over her and swung her like a rag doll into the water.

The girl disappeared, and Gray took a deep breath, diving beneath the surface, pulling himself deeper with each stroke. The heightened beat of his own heart thrummed in his ears, and the water became muddy.

Then, in the murk, she floated before him, hair billowing, arms posed like a marionette, eyes closed. He fought to propel himself toward her.

Her eyes opened.

Her mouth in a silent scream.

She grabbed him and held on as he thrashed, swallowing water as he tried to surface, his lungs screaming.

Almost there, the girl vise-gripped his neck and pulled.

Gray sat up in bed, gasping, a man's hand on his shoulder. "Mr. Hayes, it's okay. You're all right." The man turned on a light.

Gray stared. "Who are you? And why are you in my room?"

"It's Josh, Mr. Hayes. Remember? We're in a hotel. It's okay. You were dreaming."

Dubose put his paws on the bed and whined, tail wagging. Gray wiped his forehead, and something settled inside. "Holy cow. That felt real." He grabbed his legal pad and swung his legs over the edge of the bed.

"Maybe it was the fish you ate," Josh said.

"Wasn't the fish."

"Why don't you lie back and get some more rest?"

"I need to write this down. And then we need to get on the road."

"Mr. Hayes, it's not even 2 a.m. yet. Not close to daylight."

"I don't need daylight. I need to leave."

Gray finally got his seat belt buckled as Josh pulled into a gas station. He growled, "Why didn't you gas up last night?"

Josh seemed to want to say something, but he paused. "It'll only take a minute."

Gray shook his head. "I'll get coffee. Want some?"

"Sure, Mr. Hayes."

Gray walked through the harsh fluorescence that attracted a sea of moths, the night filled with screeching insects.

The dream still haunted him. All that struggle. In the distance, the resonant hum of tires and the bark of big trucks told him they were straining up an incline. So many in motion already.

Inside, he breathed in the scent of strong coffee. A heavy, short-haired woman behind Plexiglas looked as though she could take care of herself, but Gray wondered why a woman would be working at this time of night.

He poured coffee into two cups, steam swirling, and headed toward the register.

The woman was engaged with a man, venom in her voice. The man spoke in a high-pitched whine. "Please? I promise this will be the last time."

The woman picked up a cordless phone and pointed the antenna at the man, as if the phone were loaded. "I told you, put the sandwiches down and get out of here."

"Hold up," Gray said, coffee stinging his hands. He set the cups down as the man placed two wrapped sandwiches beside them. "Why are you treating him like that? He's hungry."

"None of your concern, mister," the woman said.

"Well, I beg to differ. You ought not to treat people that way. Ever hear of the image of God? We're all made in it. You and him alike."

The woman set her jaw. "That has nothing to do with it. He comes in here all the time. The manager said if I give him—"

"I don't care what the manager said! That's what's wrong with this country. A bunch of sheep who don't think for themselves. Don't care a whit about somebody looking for a little food. He could have just run out of here, but he didn't."

Now she pointed the phone at Gray. "Stop yelling at me or I'll call the police on the both of you."

"Call whoever you want," Gray said.

The man had his head down as if studying the floor. He edged away from the counter and cowered next to a display of beef jerky. A strong odor of mildew and urine hit Gray, and he realized the man looked more like a wild animal. He wore a dirty green military jacket that hung to his knees, and his bare legs were thin as matchsticks. Red blotches covered the pallid skin, and he moved from one foot to the other as if he might topple. He had long, matted hair that hung thick, as if he'd shampooed with mud.

"No free food," the woman said. "That's all there is to it. Mister? Are you listening? You want me to get fired?"

Gray turned back to the man. "That all you want? The sandwiches?"

Gray's traveling companion walked in. What was his name? "Mr. Hayes, we're ready. Let's go."

"Give me a minute. Wait, here, take the coffee to the van, um, Josh." Remembering made him feel he had accomplished something.

As Josh exited, the woman hollered at Gray. "You need to pay for those, mister!"

"Ring up the coffee and two sandwiches," Gray said. "You can keep your job."

The woman frowned and punched the register like she was in a cage match with it. The man gathered the sandwiches, and Gray saw he was just a kid. Maybe twenty. And behind the grit and grime, something reminded Gray of his dream. The pleading eyes? The innocence?

"Want some chips?" Gray said. "A candy bar?"

The man hurried out the door. Gray grabbed a package of potato chips and a cherry pastry. "Add these."

"I know you're trying to help," the woman said, her voice kinder now. "But you don't know what you're doing. He's caused all kinds of trouble around here. You're just encouraging him to come back."

"Maybe I'm just encouraging him. A little kindness can go a long way."

She handed him his change. "Kindness don't work with some people."

"Maybe one day you'll need a little."

Back in the van, Gray asked Josh if he'd seen which way the man went.

"Mr. Hayes, don't you think we ought to—"

"My van, my rules. Which way?"

It took three tries to get the van started, and by the time they pulled onto the road, the darkness had swallowed the man.

"Drive around," Gray said. "See if he went down that alley."

Josh stared at Gray.

"If you don't want to drive, let me."

Josh turned into the alley and to the dead end and had to back out. He drove toward the interstate, where the headlights shone on a figure in the shadows of the underpass.

"There he goes," Gray said. "Hurry up!"

When Josh came to a stop, Gray grabbed the bag and opened the door.

"Mr. Hayes, I don't think we can take this on."

"What are you so scared of? Is it living or something else?"

Gray slammed the door and climbed the slanted concrete, the incline so steep he had to go down on one knee. He couldn't see a thing. A light flashed. Josh had his phone out and illumined the underpass. Gray climbed on all fours to the top. Traffic rumbled overhead.

"What do you want?" a high-pitched voice called out from a space about three feet tall where Sandwich Man had climbed. He shielded his eyes from the light.

Gray held out the bag. "Thought you could use this."

The man crawled out like an animal leaving its den. A stack of flattened cardboard boxes lay on the ground. The man pushed aside a filthy blanket.

"This is where you live?" Gray said.

"Keeps me out of the rain. I've got a blanket. Warm enough. I just woke up hungry."

"You got family?" Gray said.

"Not around here."

"You ought to get back to them. I'll bet they're worried."

"Maybe." He said it low and gravelly and scratched his neck. "Someday. After I get myself cleaned up. Get back on track."

Gray turned to Josh and pointed at the van, then half crawled, half duckwalked down and opened the side door.

"What are you doing?" Josh said.

"There's a lot of things in the world I can't change. When I find something I can do, it's best to do it. Don't shove down the generous impulse. Maybe we can make his life a little better."

Gray grabbed the mattress from the back and told Josh to take the other end. It sagged and proved unwieldy, and Josh finally told Gray to let go and carried it up the incline by himself. Gray joined him, and they maneuvered the mattress over the cardboard. Josh covered his nose and backed away.

"Now you'll have a full belly and you can get a good night's sleep," Gray said.

The man stared at the mattress as if it were a magic carpet. Gray pulled out twenty dollars and handed it to him.

Sandwich Man stuffed it in a pocket. "Why are you doing this?"

"That woman ticked me off. I don't know you from Adam, and I don't know I'll ever see you again. And if I did, I probably wouldn't remember you." He twirled his fingers beside his head. "I've got some things mixed up in my hard drive. But I believe God puts people in our path for a reason. And each man has a story that intersects with those he meets. Like rivers and streams, if you know what I mean. I don't know why you're here. But I saw something in your eyes. And I'll bet there's somebody wishing you'd come home. And you don't have to clean yourself up for that."

The man's mouth opened, but nothing came out.

"Maybe God wants you to know he cares. And he just let us be his angels tonight."

The man spread the blanket on the mattress and lay down, cradling the bag of food.

"We could take you," Gray said, glancing at Josh and raising his eyebrows. "Get you to your family."

Like a child, Sandwich Man said, "I need to sleep."

Gray rubbed the back of his neck, then shoved his hands in his pockets. "You go on and sleep then, friend."

Gray nearly fell going to the van, but Josh grabbed his arm and stabilized him.

"You're not going to be able to take a nap back there now," Josh said.

Gray shrugged. "He needed it more than me."

Josh turned the key, and the van sputtered to life.

"Hold up a minute," Gray said. "Go back up there and see if he'll tell you his name. Maybe where he's from. A family member. Anything."

"What good would that do?"

"Maybe he's had enough time to change his mind about being helped."

"You really want me to go back up there?"

"Humor me."

Josh sighed and got out, and Gray reclined the seat and laid his head back. Maybe Sandwich Man couldn't see a way out. Didn't even have a nightmare to guide him.

Gray had let the woman at the gas station have it, but what had she been through? Maybe she had a sick baby at home, and that job was the only thing keeping them going. How many of the mean people he'd met in his life were just scared of something, a monster they couldn't see past?

His mind drifted to the little town and the river that ran through it, to the bridge and the girl in the dress. And he thought of Lotty. Something switched inside, like a fuse blowing or a bulb flickering. He sat up and squinted.

Why were there two coffees in the cupholders?

Dubose whined and nuzzled his hand. "You're right, boy. No reason to sit here when we could be on the road. We've had enough rest, haven't we?"

Gray moved to the driver's side and buckled in.

He hit the gas and sped away.

CHAPTER 9

GRAY SPOKE TO DUBOSE, keeping himself alert with the coffee as he drove—glad he had two cups, though the second was cold by the time he got to it. He got only static from the radio, so he told all the jokes he could remember and even sang an old Sinatra tune.

He flipped the visor down when the sun appeared. It always did a number on his eyes, and he began to squint as the traffic increased. Pickups passed him in a blur and cut him off, slowing and then speeding up again.

"Must be a sale on something, Dubose. Or maybe a fire." Another truck came so close, Gray had to slam on his brakes and jerk to the right. "Slow down!" he yelled. "You're going to kill us all!"

He smiled at the irony. He was being so careful at the moment because he was on a mission. But there would come a point where preservation would not be his highest priority. Being able to remember that gave him a warm feeling, like there was nothing that could stop him now.

"I tell you what, Dubose, we are cooking with gas. We're doing it, buddy. Just you and me. We've got the plan in place, a working van, and the road is open. I promise, you're going to run in river water before this is all over. You're going to have a high time."

Still, something bothered him. Why such uneasiness with the euphoria? Something just wasn't right, like a puzzle with a big piece in the middle missing. But this was how he felt a lot of the time, especially around others. When he said something, they would look at him as if he had spoken Swahili. His inability to recall what he had said made him feel doubly uneasy. He'd written in his journal, "Shut your mouth. If you say nothing, people won't know there's anything wrong."

When the gas gauge reached half and he felt pressure below from the coffee, he exited and found a gas station humming like a beehive. Only one pump was free, but he couldn't navigate between the other cars and a truck with tires as tall as he was. He bounced in the seat now, his bladder screaming. He waited behind a man trying to get his credit card to work. Unable to stand it anymore, Gray sped away into the country, away from the interstate. At a wide spot he pulled over. Dubose followed him and sniffed at the dirt, and within a few seconds lifted his leg and a stream flowed.

"Looks like your prostate's doing better than mine, boy."

As Gray relieved himself, a distant memory flashed. There were so many things he couldn't remember now, like faces and names, but he did recall the high-arcing streams and the laughter of boys at the riverbank. Who could create the highest arc, shoot the farthest? The image was sepia toned, the sound muted, but it was there. In those days, all of life was a contest.

He heard Lotty's voice. *Oh, Gray.* Or maybe it wasn't her voice, maybe it was just the look she gave that sounded louder than words. She always chided, as if she could counteract some irreversible flood. Cap the volcano. She made doctor's appointments and tried new herb concoctions that tasted as if she had boiled dirty socks with tree bark.

"Don't pee in a pot and tell me it's sassafras tea," he'd said to her.

Funny that he would think of her now and hear her telling him he couldn't do this in the open when he was clearly doing it. He smiled and realized what he was feeling was freedom.

Next came a hunger for something greasy. Maybe he'd find that place with the yellow sign and have a fish dinner. How long had it been since he'd had breaded fish and shrimp? He could do anything he wanted.

Eat anything he wanted. Or crawl in the back and take a nap on the mattress.

Back in the van, he made a U-turn to the interstate and cupped his hand out the window as if the wind were something he could hold. He wanted to never let go, and it almost felt as though he could. He whooped, and Dubose lolled his tongue as if he were smiling. This was the best feeling in the world.

Something overtook Gray, a companion to the freedom he loved— a chance to lose himself in a swirl of thoughts. At his desk in the morning, words would often jam in his head like a beaver dam, and he could find only a trickle—a word here and there to write. But here on the open road, with the sun shining through the trees and color bursting and the tires rolling, it felt like a breakthrough. There was a lightness to his life, the wind in his hand and his hair—nothing to hold him back.

"You feel it too, don't you, buddy?" he said as the dog licked at the wind out the other window. "Of course you do."

Gray felt no fear. This was what life was supposed to be, coasting downhill toward something he was trying to reach, instead of away from something he feared.

"The longer I live, the more I think you're supposed to be able to become yourself instead of a clone of somebody else. And the further you go, the closer you come to home. What do you think of that, Dubose?"

The dog panted, tongue out.

I ought to write that down, Gray thought. *Coming Home to Yourself*— a lifelong exercise of becoming who you really were instead of a cheap imitation. There are three people to every man. There's the man you appear to be, judged by others. He had no control over that and didn't put much stock in anybody else's view. The second man was the person he had tried all his life to become, someone different from who he was, but only a shadow he could never catch. And then there was the man emerging now, a true man comfortable in his own skin but hard to recognize in the mirror.

In the rearview, amid the wrinkles and crow's feet, his pupils looked vacant, as though the lights had been left on for someone who hadn't returned. That scared Gray until he saw tools and a large red chest and the cooler.

Lotty had slept on the mattress in the back as he drove this road in the other direction decades earlier. She was also coming home to herself, but she was taking a different route to the same destination. All that had happened, his diagnosis and her response, stretched her in ways she never could have anticipated. But she was becoming, just as he was.

He had mapped out his life like the plot of a story and factored in twists and turns. Things weren't going the way he had planned. But they were going. And who was he to say the story wasn't going well? Who was he to say the disappointments and unmet expectations of what life would be like in their twilight years might not be the best story?

If what the doctor said and what Lotty read on the internet was to come to pass because of his dementia or Alzheimer's or whatever they wanted to call it, there would come a point when he wouldn't recognize Lotty. Gray had written that down, but for the life of him, he couldn't imagine not knowing her any more than her not knowing him. But if that was true, would there also come a point when he wouldn't recognize himself? If he caught a reflection of his own face, would he wonder who in the world that handsome devil was?

Gray cursed and shook his head. The dog in the seat beside him curled up with his head on his paws, eyes closed, a picture of contentment. Not a care in the world. Why couldn't Gray live like that? Trust is what it was. The dog trusted him, and that made him smile, because the world was leaking trust like a sieve.

Someone honked as they passed, and Gray threw up a hand in frustration, seeing he was doing thirty-five. So he accelerated, thoughts still swirling. He wanted to be the kind of person who received whatever came his way, welcomed the good with the bad. This was the man he wanted to be. But part of him hoped to make sense of the distance between what he wanted for his life and what it had become. It was a chasm between his vision and reality, and that led to a deeper question.

Had he earned his diagnosis? Was the disease they claimed he had caused by divine retribution, punishment for all the things he had done or neglected to do? It seemed plausible. His life work was mostly thinking and expressing his thinking. He came alive by doing that. If he were God, the most logical way to punish a man like him would be to take away what meant the most, like a runner having his legs severed or a singer contracting cancer on her vocal chords.

If he could figure out why he was being punished, how he had fallen short, perhaps he could atone in a way that would allow his mind to return. Or was it already too late to reverse what had begun? If so, he and Lotty and everyone he knew simply had to deal with the pain that leaked from his own fountain of sorrows.

The van lurched, the engine misfiring. He pressed harder on the accelerator, and things seemed okay until it lurched again—sputtering and coughing.

"This is not good, Dubose."

He crested a hill, and the van picked up speed. Then the lights on the dashboard flickered and the engine stopped. He coasted to the bottom of the hill and halfway up another, drifting to the side of the road.

"Maybe it wasn't my fault, Dubose. Maybe I didn't do anything to deserve this. Maybe it was just my turn."

He turned off the vehicle as if it were just a tired horse that might get a second wind. But when he turned the key again, the engine turned over but didn't fire. Sounded like a fuel problem. Then he noticed the fuel gauge, and his heart fell. The arrow was way below the E, and a little yellow warning light burned brightly. It made no sense.

He banged a hand against the steering wheel, then crawled into the back, where Dubose was sniffing at something. His water dish was bone dry, and Gray couldn't recall when the dog had eaten. He poured dry food into the bowl and splashed a little water from a plastic jug into the other dish.

"Slow down, buddy. You'll chuck your lunch up if you eat too fast."

Gray and Dubose wandered past the guardrail and into the tall Johnson grass. Gray tried to remember the last town. How far back was it? He would need to walk one way or the other. Or he could wave down somebody. On a knoll in the distance sat a copse of trees surrounding a white farmhouse with a green roof, and Gray imagined the people inside and that he could write about what they were doing and where they had been and what generations before them had done to the land to make it what it was today.

Behind the house peeked the edge of a weathered barn that surely would have a gas can. If it was real. He rubbed his eyes and suddenly felt a tiredness that had snuck up on him. The wind blew across the grass and made him dizzy. He went back to the van to stretch out for a bit.

"Somebody stole the mattress, Dubose. Who would do a thing like that?"

The van swayed as a vehicle passed, and then brake lights flashed and it pulled over and stopped at the top of the hill some distance ahead. Gray felt another sway and a blurping sound. A police car with its lights on screeched to a halt behind the other car.

Gray clapped. "Would you look at that! My prayers have been answered even before I prayed!"

He stepped out and squinted. It looked as if a Black man emerged from the first car. An officer jumped from the cruiser, pointed his gun at the man, and yelled something Gray couldn't hear.

The man raised his hands but yelled something back at the officer, pointing in Gray's direction. Then he got back in his car.

Gray slid behind the wheel of the van and watched the officer move forward, his gun raised. He spoke into the transmitter clipped to his shirt.

Gray figured at some point he'd need to show his license and registration, so he opened the glove box and found a small leather holder. He smiled. It was just like Lotty to keep everything nice and neat like that.

He pulled his wallet from his pocket and found his credit card and a picture of Lotty and him in a garden somewhere. He couldn't remember where that was taken, but it gave him goose bumps. That smile of hers. What a silky-haired beauty! Anybody would look good with her beside him. He ran his thumb over her face, and something moved inside.

Now where was his driver's license? Where it should have been—in the plastic, see-through holder that flipped out—he found a card that read, in bold red letters, *Alzheimer's Identity Card*.

It listed his name and address and a contact phone number for *Charlotte Hayes, SPOUSE*. It made him feel like a child going to school with a scrap of paper pinned to his sweater: *My name is Grayson. If I get lost, please return me to Mrs. Kennington's first-grade class.*

When Gray looked up, the Black man was getting out of his car with both hands raised. What in blazes had the man done?

A feeling swept over Gray that something was wrong, but he couldn't figure out what it was. He glanced at the field and farmhouse in the distance and felt sick to his stomach. Why?

The cop approached and yelled something. Gray opened his door and stepped out.

"Do you know the man in that car?"

"I don't know him from Adam," Gray yelled back.

"He says he's been chasing you. Says he knows you."

"I don't know anybody who drives a car like that."

The officer scowled. "Get back in your vehicle until I can get this sorted out. Understand?"

Gray nodded and shuffled to the passenger side of the van and opened the door. "Dubose, get up here."

A semi rumbled by.

"Dubose, come here! Where are you, boy?"

He tried to think. Had his dog gotten out when Gray opened the door earlier?

A screech of tires on the other side of the interstate. A pickup had skidded to a stop.

Gray's chest tightened. He struggled to breathe. Everything felt out of control.

He shielded his eyes from the sun and called for Dubose.

CHAPTER 10

GRAY FOUGHT TO BREATHE as he ran along the shoulder of the interstate behind the van. The pickup sat at an angle on the median, and the driver—a ponytailed woman in a baseball cap—was out, waving to slow traffic and direct it to the outside lane.

Something lay in the road, something Gray didn't want to see. He closed his eyes and whispered, "Please don't let it be Dubose."

An air horn blew and Gray jumped back, unaware he had wandered onto the road. An eighteen-wheeler passed, and the draft nearly toppled him. He stepped onto the shoulder, craning his neck to see around the pickup. He had gone from not wanting to know to *having* to know.

In tall, black riding boots and the tight pants that disappeared into them, the woman could have just come from a horse corral. She moved into the lane, waving and bending to reach for something. Cars slowed and moved to the right into the open lane, but she disappeared from view. If she rode horses, she was probably an animal lover, and Gray believed loving an animal made you kind—willing to risk. She twisted and dragged to the side whatever was in the road.

"What you got there?" Gray yelled.

The woman stayed focused on the task, probably not hearing him because of the din of the traffic. Then she stood over the critter and wiped her hands on her shirt.

Gray yelled to her one more time, but she jumped in her truck and sped away.

Gray got down on one knee and peered through the guardrail at something furry and unmoving. What would he tell Lotty? Would he be able to hold on to what had happened? Maybe he should stop and write it down. This would break her heart. It was breaking his own, but he couldn't think about that now.

All his life he had saved emotions for later—pushed them to the back burner, let them simmer until it was convenient to feel. Was that how he had lived? He had taken the emotions, stirred and used them, each of them, in his stories. The pages absorbed his inner life so that he felt he had lived it, embraced it. But had he? Were feelings just something he used for other purposes?

All Gray felt was the emptiness that being alone brings. He had been alone when he couldn't start the van. Alone in the garage waiting for somebody to take away the things he treasured—boxes filled with things he knew he loved but couldn't recall. *You've got to figure this out on your own*, he decided. *Nobody else can do it for you.* A chill ran through him, as if he were feeling something for the first time and couldn't escape it. He didn't know whether to drag himself to the side or walk into the middle of the lane and lie down and wait.

Resolution. That's what he wanted. To resolve what he had never been able to—his own life. He had to make sense of the things that didn't.

Make it on your own. Find it yourself.

Who had said that? His father?

In the middle of this strange reverie, he heard not whispering, but someone far away calling his name.

Except it wasn't a voice.

It was a dog.

Two, actually.

Neither bark was Dubose's, though he wished it was.

On a knoll in the distance lay a copse of trees, a farmhouse, and the gravel lane that ran to it. The two barking dogs stood in the sunlight behind a chain-link fence, just fuzzy images he could make out because they were so excited. On the side of the fence closer to him stood a brown creature appearing to observe the dogs.

Then Dubose barked. Gray swore it was him, and his heart swelled and he took off for the field, yelling and waving. The ground proved uneven, and he nearly turned an ankle, concentrating so he didn't fall.

Covered in sweat, Gray reached the fence where the two dogs barked at him. He bent, hands on knees, trying to catch his breath. He yelled for Dubose and scanned the fields. No sign of him.

The farmhouse sat in the shade, and an aroma of freshly mowed grass filled the air, Kentucky bluegrass and a smattering of clover.

The sound of vehicles on the interstate reminded him of ocean waves, human and mechanical flotsam and jetsam caught in a tide and crashing on the asphalt shore in a haphazard ebb and flow.

Row, row, row your boat.

Life is but a dream.

"Dubose! Come on, boy!"

Nothing. Had Dubose grown as tired of the other dogs' barking as Gray had? Maybe he was in the field somewhere, sniffing at the corn or chasing a rabbit.

Perhaps this whole scene was an illusion, an oasis, a mirage. But the two dogs were so real, he had to cover his ears. So he couldn't be dreaming.

Or could he?

He felt in his waistband behind him for his legal pad. No luck. He suddenly felt like an astronaut who had come untethered from the ship, out of oxygen and floating toward oblivion. He turned to head back across the field to the van—that semblance of home. His shoes crunched in the gravel.

"Can I help you?"

Startled, Gray turned to see a reflection of himself maybe twenty years younger. The man let the screen door bang behind him and stood on the porch with his hands in his pockets. He wore a sweat-stained baseball cap pushed back so the bill stuck up at a ninety-degree angle. His T-shirt was so thin and holey it looked like a death shroud. His work boots and jeans hung loosely. Too loose, Gray thought. He had a patchy beard, and his face was red.

"I'm looking for my dog!" Gray yelled.

The man closed his eyes tightly, as if he could turn something off if he squeezed hard enough. He shook his head, then puckered and whistled sharply. The dogs immediately hung their heads and didn't so much as whine, ambling toward the shade.

"What's he look like?"

Gray described Dubose. "I thought I saw him near your fence."

The farmer peered into the distance at the interstate. "What's that about?"

"Not sure. There was a Black fellow in that first car. Officer pulled him over." There were two police cars on the scene now. "Might be drugs or something. You know how those people are. That's my van behind them."

"Looks old."

"What's wrong with old?"

The man came down the steps and drew closer, appearing to study Gray. "Old things break down."

Gray tried to conjure a snappy response, like dialogue in one of his stories. When nothing came, he said, "I didn't break down. I need gas. A little fuel and I'll be on my way."

"After you find your dog."

"Of course."

The farmer looked up and down the gravel drive and scratched at his beard. "Does your dog usually wander?"

"No. But my wife is the one who cares for him."

"She with you?"

"No, she's back—she didn't come."

"Where you from?"

Gray had to think hard, squinting into the sun. Then it came like a lightning bolt. "Arizona!"

"That van's taken you a long way, mister."

Gray reached out. "I'm Gray."

"Yes, you are." The man smiled and gave him a firm shake. "Kenny Ross."

"This your farm?"

He nodded. "What's left of it. What's not been sold."

"Well, what's left is nice, if you ask me. It's peaceful out here. Except for those two."

Kenny smiled. "Little one thinks he's big, and the big one doesn't care anymore. He's coming to the end of the trail."

"Looks like he's got some life left. Never underestimate an old dog, I always say."

"Or an old van, right?"

"There you go. I was thinking you might have some extra gasoline lying around. I only need enough to get me to a station."

"Let's find your dog first, Gray."

"Right. Good idea."

"What's his name?"

"Dubose."

"Come again?"

Gray repeated himself, and Kenny whistled and yelled for Dubose. Gray heard the wind and the birds and the dogs panting, and he thought he heard chickens from the barn. The whole thing sounded like a soundtrack from another life he'd lived.

"I thought I saw Dubose having a conversation with your pups. But by the time I made it through the field, he was gone."

"Why don't you come up to the porch and have something cool to drink? Maybe he'll come to us. And if not, we'll go look for him. Then we'll get you back on the road."

"I don't want to bother you."

"Too late," Kenny said with a smile. He beckoned his dogs and Gray to follow him. "Rest your bones. I'll get us something."

"I admit it's been a while since I've run like that. I'll be sore in the morning."

The dogs followed Gray to the porch, inspecting his shoes and his pant legs, then settling on either side of his chair. Gray wiped his forehead and scanned the fields for Dubose. Kenny returned with two glasses of iced tea, and the men sat facing the field and the interstate beyond.

"Is Gray your real name?"

"Grayson. Lotty calls me Gray."

"Your wife?"

"Yes, sir. Charlotte is her given name, but I use Lotty."

"Why didn't she come with you?"

"She's got her reasons."

"Where are you going?"

Gray wished again that he had his legal pad. He looked toward the van. "East. West Virginia, where I was raised. Ever been there?"

"Passed through a couple of times. Pretty country."

"Yes, it is."

Gray stared at the beads running down the side of his glass—one drop running into another and coursing down and onto his leg. So much of life felt like happenstance, and he wasn't sure why. Just the wind blowing you one way or the other, letting you bump into others just as perplexed about life as you.

"You live here by yourself, do you?"

Kenny hesitated. "My wife left. Took the kids. Said she'd had enough. I've been doing a little drinking since she left."

"How long have they been gone?"

"Two weeks."

"That's a fair amount of time to do some drinking."

Kenny nodded. "You and me are in the same boat. Your dog left you, and my wife and kids left me."

Gray chuckled, then grew somber. "You're not thinking about giving up, are you?"

"A month ago I would have said no. Now it feels like a viable option."

There it was again, the mirror. Gray had no idea why he and Kenny were so alike and dealing with the same issues.

"I wouldn't give up just yet. Sometimes you have to hit bottom before you even start asking the right questions."

"What's that supposed to mean?"

"Means you might be close to what you've been looking for."

"What do you think I'm looking for?"

Gray dipped his head. "A lifelong love. One that stands the test of time and all the storms. That's what you want, isn't it?"

"Maybe, but I'm never going to get it."

"Sometimes people leave you not because they want to but because they have to. Sometimes you need to walk away to think things through."

"You think that's what she did?"

"I don't know you or your wife. But I don't think you'll ever find what you want until you let her go."

"Give up on her?"

"The opposite. To love somebody well, you have to let go of something. Sometimes it's the person herself. And sometimes it's something that's keeping you from loving well."

Kenny appeared deep in thought, as if wrestling with something.

"When your wife said she'd had enough," Gray said, "what do you think she meant?"

"This place. Living hand to mouth. She never wanted to move here."

"Why did you?"

"I grew up here. And when my dad got sick, I felt it was something I needed to do. Keep it going."

"That's admirable. Nothing wrong with being a faithful son."

"She told me I was keeping a promise I never made. And breaking the one I made to her."

Gray nodded. "You think your mama and daddy would hold you to something like that? What would they say?"

"I don't know, Gray. I suppose they'd let me do what I thought was right." Kenny stood. "I shouldn't dump this on you when you're looking for your dog and trying to get back on the road."

"Sit down." Gray waved him back into his seat.

There was an ease to the conversation that Gray missed, and he realized something was happening. Earlier in his life, people had come to him and plied him with questions—about the writing life, mostly. And when they did, something opened up and spilled out on them that seemed to help. But no one asked him anything of import anymore.

This fellow had no expectations, however, and Gray felt no pressure to remember or fear that he wouldn't. With Lotty and others, he feared he'd say something wrong and their faces would contort. Or he would forget some detail, like his own name, and his life would be over. With Kenny he could be who he was and remember or forget all he wanted.

He wasn't trying to fool the man to make him think he was fine or that he knew what he was talking about. People would ask him how he was doing, and he would always say, "I'm fine." But had he ever known the answer to that question?

"There's a dead woman back in my hometown. Somebody killed her."

Kenny's mouth dropped open. "What happened?"

"I don't know. That's where I'm headed. And everybody is trying to keep me from it. Lotty. The doctor. He gives me these horse pills that might do more harm than good."

"Is there anything I can do, other than the gas and finding your dog? I could keep an eye out for him and let him stay here."

"I appreciate that." Gray scanned the field, then lowered his voice. "I have this dream. She's calling out for help. Sometimes I think it's not really a dream. Maybe God is showing me something, giving it to me so I can figure it out. So I can hold people accountable. Do you believe a thing like that can happen?"

"I'm not the one to ask about God. But sometimes in my dreams I see my own kids coming up the walk. Or me pushing them in the tire swing out back. Makes me want to drink some more until it comes true."

"I don't think that's the way to make it happen."

Kenny nodded. "You're probably right."

Gray slapped his legs. "Well, you asked where I'm headed. Now you know."

"So your wife let you drive out here on your own? Or did you fly the coop?"

A cloud passed over Gray, and his tone changed. "I don't need anybody's permission to live my life."

"I didn't mean anything by it. I just thought maybe you'd want your wife to know you were okay."

Gray gritted his teeth and balled his fists. He was in a corner with the man and didn't know how to get out. He had spent time pretending he understood what others were saying, trying to convince them he could remember what he couldn't because the memory was right there behind some door that didn't have a handle.

"I don't want her knowing where I am. She or that doctor. For all I know, it's the medicine that's doing this to me."

"You don't want to ease her mind?"

"What she doesn't know won't hurt her."

"You have a phone with you?"

"No." Gray narrowed his gaze, then moved a hand in a circle by his head. "I've got something going on. I don't remember like I used to."

"Like needing to stop for gas. Or letting the dog out. Easy to forget things like that."

Gray nodded.

"I'd feel a whole lot better if you let me call somebody."

"If I needed you to call somebody, I would have asked. Okay?"

Kenny held up both hands. "All right."

"Good." Gray leaned forward and cocked his head. "You know what I think? I think the point of life is to love people while you still got the chance. That means taking them for who they are instead of who they aren't."

Kenny gave a slack-jawed stare.

Something in the man's red eyes caused Gray to look under the surface. "When I say love, I'm not talking sentimental goo. I'm talking love that has another's best interests at heart. I'm talking about you and your wife now. It's easy to focus on who you want her to be—who you want her to become. Then you come up against the hard truth."

"And what truth is that?"

"That you were wrong. She wasn't who you hoped she'd be. She didn't tell you good job for taking care of your daddy's farm. She didn't value that like you did. And you feel betrayed."

"I suppose."

"Here's the hard truth: She didn't betray you. You were hoping for something she couldn't give. And that's a shame. I wish she could have given you what you wanted. It's a loss. But what's ahead might be better for the both of you. Most people love in order to get love in return."

Kenny leaned forward and put his elbows on his knees. "You a psychologist?"

"I'm a writer. I think for a living."

"And you write this kind of thing?"

"Not anymore. Everything's jumbled. I have a hard time putting down two words that make any sense. But there are flashes of the old me. That's what you're getting. And I'll tell you this: I'm going to tell this dead woman's story if it's the last thing I do. And it just might be."

"Well, I hope I'm around to read it."

"Maybe I'll put you in it somewhere."

Kenny stared at his work-worn hands. "What do you think I should do?"

"You don't need me to tell you. You're just scared to do what you know you need to."

When the man didn't respond, Gray said, "Your wife a city girl?"

Kenny shrugged and nodded.

"She thought she could change you. You thought you could change her. And here you sit on your daddy's porch."

The words flowed. Gray felt clear-minded. Maybe it was the run through the field or the caffeine from the tea.

"Go find her. Apologize. Tell her you want to love her for who she is and all she brings to the world. And if she can't stay on the farm, sell it. I can tell this gal has a hold on your heart. Tell her she's more important than some obligation to your late parents. Show her you want to fight for her heart. If she heard that, maybe she'd stay and try to make a go of it. Love is a golden key. It unlocks doors to the heart. But you have to turn the key."

Kenny stared at him. "This the kind of thing you think about as you drive?"

"I think about a lot of things. Then I try to write them down before they slip away. But most of it slips away. And so will I. Someday."

A long silence lay between them, and Gray wished he could hear Dubose bark. Kenny drained his glass, and the ice clinked at the bottom.

"Let me see how much gas I have in the barn."

CHAPTER 11

GRAY AWOKE ATOP A RAPIDLY DEFLATING AIR MATTRESS in the back of the van to the hum of the engine and the jiggle of misaligned tires. Green fields blurred past, along with the first glimpse of orange as the sun rose. He struggled to sit up, and his whole body throbbed like a muscular toothache. Up front, two eyes peered at him from the rearview mirror.

A snout sniffed his face, and a long, pink tongue licked his cheek. Hope filled his heart. "Dubose!" he said, taking the dog's face in his hands. "Hey, buddy. I'm glad to see you. I had a dream I lost you."

"Morning, Sleeping Beauty," the man driving said.

Gray squinted. A Black man. "Hey, what are you doing? Where are you taking me?"

The man turned, and Gray saw kindness in his eyes. "It's okay, Mr. Hayes. Come on up here." He patted the passenger seat.

Gray's heart pounded. *Don't you* Mr. Hayes *me.*

He rubbed his eyes until he saw stars and recalled something about a field and a farmer on a porch and police cars—a jumbled mess of a dream with barking dogs—and he had run through a field and over gravel. He stood and steadied himself on the toolbox.

"You've been out like a light," the man said as though he knew him. "Snoring like a chainsaw."

He felt the urge to find a way out of the van and get away, but the man's confidence drew Gray. This was what his life had become, some-one else driving, someone else making decisions.

Gray gingerly made his way to the passenger seat, plopped down, and tried to orient himself. He grabbed his yellow legal pad from the door pocket.

"Seat belt, please," the man said.

"What are you smiling about?"

"Put that around you and I'll tell you."

Gray finally made the buckle click, and the man held out a plastic cup with pills and a bottle of orange juice.

"I don't take medicine from people I don't know."

The man set the orange juice down and held out a hand. "Josh Chambers. Glad to be back with you, Mr. Hayes."

"What are you talking about?"

"You really don't remember?"

"I remember lots of things. You're not one of them."

"The mattress in the back. Know what happened to it?"

"That inflatable thing?"

"No, the one that was there before. Remember where we left it?"

"We?"

"Let me back up. Your wife, Charlotte, and your doctor, Barshaw, asked me to accompany you on this trip. You and I met a man sleeping on card-board boxes under a bridge. You gave him your mattress. That ring a bell?"

"Of course. What do you think I am, a numbskull?"

"No, I just know you can't remember everything."

Gray grabbed the cup and struggled to finally get the cap off the orange juice. He washed the pills down. "I had a dream about the police pulling me over."

"That was no dream. But they didn't pull you over; they pulled me over. You nearly got me hauled to jail."

"How did I do that?"

"I was trying to catch up to you. And the first officer wouldn't listen to me when I tried to explain—"

"There you go, blaming the police. You people speed, and when they pull you over, you claim racism."

"I didn't say anything about that, Mr. Hayes. I was just telling you—"

"What do you mean, catching up to me? And where are you taking me?"

"Relax. You're going back to where you grew up. I'm helping you. All right? When we gave that man the mattress, you drove off without me. I yelled for you to stop. I found a rental car place but had to wait until they opened. And then I was racing down the highway, praying you hadn't taken an exit. I sure was glad to find you on the side of the road. You ran out of gas, remember?"

Gray rubbed his forehead. "Yeah."

"I tried to make the officer understand what was going on, but he didn't believe me."

"Because you're Black." Gray shook his head.

"Let's say he didn't give me the benefit of the doubt, and yes, that upset me. Dubose bolted from the van and ran across the field. You got out and wandered onto the interstate. I thought you were going to be killed. And then you followed Dubose. I didn't know you could run that fast."

"There was a farmer . . ."

"Yes. After the officer's backup arrived, I was able to get Lotty on the phone to calm them down and prove I was who I said I was. I assured her I still had you in sight, and once I guaranteed the cops I would again take responsibility for you, they let me go. I drove to the Ross farm—that was his name, Kenny Ross. Nice guy. You were dozing on his porch. He found a can of gas and that old air mattress, and he told me where the nearest service station was. About that time, Dubose came running out of the field, looking like some explorer who had conquered the wild. He likes this part of the country, I think."

"Lotty would have had my hide if I'd have come back without him."

"Oh, I let her know. We had several conversations when I was trying to catch you. And she let me have it, no second chances about taking the keys with me from now on. Cost me a pretty penny, but I called the rental place to tell 'em where to pick up their car."

"Where are we, anyway?"

Josh pointed to a sign. "Close to Louisville."

"You must have driven all night."

"Stopped a couple of times, but you slept through Texas. Sounds like a country song, doesn't it?"

Gray laughed. "Why don't you let me take the wheel?"

"I'm good. I was thinking we could stop in Lexington and get something to eat and stay overnight there. Make our final push tomorrow. You okay with that?"

Gray waved. "Nothing in Lexington I need to see. When you get tired, I'll take it the rest of the way."

"Your wife insisted we head back to Arizona."

Gray shook his head. "Give me your phone."

Josh handed it to him, and Gray stared at the screen and all the images on it. "How do I call Lotty?"

Josh took the phone, spoke into it, then hit the speaker button and handed it back.

Lotty sounded groggy. "Josh, are you okay?"

"It's not Josh, sweetheart. It's me."

"Gray, where are you?"

"Kentucky. Can you believe it?"

"No, no! I told Josh to turn around." She was fully awake now.

"Well, he apparently listens as good as I do. I'm letting you know we're doing okay."

"Gray, why did you take off without Josh? I was out of my mind."

"I didn't do it on purpose, Lotty. I was just doing what I came to do. We're making good time. I feel ready for what's ahead."

Silence. Then he heard her crying—the loneliest, most defeating sound in the world. How was he supposed to go on with that over the phone?

"Lotty, stop. You're not helping."

"Gray, I thought this was a good idea, but just come back. Please. Have Josh turn around."

He opened the legal pad. "Listen, there's nothing to worry about. I got my plan mapped out. All right?"

"Gray, you need to prepare yourself. I don't think you know everything you're getting into."

"I know exactly what I'm getting into."

He couldn't figure out how to turn the phone off, so he handed it to Josh, who spoke to Lotty with the speaker off.

When Josh finished, Gray cocked his head. "Know what I have a hankering for? You know that fish place with the yellow sign? What's that called?"

"I know what you're talking about. We'll find one before we go to the hotel."

"I don't need any hotel. I got a lot of sleep. I'm rarin' to go."

"All right, Mr. Hayes."

"And why are you calling me that? You make me feel like my father. It's Gray."

"Gray it is. While you have your pad open, give me an idea where we're going."

Gray's handwriting wasn't the best, but at the top of the page he read: *I'm fighting a monster who wants to steal my memory. I will not let the monster win. I cannot let him win until I complete the task I've been given.*

He flipped back to the front and found a page with asterisks down the left side, a list he realized he had to read each morning when he awoke.

* Your name is Grayson Hayes.
* Your wife's name is Charlotte. You call her Lotty. You love her and she loves you. Don't mess things up.
* You have Alzheimer's, and they say you will not get any better.
* You need to take care of Charlotte. There is a plan to make that happen. First get the van started. Then see page 34.
* Somebody killed a woman on a bridge. It's up to you to find who's responsible and bring them to justice. More on page 34.
* Don't let anybody see this notebook. This is for your eyes only.
* You are a Christian. God is taking care of you. Even when you get confused and think he's not there, he is. Trust him.
* This notebook is your lifeline. Do not lose it. Keep it with you at all times, and write down anything you think you need to remember. Don't worry about repeating yourself.
* Pooch Parsons will help you find the woman's killer. He lives in the town where you grew up. You can trust him. Start the van and drive it to West Virginia and find Pooch.
* Tell Pooch the dream you had. Then ask his help with the plan to end your life. See page 34.

"What's it say in there?" Josh said. "Looks pretty interesting."

Gray closed the legal pad. "An old boy I grew up with, Pooch Parsons, lives in my hometown. Sycamore. That's where we're going."

CHAPTER 12

EARLY THE NEXT MORNING, Gray joined Josh for breakfast in the hotel and told him he wanted to drive the final leg through eastern Kentucky. But Josh convinced him, just as he had convinced him of the value of a night in the hotel, that he could see more and better experience the final miles from the passenger seat.

When they passed the city of Grayson, Gray made Josh take a picture of him in front of the sign, with his hand under it as if he were serving himself on a platter. "Lotty will get a kick out of that," he said.

The rolling Kentucky landscape ushered them toward the mountains ahead. They passed a refinery and crossed the Big Sandy River, and Gray pointed at a sign that welcomed them to *Wild, Wonderful West Virginia.* He rolled down his window and let the heavy air blow through the van. "Smell that? That's a West Virginia fall in all its glory. Like you popped open a can of Mountain Mama. Would you look at those trees? You don't see this in Arizona. It's like God took all the colors in his palette and tossed the whole thing at the canvas."

Gray paged through his legal pad, looking for anything about Josh but found nothing but his name. As the van strained up a serious incline, Gray said, "You haven't told me much about yourself."

"You haven't asked much."

"All right then, I'm asking." Gray jotted *Josh* at the top of a new page. "How did you get this job? Riding with me?"

"Your wife and Dr. Barshaw suggested me."

"Right, but how did they know you?"

"Your wife knows my wife. And I happen to be a patient of Dr. Barshaw too. They thought I'd be a good fit for you."

Gray scribbled on the page. "How does Lotty know your wife?"

"I don't know all the specifics. You should ask Charlotte."

Gray wrote, *Ask Lotty about Josh's wife* and said, "Is driving people your main job?"

"No, my degree is in IT."

"It?"

"Information Technology. Computers."

"You work for a good outfit? Successful?"

Josh shrugged. "Restructured, moved people around, downsized."

"Well, a smart guy like you, with your skin tone, shouldn't have a problem."

"What's that supposed to mean?"

"If you're even halfway qualified, everybody's looking for minorities. Equity and all that."

"So I would be hired only because of my race?"

"Don't twist my words. If there's anything that frosts my socks, it's somebody who twists what I say."

Josh topped a hill, and the van gained momentum. Memories surfaced in Gray like a door to his youth opening. Enlivened by his anger, the past stirred. He slapped the dashboard, and Josh jumped.

"What did you do that for?"

"Camden Park! I remember that place as a kid. Roller coasters and the haunted house and bumper cars. Skee-Ball. I can still taste the cotton candy and corn dogs."

Josh shook his head. "How do you remember that and not other things—things a lot more important?"

"Think I'm making it up?"

"Just trying to figure out how your mind works."

"I've given up trying to figure that out. When things come back, I just try to be grateful." Gray sat up and craned his neck. "There's the Ohio. Curving through the valley like a snake. Funny how rivers separate one state from another. Towns on one side divided from the town on the other. I ought to write that down."

He jotted on the page, struggling with the bouncing of the van. *Josh* at the top of the page reminded him of his questions, so he said, "What about your wife? What's she like? How long you been married? You are still married, right? I mean, you're wearing a ring."

"That's a difficult subject. Like jumping into the deep end of the pool."

"You two going through a rough patch?"

"You could call it that."

"What's the problem? You're not being a jerk, are you?"

"I try not to be."

"Then what? Her daddy get sent to prison? I know that happens a lot in your community."

"Would you stop that? Just because I'm Black doesn't mean—"

"A lot of Black men leave their families—that's all I'm saying. I swear, why are you so touchy? Maybe that's why you're having problems at home."

"Let's just drop it, okay?"

"No, sir. You're running, aren't you? You came on this trip to get away. You can't run. You've got to face conflict head-on."

They rode in silence for a mile. Finally, Gray said, "You talk with her since we started out?"

Josh nodded. "She wanted to know what you're like."

"I hope you lied."

Josh seemed to fight a smile.

"That's good you called. Shows strength. Maybe there's hope for you. What's your main problem?"

Josh gripped the wheel a little too tightly in Gray's estimation.

Gray pointed at a sign and said, "Get off here! I used to take this exit years ago."

Josh veered off, and the van's brakes squealed as they came to a stoplight. Gray rubbed his hands and let the surroundings wash over him. He felt drawn like a magnet as they rode past brick homes on narrow streets with ancient trees. As they drew closer to the city, boarded-up businesses and dilapidated houses lined the streets.

"I don't remember things looking this rough," Gray said.

They went under railroad tracks, and Gray pointed. "I got stuck right at the top of this hill. I was learning to drive a stick shift, and the light changed. Engine kept stalling."

"What did you do?" Josh said.

"A fellow behind me saw I was having trouble. People were honking, and I was embarrassed. He got out of his truck and drove my car up the hill for me. He could have been mean, but he helped me."

"And you remember that."

"I don't know why some things stick. Turn right here, Fifth Avenue." They passed an Italian restaurant. "Hope they never close that place. Best chocolate pie in the world."

"Chocolate pie and spaghetti?"

"Don't knock it till you try it, pal."

They came to a sprawling campus with brick buildings and enormous trees. Gray directed Josh to a parking area where the campus spread out before them. "See that fountain? They shut that off every November on the day of the plane crash. Football players and coaches and leaders in the community died that night."

"I saw the movie."

"Yeah, well, I lived it. Cold, rainy day. Leaves on the ground. Earth so wet you sank when you walked on it. Foggy, too."

Gray pulled at his ear. "People see this part of the country as a place to get through on their way to somewhere else. That's why I write about it. No matter how far I go, I can close my eyes and see it. Taste it. Pay attention to the people here. You can't know the hills until you understand the pain these people have been through."

Students strolled through the campus, some hurrying. A young man and woman walked hand in hand.

"Outsiders came and took the coal and gas and lumber, built chemical plants by the rivers. They never saw what all the taking did to the people or the land. Mines cave in and men die, and those who survive carry black in their lungs. Rain comes and rivers rise and bridges collapse.

"When a new war begins, young men leave these hills and return in body bags or as troubled shells of themselves. A plane gets close enough to the runway that you can see its landing lights. And when it clips the top of a tree, it goes nose first into the hillside.

"These people may not look like they amount to much, but they're the salt of the earth. I've tried to tell their stories all my life. They're not victims; they're survivors. They don't know the meaning of *quit*. You kick 'em to the ground and you think there's no way they can come back, and the next thing you know, they're standing. These are the people I come from."

"Why did you leave if they're such great people?"

"Fair question. I don't recall exactly. I guess there were forces at work that drove us west."

"What forces?"

"Wish I could remember. But my richest stories are about the people here. See that building on the knoll? That's Old Main. Built a few years after the Civil War and still standing. Think about that. The state of West Virginia exists because the western part of Virginia wanted nothing to do with slavery. The state itself was born in conflict and bloodshed." Gray pointed. "My office was right up there. I can still smell the hardwood floors and hear the creak of those old stairs."

"Your wife told me this was where you met."

"She did? When did she tell you that?"

"When we talked about the trip. She said you might want to come back here."

Gray scribbled in his pad.

"So I'm still wondering why you left. What forces were at work?"

Gray shrugged. "Call of the west. Leaving the past. New start. That sort of thing. I don't know." He made it sound plausible, even to himself. But something sounded off. Behind the words there was more to it, but Gray couldn't recall.

"Maybe it's more convenient to forget than to remember," Josh said.

"What do you mean by that?"

"Maybe you don't want to remember."

Gray pulled at his ear. "Want to see something I do remember?"

"Sure."

"You hungry?"

"I could eat."

Gray directed Josh back onto Fifth Avenue and to an orange shack in the middle of a parking lot. Gray's mouth watered. A server put a numbered card on the windshield, and Gray waved her to his window.

"Welcome to Stewart's. Your plate says Arizona. This your first time here?"

"First time in a long time," Gray said. "Are you a student?"

She nodded. "Psychology major."

"The world could use a good psychologist who knows how to serve a hot dog wrapped in a napkin. You still do it that way?"

"Yes, sir. Steamed buns are the best. What would you like?"

"Since you study psychology and you know how far we've come, you ought to be able to see how hungry we look. Why don't you guess?"

She seemed to study the men. "I'd say three each and two root beers."

"You must get good grades," Gray said. "But make it four each. Sauce still the same?"

"Since 1932. You eating here?"

"Yeah. You still serve the root beer in those frosted mugs?"

She winced. "Sorry, sir."

"That's a crime against nature."

She wrote on a green pad and went to get their order.

"Taste is like music," Gray said. "Something even I don't forget. I can still hear a song that was on the radio when my father drove around, and it takes me right to where I'm in the backseat looking at the back of his head and the Brylcreem. And my mother's bob haircut. She looked like Doris Day. You have no idea who that is, do you?"

Josh shook his head. "What song?"

"Something by Sinatra. I can't remember titles. I'll know it when I hear it, though."

The psychology major returned with a tray that fit over Gray's window, and Gray handed Josh a hot dog. He unwrapped it with a puzzled look, as if wondering why it would be wrapped in a napkin. He took a bite, and Gray studied his face. "Amazing, isn't it?"

"It doesn't have ketchup or mustard."

"Don't need it. You've got that special sauce." Gray took a bite of his, closed his eyes, and moaned.

When Josh finished the hot dog, Gray asked if he was ready for another.

"I'm not that hungry."

Gray ordered him a plain dog with mustard and ketchup and asked for a bag for the remaining hot dogs.

Back on the road, they drove east until they intercepted I-64.

"How much farther from here?" Josh said.

"Won't be long."

"You have family here?"

Gray nodded and focused on the legal pad, leafing through it to page 34. "That's where we'll go first. To see my family."

CHAPTER 13

GRAY'S MEMORY WAS GOOD ENOUGH only to choose the exit. Several wrong turns that led to dead ends or endlessly winding roads later, he allowed Josh to use his phone to pull up the local cemeteries. Gray chose one that sounded vaguely familiar, and a woman's voice guided them onto a two-lane road that snaked into the maw of vibrant fall colors. The air had turned cooler and heavier and felt like rain.

As the van chugged up a hill, the road narrowed and the asphalt crumbled where water had washed. The voice told them to turn left.

"She was right!" Gray said, pointing at a white church in the distance.

Mount Olive Cemetery sat behind the Mount Olive Missionary Baptist Church and was surrounded by trees that made the mountain look like a man's bald head. The church's white-gravel parking lot sat empty, so Josh parked near the chain-link fence and the first line of gravestones. A whisper of a breeze blew through the window.

"Peaceful, isn't it?" Gray said, taking in the undulation of the land due to the ebb and flow of time.

He studied a page in his legal pad, then got out and opened the side door to free Dubose. The dog sniffed at the edge of the lot and squatted as Gray entered the gate and approached the first stone. The name—*Flowers*—brought nothing to him, no face, no memory. As Josh reached him, Gray said, "Well, these people will always have flowers on their grave."

Josh grinned. "You just come up with that?"

Gray chuckled and stepped carefully around the stone. "Never walk on people who are resting. Even the dead have their decorum and deserve respect."

Josh matched his footfalls as Gray continued, "Every one of these stones bears a story. Mothers and fathers, sons and daughters. Each stone has its pain. It comes to rich and poor, like a freight train. You can try to step off the track, but sooner or later, that train will find you."

Josh nodded, looking somber. "You know, Gray, when I heard you wanted to take this trip and that you had . . ." He paused. "When the doctor told me your diagnosis, I wasn't sure what to expect."

"Afraid you'd ride a thousand miles with a fern?"

Josh appeared to stifle a smile. "Not quite that bad."

Gray waved. "That's the problem with your generation: Everything's disposable. If something shows a little age, you toss it. New phone comes along, you plunk down the money. You've got to learn to value things that have a little wear and tear."

"That's not fair. My generation learned from yours. Baby Boomers started the whole disposable thing. And if I was so gung ho to toss you out, what am I doing here?"

Gray kept walking. "You're here because you're getting paid, just like the rest."

"How dare you say that."

That made Gray stop and turn. Standing by a tombstone with a cross on top, Josh didn't seem angry as much as hurt. "You don't know a thing about why I'm here or who I really am. You've judged me, not for who I am but who you think I am. From your own limited knowledge. The surface."

Gray stood tall. "Is that so? All right then, how do you want me to judge you?"

"How about by the content of my character? That would be a start."

Gray rolled his eyes. "Oh, for crying out loud, here we go again. Playing the race card. Why do you keep going down that path, son? You're like—"

"Hey!" someone yelled.

A man behind the van peered at the license plate. He wore brown coveralls stained green and a paint-blotched, plaid shirt. John Deere hat. Hair stuck out the bottom, and his beard looked a week old. He sported a dark stain on his chin and a bump between his cheek and gum.

"Can I help you?" Gray said.

The man spat a stream of brown. "You can start by getting your dog out of there. Can't you read?"

"I didn't see any signs," Josh said.

The man glared and approached the fence. "Was I talking to you? There used to be a sign. Somebody musta stole it. You don't let a dog run among the graves. It's common sense."

Gray whistled, and Dubose came running. When he trotted out the gate, Gray closed it. "There, satisfied?"

"No, put him back in your van. He's going to mark up the church lawn."

"He's not going to hurt anything, mister," Josh said. "He's been cooped up for a thousand miles."

The man leaned and spat again, and Josh took a step back.

Gray moved through the gate and put Dubose in the van. "Happy now? We did what you asked."

The man stared at Josh. "We don't have any of your kind buried around here."

"He's with me," Gray said. "I wanted to visit some of my family. I'm from out of town."

"You don't think I can read? Arizona. So why don't you both get out of here? Let people rest in peace."

Gray noticed a house across the road. The roof's white shingles had turned black in places. The yard was freshly mowed, and behind the house sat a barn and a fenced pasture.

"You the caretaker?" Gray said.

"I keep an eye on things for the church." He looked at Josh. "There's been vandalism. Broken windows and gravestones toppled."

"Well, we're not here to vandalize. I'm looking for the Hayes plot. I can't remember where they're buried."

The man squinted. "Which Hayes you talking about?"

Gray searched for the words. The question had come too quick and pressured him.

"I can get your pad," Josh said.

"Just give me a name," the man said.

Gray pulled at his ear and closed his eyes tightly.

"All right, get in your van and—"

"Harlon!" Gray said, and the man recoiled. "My daddy was Harlon Hayes." He spelled it. "Does that ring a bell?"

The man rubbed the brown spot on his chin. "His wife was Isabel?"

"You got it," Gray said. "Family called her Izzy."

The man pointed. "They're in the shade, right behind that big oak."

"Much obliged," Gray said, and as he moved back toward the gate, Dubose scratched at the van window. Gray felt bad for him. He'd tasted a bit of freedom after the long drive, and now there he was, cooped up when there was all of creation to sniff.

The man cleared his throat. "Hold up there. What's your name?"

"Grayson. My friends call me Gray."

A nod and the man narrowed his eyes. "That's what I thought. You're that Hayes who writes the books." The man cursed. "I thought it was you. I could tell by the way you look down on everybody."

"What in the world are you talking about?"

"How long's it been, Grayson? You never even seen their grave, have you?"

"That's none of your business, pal."

"You're no pal of mine. After what you did? I wouldn't pee on you if you were on fire."

"Come on, Gray," Josh said.

"Tell me this," the man said to Gray's back. "Was it worth it? What you did to your family? Never figured I'd ever see you again. But here you are."

"This the salt of the earth you were telling me about?" Josh said.

Gray didn't know what he was referring to, but a noise drew him. He turned to find Dubose with his paws on the dash, clawing at the windshield. It wasn't right to keep him in the van when all of God's green earth was here. He walked back through the gate.

The man spat and stepped back, as if expecting Gray to pummel him. Instead, Gray opened the van, and Dubose jumped out and ran for the gate.

"I told you he can't go into the cemetery!"

Gray briskly joined Dubose and Josh, turned to close the gate, and faced the man. "Don't believe gossip. And don't judge a man by his skin tone."

The man shouted something, but Gray didn't understand him and didn't want to. He kept walking among the uneven gravestones, reading names and trying to jog some memory.

Josh caught up to him. "You told me to pay attention to the people around here. What about that guy?"

"He doesn't know any better. Don't judge a bushel by one bad apple."

"I've never had to dig far to find a bad one."

"Now, don't play the victim. It makes you a whiner. Don't give the person who wants to hold you back any more attention than you have to. Spend your energy on better things."

Josh stopped short.

"Find something?" Gray said.

"You ever walk into a department store and immediately say something to the security guard?"

"What's that got to do with the price of tea in China?"

"I do that a lot. I smile and say hello and try to put the guard at ease. Let him or her know I'm not there to steal something."

"Why would you do that?"

"Because if I don't, nine times out of ten they follow me."

"Because you're Black, right? Is that what you want me to believe?"

"I don't want you to believe anything. I'm telling the truth. Driving or shopping or just taking a stroll in a graveyard, I don't get treated the way you do. And you know why."

"That fellow didn't exactly treat me like the king of England. Besides, he wasn't taught any better. He's just trying to take care of the place. Keep out the riffraff like us."

"How would you like it if you got pulled over because you didn't look like you belonged in a certain neighborhood? Or got handcuffed because you said the guy in the van along the road . . ."

"You're saying the police cuffed you for no reason?"

"Never mind," Josh said.

As they neared the oak tree, Gray passed a freshly dug grave with red clay mounded on top. No marker. He lingered and thought how eventually everyone is reduced to a mound of clay.

"Why are we here?" Josh said, hands on his hips. "What are you looking for?"

"This is the destiny of every man, right here. Unless you get cremated and they spread your ashes over their garden. Which is not a bad thought. Maybe when I go I can at least fertilize somebody's strawberries."

"That's awful. Don't let your wife hear you talking like that. And answer the question."

"It's better to go to a house of mourning than a house of feasting. I suppose that's because you learn more from pain than from parties. That's from the Bible."

"I know. Ecclesiastes."

"That's right," Gray said. "Good for you. You want to know why we're here? You can't know the end without a beginning. That's a law in the writing trade. In the end is your beginning, and in the beginning is your end."

"I don't understand."

"To do what I came here to do, I need to see the ones I came from. And if that fellow was right, they're right over there."

A breeze made leaves fall around them. Dubose ran after something skittering along the other side of the fence. The dog had never seen this much color or the kind of soil he ran on, rich and loamy instead of desert grit that grew only cactus and ocotillo.

Josh walked on while Gray rested beside a lichen-covered obelisk that stood like a sentry, taller than him. Gray could make out *1917* and the words *foreign war*. He patted the stone. "Thank you for your service, whoever you were and wherever you died."

He wandered into the shade, where Josh was inspecting tombstones one by one. The view looked out over a picturesque valley.

"Could you take a photo of this with that phone of yours and send it to Lotty?"

"Sure."

"Looks like Eden, doesn't it? And in a week or two, all the leaves will be gone and what looks alive won't be. Seems cruel that things look so good just before everything dies."

Josh snapped a couple of pictures.

"Seems like a waste of pretty scenery to bury people here," Gray said. "You can't see the beauty when you're six feet under."

"The view isn't for them. It's for you."

The stone was a simple square of pink granite with *Hayes* at the top. Underneath were *Harlon H.* and *Isabel "Izzy"* with their birth and death dates. Gray stared, waiting for a feeling he expected would come.

"Can you give me a minute?"

Josh retreated and wandered while Gray paced at the foot of the graves, as if collecting disparate thoughts and trying to put them into words. He began to whisper.

"I know you can't hear me, but I'm going to say it. I'm sorry I wasn't here. And if I could remember why, I don't expect you would understand. I sure didn't understand you two. Why you did what you did or lived the way you did. Or didn't live. Always seemed to me you were scared. I don't know if it was the past coming up behind you or the future looming. It doesn't matter, and I can't fault you. I never spent much time trying to figure out why you were the way you were.

"Mama, I found somebody who seems to love me for who I am. She is a gift. I don't know if I've been that for her. I want to be. But I'm not sure I'm up to loving the way she does. I'm sorry I can't remember your face.

"Daddy, I've worked real hard. That would make you proud, if there was a way to make you proud. I don't do the kind of work you did, but I've never lived a day that I didn't do as much as I could. I don't think you were too happy that I was your son. It always felt like I was your lottery ticket that had all the losing numbers."

Gray stepped to where he thought he was between them now and placed a hand on the cool stone. He ought to feel some stirring of the heart after all the miles he had traveled and all the years he'd been gone.

But the well was dry, and his vision of them in the window or on the porch had faded. He wasn't sure what was real or imagined.

"I've got a disease that you both probably know about. I can't recall if you went through it or had relatives who did. It might be passed down. I can only guess. The things I want to remember I can't, and the things I want to forget won't leave me alone. But nothing's in focus. I'm having dreams that frighten me. And I thought coming back here would be a good idea.

"First I wanted to pay my respects. You both pushed a wheelbarrow of pain and sorrow uphill. I don't remember what was in it, but I know it spilled over on me a time or two. And if I could remember the bad things, I would try to forgive you. And I'd ask you to do the same for me.

"I've done the best I could. But it's never been enough. I'm always trying to climb a little higher to see what's ahead, but every time, something blocks my view."

Dubose pressed his nose against Gray's hand. And for the first time in as long as Gray could remember, the dam inside cracked and allowed something to leak through. He sat with his back against the stone, and the dog crawled onto his lap and put his head between Gray's knees. Gray stroked the dog's back.

Through the sea of stones, Gray saw Josh talking on the phone.

CHAPTER 14

GRAY SAT WRITING IN THE VAN in the cemetery parking lot while Josh found a spigot by the church and gave Dubose a drink. Josh returned with a pained look.

"What's wrong with you?"

"I'm hungry. I don't know where we're going. And I'm exhausted."

"Settle down," Gray said, holding up the yellow pad. "It's all right here. Step by step. We're going to my friend's house, the one I'm giving the tools, and then we're going for the best meal you've ever had."

"And where will we sleep tonight? Is that in the plan?"

"Have a little faith, friend."

Gray tore off a piece of paper from the back of the pad. "Use your phone to get the directions to this man's house. I don't remember all the turns."

The early afternoon sun bore down as they drove into town. A crisp, fresh smell made Gray close his eyes and cup his hand out the window, feeling as if he could almost touch things he had lost so long ago.

"We're really doing this, aren't we?" Gray said.

Josh appeared focused on the directions. When they went over a bridge, Gray said, "There it is, the Sycamore River! Can you smell it? Makes me want to catch some fish. Take the next road on the right. I'd bet my life on it."

"I'm about to pass out from hunger."

"We'll get you something." Gray rubbed his hands together. "And you're going to tell me it was worth the wait."

Josh finally reached a driveway of sparse gravel and mostly dirt and parked behind an old pickup. Gray tried to recall how the house had looked when he was a kid. The aluminum siding looked as if it had been painted recently. The roof sagged over a porch with metal chairs and a swing. The slope of the hill and the contours of the meadow below the house were deeply etched, like lines in the face of the aged.

"I need a bathroom," Josh said.

Gray rolled his eyes. "Just hold it for a minute while I pave the way."

"I need to go."

"If you can't wait, go in the woods." Gray walked to the porch, where the wood lay split and weathered. Would it hold his weight?

A dog ambled toward him from the side of the house, giving a low growl. Gray spoke to it in a gentle tone and knelt. The dog walked gingerly up the steps and sniffed his hand, and with that one act Gray felt a peace seep into his soul and believed everything was going to be okay. Funny how an animal could set his heart at ease. Then Dubose barked from the van.

The screen door hung at an angle and didn't close all the way, so when Gray knocked lightly it clacked, metal on metal.

Footsteps.

Gray had rehearsed this a thousand times, imagining how his friend would react and what he would look like after all these years.

The door opened, and a man with a mustache and gray beard stood before him, his leathery face chiseled with cracks. He was more filled out than the scrawny kid in Gray's faded memory. The eyes were the same, though—truly windows to the soul.

"Pooch," Gray said.

The man pushed the door open and narrowed his eyes, and Gray couldn't tell if there was suspicion or disapproval in them. Then Pooch tilted his head, as if studying a painting that hung crooked. "Grayson?"

Gray smiled and nodded.

"Well, look what the cat dragged in," Pooch said, but he seemed less happy than agitated and shoved his hands in his back pockets. Gray had expected a hug and a pat on the back and laughter and a million questions. Instead, Pooch appeared nervous, glanced behind him, and pulled the inside door shut. "What are you doing here?"

"That's your question? You're not glad to see me after all these years?"

"Glad? You'll have to settle for surprised." Pooch looked past him to the road. "You still have that old thing?"

"Got me here. Point A to point B."

Pooch nodded but fell short of a smile. He reached for the doorknob. "I need to get back inside."

"You look like your daddy, you know that?" Gray said.

The curtain fluttered at the front window.

"We both do." Pooch said it like an accusation. "You take care of yourself, Grayson."

"Hold up now. I've got somebody traveling with me who needs to use the facilities, if that's all right." Gray waved at Josh, who got out and approached the house.

"Where'd you find him?" Pooch said.

"Just a friend. Name's Josh."

"How far have you come?"

"From near Tucson."

"Thought you were in Colorado."

"No, Lotty and I live in the desert now. Better for my health."

The door opened behind Pooch, and a tiny woman with red hair and freckles appeared, drying her hands on a dish towel. At first glance she looked like a teenager—somebody Gray should remember. She glanced at Josh, then glared at Gray as if a lit fuse were nearing a crate of dynamite. "You've got a lot of nerve coming back here."

"Can't a man come back to his hometown to see a friend or two?"

"You remember Annie Slade, don't you?" Pooch said, as though the name had special meaning. It didn't, but Gray smiled anyway and extended a hand. "Yeah, sure. Good to see you, Annie."

She went rigid, as if she'd turned to stone. Gray pulled back and found his ear. "You two married?"

"Pooch," Annie said, "can I talk to you?"

The two retreated and closed the door, and Gray heard them arguing but couldn't decipher what they said. "I must have miscalculated, Josh. I wasn't expecting a red carpet, but . . ."

"Maybe it's not a good time. I really need to go, Gray."

Gray pointed at a rise in the land by the house. "Mr. Parsons used to have an outhouse. Or go around the house in those weeds."

Josh started down the stairs just as Pooch stepped out. "Bathroom's the last door on the right," he called out. "Down the hall."

Josh jogged back up and disappeared inside, and Pooch shut the door. He stood leaning against the house with his arms crossed.

"Your wife doesn't like me."

"Can you blame her?"

"Well, I don't have any idea what I did wrong. Did we park too close to your truck?"

Pooch gave him a funny look, as if to say, *Are you kidding me?* "What *are* you doing back here, Gray?"

"I came to ask you a favor. You were a friend to me. And I wrote down that we had a bargain."

Pooch shook his head. "You're something, you know that? You come back here and expect everybody to pretend?"

"Look, I just need you to hear me out on a couple of things. I'm taking Josh to Happy's because he's starving and I've got a hankering for catfish. Would you come with us?"

Josh stepped back out. "Thank you, sir."

Pooch introduced himself and reached to shake hands. "How did you get hooked up with this fellow?"

"Kind of a long story," Josh said. "He was dead set on coming back here. I volunteered."

"So Grayson is Miss Daisy. That's rich. You've seen that movie, haven't you, Gray?"

"Maybe," Gray said. "I can't recall a lot of things anymore."

"And why did he want to come back, Josh?"

"Come on," Gray said. "We'll leave you alone."

"No, let him answer. What did he tell you about coming back here?"

"Said there was somebody he trusted who could help him. Somebody he needed to see."

"You can pick up a phone a lot easier."

"I agree," Josh said. "And so does my backside after driving all this way. But he said some things you have to do face-to-face. Mentioned a friend who had made some agreement, and he was going to ask him to keep his side of it."

"Is that so, Gray?" Pooch said. "What favor?"

Gray suddenly felt untethered and pulled at his ear again. Something in the recesses of his mind he couldn't reach, like a dandelion in the wind. He clenched his fists, and his eyes darted.

"Be right back," Gray said.

He loped toward the van and could hear Pooch asking Josh questions. He found his legal pad. The sights and sounds of the area had stirred things, and he needed clear thinking now more than ever. He flipped through the pages, and when he looked up, Pooch and Josh were next to him, and the redheaded woman stood on the porch with her arms crossed.

"Sorry," Gray said, closing the pad. "I want to buy you dinner. Is Happy's still in business? My treat."

Pooch and Josh looked at each other as if they'd been swapping secrets. The woman on the porch said something, then darted back inside. Pooch turned to Josh. "Follow me."

Late in the afternoon they reached Happy's Catfish & Chips at the edge of town, next to the Sycamore River. As soon as Gray saw the yellow sign, he let out a whoop. Happy Sullivan had passed the place to his brother and moved to Florida. His brother didn't have the heart to change the name, and eventually his children made the same decision.

Gray recognized the exterior, like a ghost of dinners past. It had undergone repairs and an addition but maintained its shacklike appearance. Several rocking chairs and a swing sat on the wooden porch.

Josh fed Dubose and walked him while Gray and Pooch headed inside. For Gray, this was like stepping back in time. The aroma of breaded fish and shrimp made him smile and pat his stomach. Along the walls, instead of booths, sat picnic tables with plastic tablecloths checkered red and white. In the center of the dining room, heavy wooden chairs stood by heavy wooden tables. Each table carried an abundance of malt vinegar, ketchup, cocktail sauce, and tartar sauce. A counter at the front stretched before revolving stools.

Gray ordered catfish for Josh and himself and told Pooch, "This is on me. Two things I need to talk with you about. I need your help."

Pooch sat back and crossed his arms.

"First, a girl has come to me."

Pooch frowned. "A girl?"

"Well, a grown woman. She comes in my dreams."

"I don't interpret dreams, Grayson."

"She walks out on this little bridge. It looks familiar, like it's around here somewhere. I'm in the water looking up at her, and there's somebody behind her. She's struggling, but he's too strong for her. It's the strangest thing, and I'm nervous to tell you this, afraid you'll think I'm touched in the head."

"I've always known you were touched in the head, Grayson. Go on."

"This dream keeps happening. That's how I know there's something to it. And it keeps getting clearer." He put a finger to the page in his legal pad. "I wrote down the last one. She was wearing a wedding dress."

Pooch leaned forward. "On the nights you have this dream, do you recall what you had for dinner?"

"This is not about too much pepperoni. It's real. I can feel it. This mystery girl—woman—is calling out to me. Maybe she has a family and they don't know what happened to her."

"And you're the one who has to find her. Is that it?"

"Somebody is looking for her. The people who care about her need to know."

"Why do you think she came to *you* in your dream?"

"Maybe because I'm open to her now. In the past, I would have thought this was crazy and just dismissed it. Now I'm ready to listen. I need to find out who she is."

Josh appeared and apparently didn't notice they were deep in conversation.

"Pooch isn't your real name, is it?" Josh said.

"No, it's Howard. But it's one of those things that sticks when you're little. I must have looked like a basset hound as a kid."

Their food came in red plastic baskets, and Josh dove in.

"Slow down," Pooch said. "You'll inhale a bone."

"He eats like he knows what he's doing," Gray said.

Gray ate the slaw and catfish together and let the hot and cold and spicy mingle on his palate. "It's like I'm ten years old again and sitting here with . . . whoever I used to sit with. Didn't they have a jukebox?"

"I don't recall that. Maybe you're thinking of another place."

"'These Boots Are Made for Walkin.' Remember that one?"

"Sure do," Pooch said. "Nancy Sinatra."

Gray wiggled in his seat, dancing to the tune in his head. He asked Josh about Dubose.

"He had a good walk. I think he was tired from all the running at the cemetery."

"Which?" Pooch said.

"Mount Olive," Gray said. "Needed to pay my respects."

Pooch's eyes glazed. "Better late than never, right?"

Josh looked up from his food but stayed quiet.

"That's one thing I never understood, Grayson. Why wouldn't you at least come back for their funerals? Seemed like the least you could do."

Gray glanced out the window at the beauty of the trees and the verdant hillside that would soon move toward winter and dormancy. Life to death and back again. The never-ending cycle. And he was part of it.

"Don't know that I have a good answer for you."

"Because you don't remember or you don't want to?"

Gray shrugged.

"I know your daddy was mean to you. But why not come and see your mother before she died? Why not be here for her? How in the world could you leave all the details of the house and the property—"

"I told you I don't have a good answer." Gray put down his fork. "It doesn't mean there's not a reason. It means I can't think of it right now."

Pooch wiped his hands and mouth, his face grim. "Did you drive by and see Sam before you came to my place?"

It felt as if Gray's heart stopped beating.

At the awkward silence, Josh said, "Who's Sam?"

"Grayson's little brother."

Josh put down his catfish. "You have a brother here?"

"Don't look at me that way. Of course I do."

"I asked if you had family in the area. Don't you think your brother counts?"

"I didn't recall he still lived here." Gray looked to Pooch. "Did he sell the house?"

"He sold some of the property. I think he rents out the house. Last time I spoke to him was at your mother's funeral. He bought a little land outside of town and took his time building where he lives now."

Gray pushed the basket away and turned the page on his legal pad, leaving a grease mark. He wondered if he had written anything that might help him.

"You going to see him?" Josh said.

"Of course," Gray said defensively. "If it works out." Gray's eyes wandered. "But Pooch is the one I came to see."

Pooch's face contorted. "Is it that easy? Just push somebody out of your mind and never think of them again? That how you become successful?"

"I don't have to push anything anymore." He pointed to his head. "I got a leak in the pipes, and there's no plugging the hole."

"What are you saying?"

Josh said, "Alzheimer's."

Pooch looked stricken. "I had no idea."

"I don't feel any different," Gray said. "It's not like having the gout or pneumonia. I just can't remember things. And they say it's going to get worse."

Pooch's look changed. "I'm sorry, Grayson. I truly am. This changes things."

"It's changing a lot of things," Gray said.

"Must be hard on your wife."

"Lotty's got things under control. She keeps things straight." Gray waved the server over. "What's the best dessert on the menu?"

"People come for the fish, but they stay for the cheesecake."

Gray snapped his fingers. "With the cherries on top?"

"You bet."

"Set Josh here up with the biggest piece you got. He'll eat it at the counter."

"Why?" Josh said.

"I need to talk with my friend alone, if you don't mind. And if you do mind, you can eat your dessert with Dubose." Gray said it with a smile.

CHAPTER 15

GRAY SCANNED A NOTE IN HIS LEGAL PAD, knowing he had to carefully explain this to his friend.

"So you came back because of this memory thing?" Pooch said.

"I did. But I didn't mean to cause trouble between you and your wife. I'm sorry about that."

"You don't remember her, do you?"

"Should I?"

Pooch sighed. "Just keep going."

Gray wiped his fingers on a napkin and flipped a page. "Let me tell you about this woman who comes to me on a bridge over a river."

"The one in the dream, with the wedding dress."

Gray's heart fluttered. "You've had it too?"

"Grayson, you told me about her five minutes ago."

"Right." Gray blinked hard and regained composure by scanning the page. "You know anybody who's gone missing? Maybe somebody who died under mysterious circumstances? I had Lotty look online."

Pooch shifted on the bench. "More than a few have gotten hooked on drugs or been sent away. That's been a scourge of late."

Gray wrote, *Drugs. Scourge.*

"There was something else on your mind, though. Besides the woman on the bridge, right?"

Gray wiped crumbs from the table. "Yessir. So, you know my diagnosis. The doctor says even though I feel fine, things are going to accelerate. I don't mind losing my memory. He says I won't feel much of anything. I'll just be in my own little world."

"Oblivious."

"But I've done some reading about what's to come for Lotty. I'm not going to put her through this. I see it in her eyes. She sobs at night and thinks I don't hear her. Shakes the bed."

"To be expected, don't you think? Grieving ahead of time."

Gray found a page he had dog-eared. "She shouldn't have to go through that. So I've come up with a plan, but I need your help—need you to promise me something."

"I'll do whatever I can, Grayson."

Gray leaned forward and lowered his voice. "Promise that when things get bad, you'll take my life."

Pooch's face slowly changed as he squinted at Grayson. He dropped a hush puppy back into the basket.

"I can't do this myself," Gray said. "It wouldn't be right. I need you to—"

"Grayson, you're talking silly."

"It's not silly at all. It makes perfect sense."

"If you're trying to get me locked up."

"You're too smart for that."

"And you're dumber than a stump if you think for a minute I'm going to kill you."

Gray glanced around. "Keep your voice down."

"You're not thinking clear."

"I'm thinking as clear as I've ever thought. Now pipe down."

"I'm not going to be part of it. I won't try to make your pain go away by—"

"It's not my pain—I just told you that. Lotty will suffer. And I can't have that. She's the one I'm asking you to help me care for."

"Yeah, and I'll just bet she would think this is a great idea, wouldn't she?"

Gray pulled his ear. "You need to listen and stop interrupting."

"Have you talked with her about this?"

"Of course not."

"You know she'd say this is the last thing she'd want. This would bring her more pain than you could ever imagine."

Gray saw Josh had turned toward them, an untouched slice of cheesecake on the counter behind him.

"Focus," Pooch said. "You want to keep your wife from suffering, drive that rusty old van into the river."

Gray shook his head. "I'd be going against God's ways."

Pooch rolled his eyes. "And it's okay for me? I'm beginning to think you don't have Alzheimer's, you're just plain crazy." Pooch was red in the face and appeared to be trying not to be too loud.

"I'm not crazy," Gray said, pecking at the table with a finger. "If the shoe was on the other foot, I would surely do this for you."

"Hold on. Hit rewind for me. Since when have you ever cared about God's ways?"

"Lotty and I both found the Lord. Or, he found us. I've been asking him to provide for her. Nothing has turned out like I planned. I don't have a retirement fund or inheritance. This would give me peace of mind, knowing she'll get the insurance."

Pooch sat back and ran his tongue along his teeth. "All right," he said, sounding more in control. "You're scared. I get that. You love your wife. I get that, too. But this is not the way."

"Why not?"

"A million reasons. First, you know what they'd do to me?"

"Who?"

"Whoever figures it out, and you know somebody would."

"There's ways of doing it so nobody will ever know. I just don't want Lotty to go through this pain."

Pooch cursed and pointed straight at Gray. "A few people around here would pin a medal on me if I did this. You ought to ask them to do it. They'd jump at the chance."

"I don't want some ne'er-do-well. I want a friend. I know you can do this. I trust you. I wrote down in here the promise we made each other."

"What are you talking about? We never promised to kill each other. That's one of your stories, your brain playing tricks on you. Like this girl on the bridge."

"It's a woman."

"I don't care if she's a polar bear. It's a dream, for crying out loud."

"The dream pointed me back here, Pooch. And there's another thing." He gave a dramatic pause. "I want you to have the van and the tools."

"That's your payment? An old VW and some rusty tools? Will you throw in the dog and a bag of food for him? In the movies, people get thousands for a hit."

"It's not a hit. It's what a true friend does."

"You have a strange definition of friendship, Grayson. I don't want your tools. I don't want your van. I don't want the guilt, either. Imagine they *don't* catch me. I spend the rest of my life thinking about what I did?"

"You'll be grateful that you helped—"

"Can I get you gentlemen some dessert?" the server said, startling Gray. "I'm sorry, hon," she added, gathering up the baskets.

"We're good," Pooch said.

"Hang on," Gray said. "How about a couple of pieces of cheesecake like you served our friend?"

"Might as well bring two coffees, too," Pooch said, then lowered his voice. "Not that I can eat or drink after what I just heard."

When the desserts arrived, Gray grinned. "Lotty doesn't let me eat sugar or any of this fried stuff. But this is a celebration, the end of a long journey. And you're going to help me, aren't you?"

"Not this way."

"You're the only one I can count on."

Pooch put his elbows on the table. "You know I could say yes, tell you I'll come up with a plan, and then let it go. You'd never know the difference. You'll forget we even had this conversation."

"More than likely. But you'll remember it the rest of your life."

"I don't doubt it."

Gray knew, right then, he had the man. He was mulling over the plan and its ramifications. They were negotiating.

"That's why I write things on my pad. Helps me keep things straight."

"And then somebody finds my name in there and I live out my days in a penitentiary. You're not thinking of me; you're thinking only of you."

"I'm thinking of Lotty, of not putting her through this."

"Grayson, you have to face the fact that some things are out of your control. You have to play the cards you're dealt. And you can't play other people's cards for them. That's what you're asking me to do to get your life to come out the way you've planned it. But in the real world, it's going to be worse for your wife and for me."

"Not if you put your mind to it. You can make it painless for me and easier on her."

"Am I the first you've asked?"

"You can't trust something like this with just anybody. Listen, nobody is going to find this notebook. I'm taking care of that. And you're right that you could lie to me and I would never know. But you would know. You'd know you could have helped. And when they lock me away and I'm drooling down my chin, you'll think, *I should have helped him.* But I don't think you're the kind of man who plugs his ears to the cry of a desperate heart."

"But I'm the kind of man who would murder an old friend?"

"It's not murder."

"Tell that to the judge. Oh, wait, you'll be dead. My defense will be, 'Your honor, I just wanted to show him I cared.'"

"You'll figure a way where I won't feel a thing. You and me took an oath—said we'd be there for each other."

"I have no recollection of that. Show me the papers I signed."

"It was an understanding, a verbal agreement."

"And how can you remember that?"

Gray shrugged. "Some things can't be scrubbed from the bottom of the pan. It would bring me peace of mind to hear you say you're on board."

"Would it really?"

Gray nodded.

"Then hear me loud and clear. Ready?"

"Go on."

"I'll help you. But not the way you want. I'll help your wife take care of you when you can't remember anything and things get hard."

"That's an empty promise, and you know it."

"I'll find a way."

"No, I can't have a slow death in my own house, sleeping next to a stranger." Gray studied his cheesecake, picking at the crust with a fork. "Don't make me do this myself."

"Grayson, why won't you let the people who care about you love you?"

"Lotty is dying inside. I see it in her eyes. And it's my fault. I can't put her through more of this."

"So put the shoe on the other foot. Is this what you would want her to do?"

"It's not the same."

"You think you're protecting her and providing for her with your insurance."

"Bingo."

"What you're really doing is stealing the chance for her to do something good, to show love to you and care for you. Why won't you just accept that?"

Gray put down his fork and clenched his teeth. "I came back here because of you. And you accuse me of being a thief."

Pooch's face softened. "I'm talking straight to you, Grayson. You wouldn't want it any other way."

"So you won't even think about it?"

"I told you. I'll do everything I can, but not what you're asking."

Gray pulled at his ear and pushed his plate away, lowering his voice again. "I shouldn't have sprung this on you. I should have warned you; I see that now. So I apologize. But let's say a month from now, a year from now—I don't know how long—you take me hunting or fishing. We're walking along some mountain trail, and I slip and fall. It doesn't have to be—"

"Stop it, Grayson."

"You have to decide, Pooch."

"I'm sorry you're having a tough time understanding me, Grayson. But I've already decided. I get it that you don't want to be a burden."

"Now you're getting it."

"But life is sacred. Surely you believe that. You're playing God."

"Showing love is not playing God."

"Showing love to us is exactly what God does. And I'm no preacher, but from what I hear, what he asks of us is to receive it. So why won't you let the people who love you give it to you? Love is not just something you give. It's also something you receive."

"And I want you to care enough to let me receive what I'm asking you for."

"This is like Abbott and Costello," Pooch said. "We always get back to third base."

"Third base?"

"What if you could reduce your wife's pain by moving in with somebody when things get bad?"

"I won't go to a facility and wander the halls. I've told you the only way to fix this."

"What if you lived with Annie and me?"

Gray blew air through his lips. "Your wife would divorce you on the spot."

Pooch scratched the back of his head. "Have you considered that maybe the reason you came all the way back here was not to ask this of me, but because you need to see somebody else?"

"Who?"

"Your brother."

Gray searched Pooch's eyes, and his voice caught. "You think he'd do it for me?"

Pooch closed his eyes and sighed. "No, but maybe he's the answer to all of this."

Gray pulled his ear and raked his arm across the table, coffee and cheesecake crashing to the floor.

"Goodness," the server said. "What happened?"

A heavy man in shirt and tie rushed out of the kitchen, wiping his hands on a dish towel. His eyes locked on Gray as if he were a jury foreman ready to read the guilty verdict. "Mister, you're going to pay for the damages."

Gray stood and turned to Josh. "You coming or not?"

CHAPTER 16

GRAY INSISTED ON DRIVING. Belly full of catfish, his head spun like the gravel beneath his tires as he sped away.

"What was that all about?" Josh said.

"I overestimated our friendship."

"You didn't pay," Josh said. "You said dinner was on you."

Gray took his foot off the accelerator, then sped up again, waving and mumbling. The sun had set, and a soft glow spread across the graying sky. Twenty minutes later, he pulled to the side of the road, dust pluming, and craned his neck. "I could have sworn the Sycamore Inn was right around here. There was a grocery store next to it. And there were railroad tracks."

Josh pulled out his phone. "I don't see anything by that name. The closest hotel is back up the interstate maybe twenty miles."

"A grocery and a gas station," Gray said absently. "We rode our bikes there as kids. Bottle of Nehi Grape and candy—Mallo Cups and Zagnut bars." He pursed his lips and let the memory of marshmallow and chocolate linger, then pulled back onto the road and drove through the fading light and trees even more colorful in the gloaming. Cool air blew through the van.

Josh pointed to a clearing. "Railroad tracks."

The road rose and crossed the rail bed, and Gray banged on the steering wheel. "There it is!"

He pulled into the grocery store parking lot, empty except for a few cars close to the building. "Stay here, Dubose," Gray said as he and Josh got out. At the edge of the lot, the ravine behind it led to the creek that ran brown and muddy, one of the many tributaries of the Sycamore. The brush and autumn olive shrubs were so thick he couldn't see much, but he spotted black shingles and cinder blocks, the detritus of a childhood landmark.

"They tore it down, Grayson," someone said behind him. He turned as Pooch wandered toward them. They stood shoulder to shoulder. "They auctioned off all the beds and furniture still in one piece. Wasn't much. Old TVs. Wobbly nightstands on spindly legs. Lamps from the 1950s. The place was falling apart and infested. They bulldozed the rest. Repaved the lot and shoved everything into the ravine. That was a long time ago."

Gray couldn't take his eyes off the rubble and tangled roots of shrubs and thistle. It felt like looking down at his own life, and he wondered if he could dig far enough to find anything of value. On the edge of something he would never retrieve, he couldn't remember what it was.

A train whistle blew. Then a police car pulled into the lot and parked askew behind the van.

"That restaurant manager called the police," Pooch said. "I'll talk with him."

"You'll do no such thing. I can handle my own problems."

"Gray," Josh said in a pleading tone.

"Stop calling me that," Gray said. "Show some respect for your elders."

Gray walked to the cruiser, Pooch following. "Evening, officer."

The man got out warily, as if gauging the threat and trying to exude superiority. His jaw jutted as if he might have had a few extra molars. "Got a call about some damage up at Happy's. Know anything about that, sir?"

"I can explain it," Pooch said.

"Shut up, Howard. He's talking to me. Right, officer?"

"Yes, sir. What happened?"

"It was a misunderstanding. No need to make a federal case out of it."

"There was some damage."

"I told the manager I'd take care of that," Pooch said.

"Would you stop it, Pooch? I'm not some child you need to diaper."

The officer asked for ID, and Gray gave him what he had. The officer studied the card and glanced up at Pooch and Josh.

"Now I've got a question for you, lawman. Are you working any missing person cases? Females? Drowning victims, that kind of thing?"

"Why do you ask?"

"That's why I'm here. Either somebody's in trouble or somebody's guilty."

"Sir, I hope you're not driving without a license."

"So you're not going to answer my question? You got something to hide?"

The officer handed the card back to Gray and said to Pooch, "Keep a tighter rein on him, will you?"

When the cruiser pulled out, Gray said, "That's a sign, Josh. I'm onto something."

"Grayson," Pooch said, "why don't you get in my truck? Josh can follow us back to my house. You can get cleaned up and get some rest. We can go down to the Sycamore and fish. It'll be like old times."

"You've already told me you don't want to help. So you can leave. I'll figure this out on my own."

"Grayson, come on," Pooch said. "You've got no place to stay tonight."

"There's a hotel down the road. Go tell your wife she doesn't have to deal with me anymore."

Pooch shoved his hands into his back pockets and sighed, his cheeks puffing. "What are you going to do with your dog?"

"That's no business of yours."

"Let me take him. The hotel won't allow pets. He'll have plenty to do with my dog. You can leave him as long as you need."

"That's a good idea," Josh said. "You don't want him in the van overnight."

Gray chewed the inside of his cheek. "All right, fine."

At the hotel, while Josh showered, Gray wrote everything he could recall from talking with Pooch. When Josh came out, Gray went in and let the water cascade over him. Something about water always seemed to clear his head and give him a new lease on life. He stayed there a good twenty minutes, then put on his boxers and took his legal pad back into where Josh was watching TV with the sound low. Josh looked embarrassed, then held out his phone. "It's your wife."

Lotty's voice cheered him. He imagined her smile and that long black hair she was allowing to turn gray. She had never wanted her hair colored.

"Tell me about your day," she said.

He looked at his pad and chose his words carefully, turning away so Josh couldn't hear. "Lotty, you would not have approved, but I tell you what, as I ate catfish at Happy's, all these memories came back like lightning. You know the little flowers you see at the side of the road when you're passing and you just catch them out of the corner of your eye because you're going so fast? That's what it was like."

"I'm glad, Gray. And you enjoyed your time with your friend?"

"Pooch is Pooch, you know. He hasn't changed a lot. We're different, the two of us. I don't think I recalled how different. But it was good to see him."

"And he's taking care of Dubose?"

"He's got the room. It'll be like a vacation for old Dubose."

"I'm relieved you made it. And the van did too."

"Running like a top. I don't know why it wouldn't start, and now it won't stop."

She paused, and something prickled on the back of Gray's neck. Her silence could do that to him, but he didn't know it could happen from this distance. And he felt an awe at the power of her love, if that was what it was.

"Gray, I want to ask you to do something for me. Write this down."

"Anything for a pretty thing like you, Lotty. Say the words."

"I want you to be kind to Josh."

"Who says I haven't been?"

"Nobody. I just know how you can get."

"That sounds like an accusation."

"Would you write that for me? Now?"

"Hang on." He wrote, *Be kind to Josh.* On the bed next to him, Josh flipped through channels and stretched.

"All right, I put it down. Anything else? Old sleepyhead is yawning, and I need to be kind and let him get his beauty rest."

A pause. "I love you, Gray."

He let the words hang between them and smiled. "And I believe you, sweetheart."

That was a perennial line that always lightened her mood, no matter what. She laughed. Gray knew he was obligated to say, "I love you, too." Instead, he absorbed the words and had made her laugh, and how he loved to hear Lotty laugh.

Later Gray flipped through his legal pad and trailed the words with a finger, the flicker of the TV illumining the page. "So I haven't asked you about yourself. Is that right?"

"What?" Josh jolted on the bed, his eyes wide, and then calmed. "No, you're fine, Mr. Hayes. You don't need to ask anything."

"Why so formal? Call me Gray."

Josh sighed. "All right, Gray."

"So humor me. Before you drift off to la-la land, tell me something about yourself."

"Grew up in Ohio. Just outside of Cleveland."

"Aha, so you cheered for the Browns and the Indians?"

"I tried. It was a challenge."

Gray chuckled. "Did your daddy take you to games?"

Josh turned the TV off, and they were left in the dim light of one bedside lamp. "That's a sore subject. My father wasn't around. I'll put it that way."

"Mm-hmm. Well, mine was, and I wish he hadn't been. So we've both got a sore subject there, don't we?" Gray closed the pad. "Tell me how you're doing this. Spending time on the road. You taking vacation time?"

"Personal time. Same thing."

"What do you do?"

"IT."

"It," Gray said, trying to figure it out.

"Websites. Computers. Online stuff."

"You're one of those, then."

"One of those what?"

"People enslaving us. Kids with bent necks staring at their little screens. Grownups who don't talk to each other."

"That's a good one, Gray. A Black man enslaving people. You like to put people in boxes, don't you? I tell you I work with computers and you make me an evil person because technology scares you."

"And you put me in the old-guy-who's-scared-of-computers box. How is that any different?"

Josh bit his cheek. "Actually, I see the danger probably more than you, if you want the truth. I'm not going to let my kids get hooked like that."

"Well, all right. Something we agree on. So, you have children?"

"A little girl." He hesitated. "And a boy on the way."

"Well, congratulations. That's a fine thing, starting a family." Gray put his tongue out the side of his mouth. "You know, Lotty and I, we never had kids. That's been a painful thing for her. For both of us, but for her especially."

Josh nodded.

"So you're going to have one of each. You're all set. Your wife happy about the new one?"

Josh stared at the ceiling, then draped his arm over his face.

The room phone rang, and Gray nearly jumped off the bed. He picked up and heard only silence, then a dial tone. He shrugged. "Probably a wrong number."

Josh stood and walked toward the door. "I'm thirsty. Going to the lobby. You want anything?"

"Did I say something wrong? Something that upset you?"

"No, just thirsty."

When Gray awoke, the bed next to him was empty. He called for Dubose. He had his legal pad open when a man came in and handed him a cup of coffee. Black, just as he liked it, but who was this guy?

"Time to get up, Gray," the man said. "Pooch has something he wants to show you."

Gray stood and moved to the desk by the TV. "I need a few minutes to collect myself, if you don't mind."

"Not a problem. Pooch said not to eat the stale donuts and lukewarm oatmeal here. We'll eat at his house."

"Where's Dubose?"

"He stayed at Pooch's, remember?"

"Yeah, that's right." Gray sat and flipped through the legal pad. Josh! On the hillside out the window, gray skies leaked a soft October rain that wet the earth, and a gentle breeze stirred stubborn leaves that still clung to life. He slowly realized where he was. Pooch was his friend. He was going to get some help.

When Gray had dressed, Josh gave him his medication and they headed out. The wet morning air was so crisp it nearly took Gray's breath away, and he put his hand up to block the sprinkles. He breathed a little deeper and was right back in his childhood. This was sleeping weather.

Josh cursed, bringing Gray out of his reverie. All four van tires sat flat on the pavement, rips in their sidewalls. As if that weren't enough, spray-painted on the driver's side was *Merderer*. On the other side it said, *Go home*.

Gray scanned the lot. "Why would vandals pick my van and leave everybody else alone?"

"This isn't random," Josh said. "We should call the police."

"No, that's only going to slow us down. Find out where the closest tire place is."

Josh had his phone out taking pictures. He found a place less than a mile away. "You have towing on your insurance, Gray?"

"Lotty handles that. Ask her." Gray shook his head at the van. "The world's been going to hell all my life, but it feels like we're rolling downhill. This is the last place you'd expect this kind of foolishness."

CHAPTER 17

GRAY AND JOSH WERE WAITING for the tow truck when Pooch arrived. The rain had subsided, and a fog hung over the area as Pooch walked around the van, shaking his head. "That's a real shame, Grayson. After all the work you put into this."

"I'm just glad they didn't steal the tools. Who do you think would do a thing like this?"

The man studied the writing. "Probably not a Chevy owner with a vendetta against VWs. Grayson, this was a message."

"Nobody but you knows I'm here."

Josh reached out his phone. "Apparently this is going around on social media." Gray watched a video someone had taken at Happy's. At first, Gray didn't recognize himself. After the plates and mugs went flying, the camera followed him out with Josh behind him. The video ended with the red license plate on the van.

The post read, "Evidently Grayson Hayes didn't care for his meal . . ."

"You think the person who shot this slashed my tires?"

"I doubt it," Josh said. "This lady knows how to spell a lot better than whoever used the spray paint. But somebody saw it and tracked you down. Remember last night you had a call and somebody hung up."

Gray hadn't remembered.

Pooch sighed. "Josh, you want to stay with the van and I'll take Grayson to the house?"

"I'm staying with it," Gray said. "You take Josh and get him something to eat."

Josh paused. "I'll come when it's fixed. You go on, Gray."

Gray argued more, then got in Pooch's truck but couldn't get his belt buckled. Pooch helped him.

"We didn't wear these as kids, did we?"

"I rode in my daddy's Chevelle standing up," Pooch said.

Pooch tuned the radio to a country station, and the morning sunlight finally peeked through and spread over the valley on either side of the interstate. "You came at the best time of the year."

"Looks like Eden, doesn't it?"

"But you knew the risk coming back, right?"

"What risk?"

"Not everybody has a high opinion of you, Grayson. I thought that's why you stayed away all these years."

"I stayed away because . . . I'm not really sure. Some author said you can't go home again. Tom somebody. And Jesus talked about not being welcome in his hometown. Maybe I'm in good company."

"You think you're a prophet?"

Gray clutched his legal pad. "I'm just looking for answers and maybe a friend who will help me."

They passed a billboard for a gentlemen's club, and Gray shook his head. "This is not the innocent little town I grew up in."

"I don't think it ever was."

When Pooch took the exit, Gray turned to him. "You were the one I was yelling at in that video. What were we arguing about?"

"Just a disagreement that got out of hand."

"Did you pay for the damage?"

"I'll work it out with the manager. Don't worry."

Another sign at the end of the exit showed a scantily clad woman and pointed to a road behind a gas station and a building set apart from the neighborhood.

"Did I tell you about the dream I've been having?"

"The woman on the bridge? You did."

"You think whoever's guilty might have done that to my van?"

"Guilty of what?"

"Of killing the girl, the one who's asking for help. If somebody here did something to her, they don't want me finding out."

"I don't know about that. But there are people here who wouldn't mind getting even with you."

"And who would that be?"

"You remember Alvin Slade?"

"Doesn't ring a bell. What's he got against me?"

"Nothing now. Alvin is dead. We'll talk more later. Let's get you fed, and then I want to show you something."

When they pulled up to the house, Dubose ran with Pooch's dog to the truck and looked happy and well fed. When Gray got out, Dubose jumped on him with muddy paws, then scampered back to the barn.

"Looks happy as a coon in a cornfield, doesn't he?" Gray said, wiping off his clothes.

Pooch opened the front door. "You met Annie yesterday."

"Hello there, Annie," Gray said, extending a hand.

She looked at Pooch as if the two of them had conferred about how all this needed to go. She shook Gray's hand limply, as if she would have rather skinned a live copperhead.

"Something sure smells good," Gray said.

"Annie's got a full spread for you, Grayson. Go on into the kitchen."

Gray wandered through the living room with its hardwood floors and an occasional rag rug. Built-in shelves along one wall bore glassware, family pictures, and porcelain figurines. On the top shelf sat an old family Bible thicker than three phone books. Gray sauntered into the kitchen.

"Wish you'd have stayed with us last night," Pooch said. "You could've avoided the trouble with your van."

Annie spoke in a gravelly voice. "People have a way of gaining their revenge."

Gray sat in one of the mismatched chairs. On the stove lay a cast-iron skillet like one he remembered from his childhood that weighed enough to hold down a house in a tornado. Annie removed from the oven a plate covered with aluminum foil and set it in front of Gray.

Gray removed the foil, and steam rose from a plate so full he could barely see the pattern around the edges. He wondered if this was their good wedding china. Eggs with diced onions and hash browns and several sausage links covered every inch, plus a biscuit the size of a box turtle with sausage gravy on top so thick it hung on the sides and didn't mix with the rest of the food.

Annie produced a mug in the shape of a barrel. "Can you have coffee? In your condition?"

"If I can't, don't tell me. Pour away."

She moved effortlessly, as if she might have been a dancer when she was younger. But she didn't look at him, and her voice sounded pained, as if she were being forced to do something against her will. Had she and Pooch fought about his eating with them?

Gray took a bite of the biscuit and closed his eyes in pleasure. He poured Heinz ketchup on his hash browns. Then he slowly salted and peppered his food, figuring he wouldn't have to talk if he was concentrating on such things.

"Who was that fellow with you yesterday?" Annie said. "Your chauffer?"

Gray laughed. "That's funny. No, he's a friend of Lotty and my doctor. Volunteered to drive."

Annie glanced at Pooch, and something passed between them.

Pooch pushed a glass jar toward him. "Try a little homemade apple butter on the edge of your biscuit there. You've never tasted anything better."

Gray put a dollop on the biscuit and took a bite. He thought Pooch was right.

"My grandmother used to make it like this," Gray said. "So thick you could stand a wooden spoon in the jar."

Annie stood over the sink with her back to him and stiffened. She wiped her hands and turned. Something in her eyes had changed. "How can you remember apple butter and not know who I am?"

Pooch appeared to study the linoleum.

"I have what they call Alzheimer's. At least, that's what the doctor says. I don't feel it myself—"

"I know what you have. Howard told me."

"Annie, please," Pooch said.

"Aw, keep your *please* to yourself. I swear this makes no sense at all."

"That's exactly what it is," Pooch said. "The senses. Some things come back; some don't. You can't control it; it just is."

Annie bit her lip and turned back to the sink.

"That happened with my own mother," Pooch continued. "I've told you this, Annie. You know what she went through when she was little. She and her family knew real hunger, experienced it firsthand. But she said her mama could do magic with cow butter and cornmeal. And every time she made cornbread through the years, Mama would get this far-off look, staring out the window by the stove. She went through something in her later years that's a lot like what you're going through, Grayson, as well as your daddy. And toward the end, my mother sat bolt upright in bed and yelled at the top of her lungs, 'Save some of that cornbread for me, Mama!'"

Pooch laughed and shook his head. "All I need is a little taste of cornbread and it comes back. The good and the bad. I can only imagine what was going through her mind as she stared out that window."

Annie put the skillet in the drying rack. Her voice was thin. "I just find it hard to believe he can remember something like apple butter and not what he did to my family."

"Annie, you promised."

"Promised what?" Gray said.

"It's all right, Grayson," Pooch said. "This is not about you. This is—"

"It is too about him!"

Pooch took Annie by the elbow, but she wrenched away. "Don't touch me!"

"Let her talk," Gray said. "Tell me what I did to your family, Annie."

"What good would it do?" she yelled, her face red and a vein sticking out on her forehead. "You'd just forget it and be right back to the apple butter. And Howard would be trying to help you."

She stalked out, her flats striking the linoleum in a staccato rhythm. Gray took a bite of hash browns and enjoyed the crunch. A door slammed in the back of the house. Then came the sound of a woman wailing and gasping.

"Poor thing," Gray said. "Sounds like she's dying in there. Why don't you go to her?"

Pooch put his head down, like this wasn't his first crying rodeo. "Best to just let her cry it out."

"Doesn't affect her cooking," Gray said. "Unless she put arsenic in my eggs. And if she did, it's the best arsenic I've ever tasted. She outdid herself making this plate for me."

"She's got a good heart. I think she wants to forgive you. It's just that sometimes there are so many broken places, you can't glue everything back together."

"For the life of me, I don't know what I did wrong. Forgive me for what?"

A dog barked, and a noisy muffler rumbled from the driveway. Pooch looked horrified and rushed to the front window, peeking around the curtains.

The vehicle stopped, but the engine chugged a good fifteen more seconds.

"Is he in there?" a voice shouted. "Pooch? Send him out!"

The dog was going crazy now.

"Annie," Pooch whispered, "call the sheriff."

"You call him," she said from behind her door.

"Annie, it's Del, and he's got a gun."

CHAPTER 18

GRAY PEERED THROUGH THE SPATTER on the pane and the torn screen of the front room window at the blurry figure of a man standing by the driver's side of a rusty pickup. Dubose and another dog were barking their heads off at him, not normal for Dubose.

"Who is that?" Gray said.

"He'll see you," Pooch said, grabbing Gray by the shirt and pulling him away. "You asked me what you did wrong. Delbert's part of the answer."

"Who is he?"

"Annie's brother. One of the Slades."

"You ripped my collar. This is my favorite shirt."

"Better that than a hole from Delbert's gun."

"What's he want?"

"Pooch!" Del yelled. "I'm not going to tell you again! Get him out here!"

Annie marched out of her room, a hard look on her face. She stepped out of her shoes and moved barefoot toward the window.

"He wants you, Grayson," Pooch said.

"Del!" Annie yelled. "Have you been drinking again?" Then to Pooch, "It's not even ten o'clock."

"I told you to call the sheriff," Pooch said.

"Stay out of this, Annie!" Del hollered. He was near the porch now.

122

Annie swept aside the curtain and cursed. "Del, you're drunk! Get back in your truck before you do something stupid!"

"Too late," Pooch said.

"If a deputy comes out here and finds you with a gun, they're going to lock you up again! Is that what you want?"

"Again?" Gray said.

"Long story," Pooch said.

"Send him out here, Annie! If you don't, you're just as guilty as he is!"

"You told me to stay out of it!" Annie yelled. "Now you want me in the middle of it. He's not here. Somebody slashed his tires at the hotel last night. Sheriff's looking for somebody who can't spell *murder*. So get out of here."

"A little bird told me Pooch brought him here. You of all people, Annie, letting somebody like that in your own house. Bring him out."

Annie turned to Pooch. "Take him out the back toward the river. I'll stall Del and come get you when he leaves."

"No, you take him to the river," Pooch whispered. "I'll talk your brother down. He won't hurt me."

"I'm not scared of him," Gray said full-voiced. "Why should I be?"

"I hear him!" Del shouted. "Don't you lie to me, Annie!"

She glared at Gray. "Del, get out of here before somebody gets hurt!"

Annie motioned for Gray to follow her to the back door, not turning around, as if her confidence might change his mind.

"We're going fishing?"

"Yeah, that's it," Pooch said. "I'll bring the gear after things settle down. Just be quiet about it, okay?"

"I need Dubose. He'll be all over that riverbank."

"We'll get him later," Annie said from the back door. "Just come on."

She held the door open for him. He was nearly out when a yelp made him stop and turn.

"Grayson, I got your dog out here! His tag has an Arizona address. Better come say goodbye."

Gray stepped back inside, something primal sparking. Annie hissed behind him, but he rushed toward the front door, Pooch yelling and trying to block his way. Gray got past him and out to the yard, where

Del had Dubose by the collar, his meaty hand all the way inside it so the dog's air was cut off. In his free hand, Del held a .22 squirrel gun with a scope and bolt action. Pooch reached them as Dubose struggled to get away, his tongue lolling, eyes bulging.

"You wanted me. Here I am. Now let my dog go."

"I'm going to hurt you, Grayson. Gonna give you back a little taste of what you gave my family."

Del pulled Dubose up so his front feet hung in the air, his hind legs trying to gain purchase. He couldn't bark or move his head.

"What in the world are you talking about?" Gray said. "I didn't do anything to you or your family."

"Del, listen," Pooch said. "This is not going to help. You can't bring Alvin back this way."

"I know I can't. But I can sure give this good-for-nothing a little pain."

Del lifted Dubose completely off the ground and pressed the barrel against the dog's head. "This is for my brother!"

Annie, barefoot and running as if shot from a cannon, rounded the corner of the house and launched all her 115 pounds airborne, hitting her brother square in the back with her shoulder. Del's head snapped back so hard his John Deere cap flew off, showing a mane of red. His gun flew out of his hand, and Dubose hit the ground running.

Pooch retrieved the .22 and emptied the shells from the chamber. "I swear, Del, you beat all. What were you thinking?"

Del arched his back, gasping, as if his sister had knocked every ounce of air from his lungs. He brayed like a donkey as he squirmed. "Why'd you do that, Annie?"

Annie was on her knees, panting herself, holding her shoulder. Gray moved to help her up.

"Leave me alone!"

She stood on her own, and Gray could tell she was in pain.

"Get him out of here," Annie told Pooch.

Pooch put the gun in his truck. "Come on, Grayson."

Gray got in, and Dubose jumped onto his lap. As Pooch sped up the hill, Del managed to stand and flip two middle fingers at them. "I'm going to get you, Grayson, if it's the last thing I do!"

The road narrowed, and the trees reached out from both sides, enveloping Pooch's truck in a leafy rainbow. Gray patted Dubose's head, and he didn't seem injured.

"Where'd that wife of yours learn to play football?" Gray said. "Looked like a redheaded linebacker goin' for the quarterback."

"She had three older brothers, so she learned how to dish it out."

"Looked like she hurt her collarbone."

"Maybe. This isn't the first time she's had to corral Del. I don't know if she would have run at him like that if he was holding *you* up by the collar, though. She's got a love for animals."

Gray began searching the truck. "I need my legal pad." He had been looking for someone who would take his life, and he realized he'd just walked away from a great opportunity. Del Slade was ready. He'd have to write that down before he forgot.

"We'll get it later. What do you need it for?"

"What was that fellow talking about? What did I do to his family?"

They were in deep shadows now, and the road topped a hill. The blacktop ended, and gravel flew under the truck's wheels, pinging the undercarriage. Then it turned to dirt, dust pluming behind them. As they drove farther into the woods, Gray felt as if he were returning to some backroad of his memory.

"You wrote something about them," Pooch said.

"I did?"

"At least, that's what everybody thought."

"I never wrote about any of the Slades."

Pooch gave him a sideways glance. "And how would you know if you did or didn't?"

"I would remember something like that."

"This was years ago, Grayson. And whether you meant to or not doesn't matter. People recognized them in your story. Annie told me it was about a man who leaves the hills and becomes a hotshot detective in a big town. He comes back for the funeral of his best friend, which everybody thought was a suicide. You remember that one?"

"Yeah, sure," Gray said tentatively.

Pooch rolled his eyes. "Turned out it was a murder, and the detective found the guilty man, who was part of a backwoods family with a vendetta against the fellow who died. He was not only accused of murder, but also of abusing his sisters and something about meth.

"Annie said that people in town immediately thought of the Slades and that your description of Alvin was spot on. He was never a big reader, but he also wasn't wrapped real tight to begin with. It's not fair for Del to blame you, but Alvin had a bunch of things going on that sent him over the edge, and one day he took his own life."

"So Del wants to get back at me for something I didn't do."

"Del was in the state pen while all this was happening."

"What for?"

"Drugs and weapons charges. Annie said he blamed himself for not being there for his brother. To be honest, I'm surprised he never tracked you down out there in the desert."

"No wonder Annie was put out with me."

"She and the family have been through their share of pain."

Pooch pulled off the dirt road at a place where the trees were so thick they pressed against the side window. Gray couldn't see five feet through the dense undergrowth.

"This is as far as we can go and still be able to turn around."

"Why did you bring me here?" Gray said.

"Get out and let's take a look. The river's right down there, along with what's left of the bridge we built. Across from that is where you grew up."

"You built a bridge?"

"You and me, your brother, your daddy, and my daddy." Pooch opened his door. "Come on."

Gray and Dubose had to stay near the truck because of the foliage. He followed Pooch toward an overgrown path leading down the hill.

"Watch your step," Pooch said. "The rocks are loose, and there's poison ivy."

The smell of the river and the sound of water over the rocks touched something inside Gray that felt close to biblical. The Bible's story started in a garden, and Gray always thought of his life beginning close to the soil, touching nature and accustomed to the rhythm of its seasons.

Climbing down toward the river was like stepping into his childhood, becoming himself again.

Dubose ran ahead and stopped on a knoll overlooking the water. The sights and sounds seemed almost straight out of Gray's dreams—the strong current, the depth of the river, the ripples and foam as the water licked rocks near the bank, and the muted crickets and frogs.

A crudely built bridge spanned the narrowest section of the river, its wood slats falling apart. Rusted metal cables stretched over the water, fastened to trees on either side.

"Last flood almost washed it away," Pooch said. "It's not safe. I repaired it a couple times through the years, but it needs to be torn down before kids discover it. I just haven't had the heart yet. It's kind of a marker of our lives."

Gray wished he had his legal pad. "Why did we build it?"

"To connect us. To ride your bike to my place, you had to go all the way into town to get across the river and then head back this way. So we started building a bridge ourselves, but that didn't go over well with our parents. My daddy thought up the cables. He helped the most."

"Your daddy was a lot kinder than mine."

Pooch nodded. "Remember sitting in the middle and dropping a line in the water? We'd sit for hours in the summer, the shade of the trees covering us, waiting for a fish to rise. I wanted to dive into the coolness, but we both knew the river's too dangerous. It's worse now."

"You and I did that?"

"Camped out right over there. Put up a tent. Cooked fish. It was like a scene out of Huck Finn, which you read at night. You'd tell stories till you were blue in the face. I knew you'd do something with that, I just didn't know what."

Dubose scampered down the hillside, and Gray sighed. "This is it, Pooch. You brought me to the bridge I see in my dream. And the girl is right up there. And I'm down in the water. It's just as real as the two of us standing here."

"You're not down in that water in real life, because it's way too deep and the current too swift."

"I'm telling you how it is in the dream. And somebody comes along from that side, and she looks scared, and he puts something over her, like a sack, and then he picks her up and tosses her in. And it's up to me to save her."

"Do you?"

Gray looked at the ground. "I don't know. Do you think I'm responsible for that Slade fellow?"

"All kinds of people blame other people for bad things. I guess it makes them feel better to have somebody on the hook. I say look in the mirror. Each of us has enough guilt to deal with."

"Me? What guilt do I have?"

Pooch seemed to study Gray. "You don't remember that day on the bridge, do you?"

"What are you talking about?"

Pooch shoved his hands in his pockets. "Does your doctor say anything about your dreams? Does he think they're tied to something that happened, or are they just something your brain is cooking up?"

"I don't think he knows. It might be a warning. Something that's going to happen. Or maybe I'm being told something important. All my life I've been following mysteries, uncovering things real or imagined and writing them down. I feel like this is something I need to follow."

"Obviously, if you came all the way back here."

Gray stepped off the knoll onto the path that led to the river. Pooch reached to stop him, but Gray's foot caught on a tree root and he tumbled down the hill, bouncing through the dirt and leaves and rocks, rolling like a tire. He felt a sickening crack in his side and a sharp pain, and he didn't stop until he was almost in the water.

Soon Pooch was standing over him, telling him to stay still, that he would get an ambulance.

"No, you're not getting an ambulance," Gray said. He stretched his legs and tried to sit up, but his head was spinning.

"Did you hit your noggin?"

"I hit everything. Maybe it knocked some sense into me."

He lay back and squinted, as if he had just gotten off a twisting amusement park ride. He frantically glanced around.

"Your legal pad is back at the house."

"Well, help me up. I have to go up on the bridge."

"Are you crazy, Grayson? That thing won't hold you."

"I just need to go out a little ways to see the river. I want to see what she sees."

"You can see it fine from here."

"No, I've got to look down from up there. You don't understand."

"I understand you're talking crazy."

"Just help me up."

"If you fall, I'm not jumping in after you. You hear me?"

"I never asked you to."

Pooch grabbed him under his arms, and Gray dug his heels into the loamy soil. When he was standing, he blinked hard, the world still whirling. Gray stretched, as if he could inspect each bone, wincing at the pain in his side.

"That almost knocked that cathead biscuit out of me," Gray said. "I might have lost some gravy on my way down."

"You probably broke a rib," Pooch said. "I heard something snap."

"Hurt my pride more than anything."

"Forget about the bridge, Grayson. Let go of this death wish."

Gray tried to stare a hole through the man, then limped to the tree where several boards were nailed to the side leading up to the bridge.

"I know what you're trying to do," Pooch said. "This is not one of your stories. You're not going to find a happy ending or even make sense out of it by climbing up there."

Gray ascended a foot above the ground, but it felt like a hundred. He wondered how in the world he had done this as a kid. Maybe he'd lost all his nerve with age.

A motor sounded in the distance, and dust wafted on the leaves. He recognized the sound of the VW van. He stepped back down and held on until he saw a Black man at the top of the knoll and heard him calling his name.

CHAPTER 19

DEL'S PICKUP WAS GONE FROM POOCH'S HOUSE, and so was Annie. Josh said he could hardly believe the drama they'd been through. "So Del painted those words on the van?"

Pooch said that was his best guess. "Though most of the Slades have spelling issues."

Gray jotted a note on his legal pad to add the new tires to Josh's payment. Josh had also found spray paint close to the van's color and crudely covered the graffiti.

"I'm hungry," Gray said. "Do they still have that fish place in town?"

Pooch glanced at Josh. "They do, but it's probably better to get takeout this time of day."

"I don't mind a crowd," Gray said. "There's something I want to talk to you about."

"I'll call in an order, and we can have Josh run over for us."

"Okay, I guess we can talk here while he's gone."

Gray was in a funk the rest of the afternoon because things didn't go the way he planned with Pooch. "I need to tell you about a dream I've been having and also ask you a huge favor, okay?"

"You've already done that, Grayson. You even took notes on it, if you want to check your pad."

"But I traveled all the way across the country for your help. Don't you believe everything in life happens for a reason?"

"I do, but I'm not about to—"

"You don't even know what I'm going to ask."

"Grayson, check your notes."

Gray flipped through the pages and read quickly. "So we did talk about this . . ."

"We did."

"Since when did you turn into a theologian, Pooch?"

"I just pointed out something you already know. If God is all-powerful and all-knowing, which I know you were taught as a child, it would be a sin to take out of this world a mind like yours."

Josh returned in the middle of their heated exchange, and Gray retreated to the bathroom to wash his hands. But he was really just trying to process the betrayal and the difference between what he had expected and what he got from his friend.

The shrimp proved soggy and the scallops cold, but still the food hit the spot, and Gray's day brightened. Careful not to turn the pages of his pad with greasy fingers, he studied something he had written.

"Josh, you said your wife is having a baby. So why are you here with me? Is she okay with you being on this trip?"

Josh glanced at Pooch and hesitated. "I think part of her is glad I'm here."

"So you can get paid? Or just to get you out of the house?"

"You're projecting, Gray," Pooch said. "That's probably what *your* wife is thinking."

"Not Lotty. She did everything she could to keep me from coming here. Until we found this fellow . . ." Gray's voice trailed. He wanted to write that down, but he didn't want to reach into his shirt pocket for his pen with greasy fingers.

"My wife is glad for different reasons," Josh said, snapping Gray back to attention. "But . . . well, life is like that, isn't it? Complicated."

"You can say that again," Pooch said.

"Complicated how?" Gray said.

"Just things the doctor has said."

"Is there something wrong with your wife?"

"No, the baby she's carrying."

"What's wrong?" Gray said.

Josh raised his eyebrows as if the question had surprised him. "The doctor says there are abnormalities."

Gray pursed his lips and nodded. "Well, we've all got abnormalities. I'm a walking abnormality. Is it something they can fix?"

Josh stopped eating. "The doctor says no."

Gray put down his fish. "What is he suggesting?"

"Grayson," Pooch said, "maybe we ought to talk about something else."

"Why? This is obviously bothering him." Gray zeroed in on Josh like a laser. "What's this doctor suggesting?"

"He thinks we ought to end the pregnancy."

"Does that mean what I think it does?"

Josh nodded.

Pooch sighed. "I'm sorry, Josh. That's too bad."

Gray sat back. "Too bad? That's more than too bad. This is life or death. That child's a creation of God. Do you trust this doctor?"

The muscles in Josh's cheek moved. "I don't know who to trust anymore."

"What about a second opinion? That's the first thing Lotty did—found somebody else to look me over. The first doctor encouraged it."

Josh pushed his food away. "I kind of lean toward what the doctor is saying. There could be a danger to my wife in this. And then she'll be the one who has to care for the boy. It's not fair with everything else she's dealing with."

"What does she think?" Gray said.

"She doesn't want to end it."

"And you do?"

"No. But I'm scared. I want what's best for our family. It's hard enough to raise a normal child, let alone one with a lot of problems."

"Normal?" Gray said. "What is that, exactly?"

"He's just being honest, Grayson," Pooch said.

"I know, but if you let normal become your reason for living, you'll never really live. You'll always be trying to avoid whatever hard thing you come across."

"Like you, Grayson?" Pooch said.

"What are you talking about?"

Pooch shook his head and waved him off.

"Listen, son," Gray said. "Trying to keep things normal and manageable is not going to end up good for anybody. In my heart, I know this. Don't do something you'll regret for the rest of your life. Now, I'm no doctor, but I know life is precious, a gift you need to treasure. And if God gives you some hard road, I have to believe he'll provide a way." He sat back. "Lotty and I never had kids, but at our church there's a few kids who have . . . I can't remember what it's called, but they look different. But I don't know of a single one of those parents who regret having a child like you're talking about."

Josh rubbed his face with a hand, and Gray wondered if he had stepped over some kind of line.

"You being here, traveling with me," Gray continued, "does that complicate things with your wife?"

Josh shrugged. "She didn't want me to come. She made that clear."

"That's where you and I are different. If Lotty doesn't want something, I close the door on it."

"She didn't want you to come on this trip, remember? But you found a way."

"That's different."

"Why is that?"

"It just is; trust me. But let's stick with you. If your wife didn't want you to come, why'd you do it?"

Josh glanced at Pooch. "I wanted to. Something inside said I needed to take advantage of the opportunity."

"Opportunity?"

"That's how I see it. It gives you a chance to go home again. And it helps your wife. She's busy moving. I wanted to be part of it."

"But why? You don't know me from Adam."

"I felt bad you couldn't get the van started. Hearing about this mystery woman who visits your dreams. I wanted to help."

Gray squinted at him and flipped through his legal pad, wiping his fingers on his pants.

"What's wrong?"

"Something's not adding up. I can feel it."

"What do you mean?" Pooch said.

"I have to trust the people I spend time with," Gray said. "Something's not right."

Josh leaned forward. "Gray, I think you might be——"

"Don't call me that. It's Mr. Hayes. Show a little respect." He pushed away from the table and stood.

"Grayson, settle down," Pooch said. "You can trust us."

"I can't trust either of you. You won't help me do what I need to do, and Josh here is going to end the life of his own child without a second thought."

"That's not what I said," Josh said. "Don't put words in my mouth."

"It's true," Gray said. "You toss out a child like recycling a newspaper."

"You lecture me about tossing a life away? You've got a lot of nerve, Mr. Hayes." Josh stood and slammed his chair against the table. "Find somebody else to drive you."

"I never needed you in the first place," Gray said to Josh's back as he stormed out. "I was trying to do you a favor, and look what it got me."

"Gray, come on," Pooch said. "Sit down and we'll work this out."

"Stop telling me what to do. You're not the boss of me."

Gray returned to the bathroom. He turned on the cold water and splashed it on his face. Something about sloshing water always awakened him. In the mirror, his eyes were bloodshot and new wrinkles surprised him.

The kitchen was empty when he returned, and so was the living room until Pooch walked up the front steps with a big smile on his face. "What do you say we go fishing?"

Pooch drove him to a curve on the river where the water whispered over rocks and spoke like a friend. Gray wore Pooch's hip waders and a hat with ties on it. He crept into the water gingerly at first, content to stay at the edge in the calm. He held the fly rod like a scepter and tested his skills by bringing it back and beginning the motion that returned like a lover in the night. So much of his life had left and wouldn't return, but this muscle memory had never gone away. He felt like part of the river as the fly moved forward and back, curling above him.

In the effortless movement, albeit with an occasional twinge in his wounded side, everything else receded, and Gray felt as if he were made to do this one thing well—not as a performance but simply because he could. And with one hand feeding the line and the other guiding the rod and fly, he felt warm and tingly. It was like when he was immersed in a story, caught up with the words that flowed from his heart.

Oh, if I could just do this with my writing again. If I could just sit and let it unfurl this same way.

He'd blocked everything now. The trip. The van. Lotty. Josh. Pooch. Any tension. Peace washed over him, and his mind felt free.

Is it enough to do one thing well? To live a quiet life without desiring more or needing things to work out the way I want?

Gray had lived for validation and fame and fortune. Even love was a byproduct of his effort. But could the whole purpose of existence be reduced to simply casting well and becoming part of the river, whether or not the fish rose and took the bait? Could life be less about outcome and more about simply being?

Gray moved farther into the stream, the water rising to his waist.

Could a man make up for sins he couldn't remember, make restitution for things he could no longer grasp?

Gray kept moving, slowly becoming lost in the river. In his mind he turned to the Almighty. "Maybe you're getting back at me for the things I've done and the things I haven't."

That sounds more like karma than grace, God seemed to whisper. *Is that how you think it works?*

"I don't know how it works. *Grace* and *love* are tossed around like chicken feed. Add *forgiveness* and people scatter it willy-nilly, without a thought to the cost. We reap what we sow, don't we?"

So you must earn the love you receive?

"Of course. You have to work hard to make up for all the bad."

What if you never fully grasp all the bad you've done? What if knowing that would crush you and steal the life from you?

"I'd still want to know. Not knowing would be worse."

So all you're going through is punishment? And all the pain you feel is leaking onto others who love you because you haven't measured up?

The river rose to his chest, and each step became a search for solid footing.

"Maybe it's punishment, or maybe it's just the consequences of my bad choices. Kind of like the way the river erodes the bank a little each day."

Name something—one thing—outside the reach of grace.

Gray closed his eyes and continued fly casting. "Her. At night I wake up because I hear her. And I see her silhouette in the moonlight."

You see who?

"The girl. The woman on the bridge who gets tossed over. I don't know why she's calling me. But I feel guilty as sin."

Nothing existed now but the sound of the water, the beat of his heart, the *swish* of the line, and the soft *pfft* of the fly hitting the surface. Gray finally felt he was home—that he had inadvertently achieved something he hadn't factored into his plan. In the warmth of the sun and the cool of the water, it was as if he were writing again, lost in a story, hearing dialogue, and creating something never before conceived. And instead of feeling immersed, he had simply become part of the whole. Stories that had been only ideas were now in the world, and he had lost control of them. He had created every story on his own, shaping and nurturing it into something that spoke to him as he listened to his life. If it didn't work, he changed it, cut it, fixed it, and tried to get it right, tried to write it true.

Here in the river, with the wind and the wildlife and the color around him, all his senses engaged, and he clearly saw his life and what he could no longer do. Too many pages had turned. He could no longer edit any earlier chapter. All he had were the pages ahead of him.

And the motion of the line and moving his arm like an orchestra conductor scared him, because this was all he could control. On the bank, his childhood friend and his dog reminded him he would spend the rest of his days with others making decisions for him.

He stopped and felt the pressure of the current swaying his body.

And instead of a fish rising, a thought surfaced, like some forgotten story he never told.

At some point in life, every man is called to forgive someone he cannot. Every man sees the unforgivable debt of another. And every man owes a debt he cannot repay.

"You all right, Grayson?"

Gray turned and faced his friend and the dog with its tail wagging. Dubose whined.

"Just enjoying the view."

He moved the baton again, and the orchestra responded, the line settled on the water, and the fly landed softly on the surface and floated in the current. He saw his own reflection in the water, but he couldn't see more because of the murk.

The hardest person you will ever try to forgive is yourself. Most try and never succeed. They try to do enough good to outweigh the bad in hopes that they can feel *again.*

"That must be what I want, Lord. More than anything. I want to be free of this weight. And maybe that's why you've sent her to me."

He heard the whisper again, and the water and wind in the trees.

It takes courage to receive what isn't earned, to stay in the flow of the pain and hurt you've caused.

"I'm willing," Gray whispered.

And then, as if orchestrated by providence, a fish rose and took the fly and ran, surprising Gray. The reel sang, and he clicked it tight and felt the bow of the rod. From the bank, someone called his name and the dog barked in eager anticipation. He turned and smiled, reeling as he stepped deeper into the river.

Many can't conceive that forgiveness is not earned, that it's a gift.

A gift. Not earned. Something dropped into his lap he didn't deserve. Like a monster on the line that took the hook and ran.

Gray, will you allow yourself to be loved even if you can't provide? Will you allow others to love you for who you are and not who you want to be?

Gray reeled in the fish, and Pooch whooped, "Bet it's a catfish!"

And it was—a thick green leviathan, white underneath, with a full set of whiskers below a mouth big enough for Gray to fit his fist inside. Had he ever caught something bigger? He retreated to the edge and held up the fish.

"Moby Catfish," Pooch said. "You've still got the touch, Grayson."

Dubose barked and ran back and forth along the bank. Gray removed the fly and held the fish out for Dubose to sniff. When it wriggled, the dog jumped back and Gray laughed.

"That fellow's been here quite a while," Pooch said.

"And we're going to keep it that way." Gray put the fish in the water with both hands, allowing it to move on its own and swim away. With his reflection superimposed on the fish's freedom, he felt something inside. He didn't understand it, but he knew he was simply in the flow now, and freedom felt possible.

CHAPTER 20

GRAY AWOKE IN DARKNESS AND SAT UP, cringing at the pain in his side. Hmm. He'd pulled off his shoes and socks but slept in his clothes. He stilled himself, not wanting to wake Lotty, and he listened for her rhythmic breathing but heard only the bed creak under his own weight as he swung his legs over the side. The floor felt different to his bare feet. So did the air. The smell of the room was off, something like musty covers from an attic. Everything felt strange, as if he were somewhere he shouldn't be and couldn't figure out why. The only light came from a clock radio, its glowing red numbers fuzzy. He found his legal pad and stood.

A whine from the corner. Something brushed against Gray's leg and he flinched, reigniting the pain. Why hadn't he put Dubose in his crate? "Come on, boy," Gray whispered.

He gingerly felt his way toward the door but felt only the spines of books along the wall. He finally found a light switch. The bed was empty. Where was Lotty? Where was he?

He stepped into the hall, Dubose at his heels. If he could get to the garage, he could work on the van. He had to get it started. But the door he thought led to the garage actually led outside.

A symphony of frogs, crickets, and other insects swelled around him as tiny lights blinked in the air, like earthbound lanterns freed. The night felt magical, as if this might be a dream, but Dubose licked at Gray's hand as he moved barefoot across the dewy grass. He reached the driveway, where the gravel bit his feet, and he stepped back onto the cool clover in the yard.

The moon lit the way down the hill to paved road. Once there, Dubose headed left and Gray followed him up the hill. The pavement gave way to dirt, and Gray felt drawn by some unseen force.

He walked twenty minutes, stubbing his toe on a large rock and stumbling, but mostly shuffling, trying to stay on the road, his legal pad tucked under his arm. Soon he also heard the river below, to his right. Dubose scampered onto a path that led down.

Gray followed but realized too late that Dubose had stopped. The dog yelped as Gray fell headfirst and hurtled down the hill, suffering a horrible feeling of déjà vu.

When Gray stopped, each attempt to draw a breath brought that sharp pain in his side. He lay struggling, finally able to get a whisper of a breath to ease his panic.

The moon shone through a canopy of trees onto the water. Making out the bridge suspended above him, he knew what he had to do. He pushed himself up to his knees, swooning with the pain and resting there until he caught his breath and forced himself to stand.

He made it to the tree and agonizingly climbed the boards nailed there, making the wood whine. Dubose's bark echoed through the hills and downriver, and Gray hissed at him to stop.

When he grasped the top cable of the bridge, he sighed with relief and pulled himself onto the makeshift platform. Peering down, he felt liberated from something and recalled the feeling of driving the VW away from Tucson. It was freedom mixed with some strange force, Providence calling.

He held the cables on both sides of the bridge and stepped onto the first slat, the structure swaying. A song from childhood bubbled from some forgotten spring. Why now? Why here? An image of a silver transistor radio flashed in his mind, and he heard the riff of a twelve-string guitar and a group singing a passage from Ecclesiastes. There was a time and season for everything. Turn, turn, turn.

"A time to be born and a time to die," he whispered aloud. "A time to stand on a bridge and stare into the water."

He chuckled and took another tentative step, the river a moving shadow below like time itself passing as an ever-rolling stream. He tried to judge the distance between him and the flow. How far would he fall?

Dubose barked again, startling Gray.

Why hadn't he left the dog? He was going to wake someone and ruin everything, ruin Gray's purpose.

Purpose. What a word.

Gray had always sensed, even as a child before he had fully believed in God the way he did now, that there was a "time to every purpose" for all. Like the stories he loved, there seemed to be a grand design, a way to fit together life's unexplainable twists and turns so a person could see how each small event contributed to the whole.

There was no comprehensive understanding of all the implications of choices, all the outward ripples of a soul dropped into the deep end of living. There was only so much he could comprehend, but he could understand enough to make life bearable. This was why he loved stories, because he could control outcomes of choices, even when he could not do the same with his own life. It comforted him to see cause and effect on the page. And he forced the people who populated his stories to look into the abyss and see themselves, forcing his readers to do the same.

He traced the conflict of each life on the page, and the question that guided him was when those characters would be willing to finally see themselves. Would they open or stay closed?

Would he open or stay closed?

In the end, life was like a patchwork quilt—beauty you couldn't see while it was being stitched. Pivotal settings graced every story, locations of the heart. Where he now stood, swaying above the dark river, was one in his own. It was a Calvary, where past and present hinged, and none of the events that had led him here were happenstance. This was designed not by himself, but by a much greater force.

He reached for his legal pad to get these thoughts on the page, because they seemed to come as a gift he wanted to give others.

But the pad was no longer under his arm, and panic seized him. He grabbed the right cable with both hands, and the bridge shifted and tipped and frightened him. He reached for the other cable and managed to right himself.

His breathing and heartbeat slowed as he looked to the other side of the river, as if the man might appear from the darkness and begin pushing the woman toward the middle of the bridge.

He took another cautious step, and a sound touched a nerve that gave him pause. A whimper? Lotty always tried to stifle her weeping and still her shaking, but he felt her, even here. And he smiled at the thought of her beauty and all he had known that was slipping from him.

He wasn't home. Lotty wasn't beside him. This wasn't a dream. And yet, from the bridge of his dreams, the bank seemed so far away. Cables swayed. The fecund aroma of the river made the sky and earth spin, a scrolling vertigo that lifted and reset and started again.

Dubose barked.

That was the noise.

It wasn't Lotty or the woman being dragged onto the bridge.

"I'm okay, buddy. Quiet down."

Dubose paced in the moonlight, whimpering, his tail like a windshield wiper.

"I need to do this, pal. You stay there, okay?"

The vertigo lifted, replaced by a gentle sway. When would the man and woman appear? When would he see the way he wanted his characters to see?

Behind him lay the past. Ahead, the future. And Gray knew it took courage to stand in the middle and be where he was instead of where he thought he should be.

"Maybe I'm getting better, Dubose. Maybe God's not through with me. Maybe my mind is clearing. I can feel it."

Something flapped above him, and in the moonlight three crows stretched their wings in the trees. One cawed, and all three bowed the high limbs. He shivered at the spectral creatures who feasted on dead flesh. They were watching him. They were a sign.

The next board crumbled beneath him, and he tried to hold on to the cable, his legs swinging wildly. Something told him to fight, but he simply couldn't hold on any longer. He lunged toward the nearest slat, the pain unbearable.

His fingers slipped, and as he fell he heard Dubose's incessant barking from the shore and wondered if his wife and friends would think he'd jumped.

He plunged into the water, swallowing the river.

PART 2

CHAPTER 21

JOSH CHAMBERS STUMBLED INTO THE KITCHEN at sunup and found Annie replacing the filter from the coffee maker. The skillet sizzled.

"How's the shoulder?" he said. "What's the doctor say?"

"Never trusted doctors. I was taught you don't go to one unless you're dying or close to it."

"Any stirrings from Gray yet?"

"Not a peep," she said. "The longer he sleeps, the better chance I have of keeping my sanity."

"What about your brother?"

"I assume Del's as sore as I am. He had too much to drink when he vandalized the VW. Too much Budweiser will make you do things you regret. Must've drunk some more to get up the courage to face Grayson. Lucky none of the neighbors called the sheriff."

"He threaten people often?"

She kept working and didn't answer.

"Can I ask you about . . . your other brother? Alvin? You think what Gray wrote in his book caused him to . . ."

"Kill himself?" she said matter-of-factly. Annie shrugged. "Who knows? Alvin always had a little crazy in him. He'd brood at his own birthday party. He was just different. He'd laugh at things that weren't funny. Always seemed about five minutes behind everybody else. And when people started comparing him to the character in Gray's book . . ."

She paused. "I doubt ten people in town read that book. But they sure liked to talk about how old Grayson got Alvin good, right down to the color of his eyes—one brown and the other blue. I told him I'd help him find a lawyer to sue Grayson, but he never took me up on it. Other things bothered him more than that. It just got added to the pile. It finally got to him. Our family never recovered, really."

Pooch shuffled into the kitchen in a tattered T-shirt and flannel pajama pants, rubbing his eyes. "Heard anything from Grayson yet?" he said as he sat.

Josh shook his head. "Waiting for the next storm."

"I'm sorry about what he said to you yesterday."

Josh shrugged. "I doubt he'll remember it."

Sadness crossed Pooch's face. "I need to tell you something I've not told anybody my whole life. Not even you, Annie." Pooch leaned forward with his elbows on his knees, his work-worn hands clasped in front of him. "You both know about Grayson's dream, the main reason he came back here."

Josh figured Pooch had told Annie all about it, probably even what Grayson wanted Pooch to do for him.

"Well, this goes way back to when we were just kids," Pooch continued. "Grayson was probably ten. We'd worked on the bridge together alone, trying a couple of ideas that nearly got both of us drowned before we finally got help." Pooch shook his head and continued. "You have to understand what kind of man Grayson's daddy was—the kind you might see from a distance and think was all right. He could smile at you and act cordial but then turn on a dime. His true colors came out when he was home."

"Abusive?" Josh said.

"That doesn't begin to describe him. But yes, he knocked his wife and sons around. Especially Grayson. But it wasn't so much the beatings as the mental torture. Grayson would sit on that bridge and tell me things he'd been through that would make you weep. He described his house like Stalag 17 in a World War II movie."

"Go on," Josh said.

Pooch had a far-off look. "It was close to summertime when Grayson found him. The bus stop was toward the end of the road, and Grayson had to walk—"

"Found who?" Josh said.

Pooch held up a hand. "I'll get there. He was walking home from the bus when—"

A commotion rose outside, the dog barking, making Pooch and Annie go see what was going on. She returned with a look of horror and ran through the kitchen and down the hall to Gray's room.

Josh followed Pooch to the door and noticed Dubose.

Annie ran back into the kitchen, her face ashen. "Gray's gone."

Gray's legal pad was gone. His shoes were by the front door, which gave Josh hope. But he and Pooch and Annie scoured the house, the barn, and the fields and woods, yelling for Gray.

"He could be anywhere," Annie said. "No telling how long he's been gone."

"He took his pad with him," Josh said. "It's kind of his guide."

Pooch headed for the hill behind, but Josh stopped him. In the confusion, he had forgotten the device in Gray's belt. He pulled up the app on his phone. He explained the device Charlotte had hidden to locate Gray if he strayed. "That's weird," Josh said.

"What's wrong?" Pooch said.

"No signal. I usually see a blue dot where he is."

"Maybe he's too far away."

"No, even Charlotte can follow the signal from Tucson. I'm going to reinstall the app."

"Don't waste time," Annie said. "Just call his wife."

"I don't want to worry her," Josh said. "I lost Gray earlier and promised it wouldn't happen again."

"Swallow your pride," Annie said.

Josh quickly reinstalled the app but couldn't find the code he'd written on a scrap of paper. He called Charlotte. "Sorry to bother you so early. Could you check Gray's location? My phone isn't working."

"Isn't he with you?"

"We're at Pooch's house, and he and Dubose were sleeping in the same room. Looks like he got up and took the dog outside."

"How long has he been gone?"

"I'm not sure. I'm hoping he'll show up any minute, but . . ."

"Just let me concentrate."

He prayed she would see the blue dot. Or that Gray would come walking out of the woods. "I'm really sorry, Charlotte. Believe me, I didn't want to—"

"Listen to me, Josh. I can't take any more of this. When you find him, you're heading back. Do you understand?"

"I'm really sorry."

"Tell me you understand and that you'll do it. I want to hear you say it."

"I understand. I'll do whatever you want."

"I'm opening it now," she said.

It felt like an hour before Charlotte spoke. "I'm not getting a signal."

There were only a couple of reasons the transmitter would fail.

A desperate cry on the other end, like something breaking. "The battery is new. It can't be that. Is there water—"

"There's a river that runs near the house."

"Please, God, no!" Charlotte cried, and Josh had to pull the phone from his ear.

"What is it?" Pooch said.

"If the transmitter gets submerged," he whispered, "it fails. Let me try to pull up the last ping." He found the blue dot in an area just up the road a mile or two. "Where is this?"

"Near the bridge," Pooch said, "where we were yesterday. Annie, call the sheriff."

Josh leapt from Pooch's truck before it stopped and found the path down the hill. He slipped and slid, wondering if Gray had tried to navigate it in the dark. He reached a plateau over the river and headed down toward the edge, scanning the rushing water.

Pooch came running behind him and yelled, "I found his legal pad!" Josh continued downstream to a knoll that offered a better view. Among the branches, leaves, and collected detritus where the river curved lay something out of place: a wad of blue.

He hurried close to the edge but still couldn't see clearly because the wad was partially submerged. Pooch joined him, grabbed a stick, and tried to reach it from the muddy bank.

"His pants," Pooch said, finally removing them from the debris.

Josh grabbed them, removed the belt, and dug out the chip Charlotte had embedded in it. "How would he lose his pants?"

"They were loose, and that current is strong." Pooch cursed and looked downriver. "I should never have brought him to see the old bridge up there."

"Show me," Josh said.

They backtracked up the hill to the tree where the top and bottom rusty cables were secured.

"See that slat hanging and one missing in the middle? Bet we'll find that downstream."

Josh shook his head. "You think he'd climb all the way up there?"

"He threatened to. Says that's the bridge in his dreams. I talked him out of it. He must have written it down and come back. Or . . ."

"Or what?"

Pooch hung his head. "I told you what Grayson asked me to do for him. Which I would never do, of course."

To Josh, the movement of the water sounded like regret. "I don't know what to do."

Pooch sighed. "Only what we can. I'm afraid we're dealing with a recovery, not a rescue."

"He couldn't have made it to the other side?"

Pooch frowned. "If he fell and didn't jump, he would have been confused when he hit. And if he jumped, he would have just surrendered."

Josh studied the river. How could he tell Charlotte? How could he live with himself?

"I told you he was determined to spare his wife the pain. I guess he decided to do it himself."

Josh shook his head. "No. This was an accident. He didn't jump. He wouldn't do that."

"That works for me. Nobody needs to know any different. Don't be hard on yourself, you hear?"

CHAPTER 22

SOMETHING ROUSED SAM HAYES as he lay on a bare mattress without a pillow, unable to open his eyes because his alcohol-clouded head pounded as if it might explode. He tried to sit up, but that felt like climbing Everest in his flip-flops. If he could just lie still enough to quiet the storm inside . . .

It was his phone. He made a valiant effort to stand but wound up on his knees, head hanging, feeling he might ralph right there on the hardwood. He inched along the wall and pulled the phone from his pocket.

"Sorry to call so early. It's Wendell."

Who in the world was Wendell?

"Wendell Martin. We're renting your house."

Oh, yeah. Wendell and his wife, Judy. Or Jill. Or something. He'd regretted renting the old house as soon as he'd signed the lease, but he couldn't bring himself to sell the place.

"What can I do for you?" Sam slurred, bracing for the answer. Septic backup? Leaky roof? Flooded basement?

"It's kind of hard to explain on the phone," Wendell said. "Would you mind coming over here?"

"I'm not feeling myself this morning, Wendell. Can you just tell me?"

"You're going to want to see what we found."

Found. The word reverberated inside. Like buried treasure or oil bubbling up from the ground like Jed Clampett?

Half an hour later, with the bite of corner store black coffee fresh on his tongue, Sam pulled up to the house he had left behind. The way it sat in the bottomland, vulnerable to floodwaters, always gave him a queasy feeling. It was a work in progress his father never quite finished. The wiring was never up to code and the walls never quite plumb, so Spackle filled the cracks and some of the doors never quite closed. He had been advised to sell it and move on.

Sam sat in the driveway, which wasn't really a driveway anymore—the gravel having been swallowed by the soil and grass. Behind the house sat the barn with the tin roof a strong wind should have blown away years ago. A tire swing hung on the hickory nut tree in the back, reminding Sam of summer vacations in the shade, trying to come up with something to do. His life had become an exercise in trying to figure out what to do when other plans failed.

He recalled a mismatched croquet set that didn't have all its wickets. A promised outing to a Charleston Charlies game, the Pittsburgh Pirates' farm team. His father had made it all the way to the parking lot, so close Sam could see the lights of Watt Powell Park, could taste the popcorn and Cracker Jack. But Sam's brother, Grayson, probably said or did something, because their father turned around and drove home. Years later, Sam had asked his father about that night. The man claimed no recollection.

The renters hadn't changed the house and certainly hadn't mowed. Ivy seemed to have taken over the chimney, and autumn olives smothered the fence by the field. Two rusty bikes leaned against the side of the house, and a newer tricycle sat askew near the front steps. Where death had inexorably encroached, life had found a way.

That was the way of the hills, the way homes could be transformed. Old men sleeping in rocking chairs gave way to children's muddy feet clambering over hardwood. And while fall was seen by many as the most beautiful season of the year, to Sam it signaled dormancy. Leaves that turned bright colors were near death and would accumulate on the ground as branches emptied, like the arms of a barren woman longing for a child. But somehow, each year, seasons found a way to resurrect, to exchange death for life, empty for full. And the hills again filled with green.

Wendell waddled barefoot onto the porch, his hair tousled. He had gained weight, which Sam hadn't thought possible, and moved like a balloon in a parade. He beckoned Sam, as if whatever he needed to show him might scamper away if he didn't hurry.

"Thank you for coming," Wendell said, his jowls fluttering, his breathing heavy. He spoke with a cackle, as if his weight pulled hard and kept his voice at bay. "Sorry I was a little vague on the phone. I didn't know what to do. Janie said we should call the sheriff, but I thought you might be able to sort it out."

Wendell opened what was left of the screen door, which hung precariously on hinges screwed into moist, rotting wood. There wasn't a fly in the county that couldn't navigate the holes in the screen. Sam tried not to look at the living room, but it was hard to ignore. Stacked newspapers and magazines and piles of unfolded clothes evidenced a couple plainly unfazed by clutter.

In the kitchen, Janie leaned against the oven, cupping a faded green mug. Her hair dripped on her T-shirt, and she had the same look on her face as a cat he once tossed into a pond that had climbed out the other side and looked back.

A man sat at the table that took up too much of the room. All Sam could see was the back of his head and a heavy blanket pulled around him like a superhero's cape. He could have sworn his own father had stepped out of the grave and returned for breakfast. The man had the same shaggy gray hair Sam remembered, thick and cowlicked.

When his dad's health took a final turn, Sam and his mother had spent most of their energy trying to make him comfortable. His father had never found comfort in much of anything except meanness, so the whole exercise was a losing proposition.

This man had a full mug of black coffee and a microwave breakfast bowl in front of him. He put a fork in the bowl and twirled the melted cheese. A dwindling bottle of Heinz ketchup stood upside down next to the bowl.

Sam edged around the table to get a look at the man's face. His stomach soured afresh. The boyish good looks had given way to a handsome maturity. The smooth-faced man with the knock-em-dead looks had become lined. But he couldn't hide those piercing blue eyes.

"Grayson," Sam said.

"Says he's from Arizona," Janie said.

Grayson put down his fork and narrowed his gaze. "Who are you?"

The voice sent a shiver through Sam, and he heard echoes of Christmas mornings, bike rides, and angry words exchanged with their father. Grayson had lost a bit of the twang, but the timbre was the same, smooth and inviting and confident. There had always been a musicality to his voice, a song you want to hear—every word. Summer campfires with marshmallows on sharpened willow branches, and that voice telling another story.

"I said, 'Who are you?'"

Sam took a deep breath through his nose. "The fellow they called to look after you."

"You with the sheriff?"

"No."

"You don't know who this is?" Janie said.

Sam gave the woman a hard look, and she seemed to understand. Grayson's eyes wandered back to his food and then to Sam. "Should I know you?" He pushed back from the table and stood. "I don't know any of you people."

"Sit down, Grayson," Sam said firmly.

Grayson sat like an obedient dog. He seemed to see the bowl in front of him as if for the first time and picked up the fork again.

"Do you recognize this house?" Sam said.

"I remember growing up somewhere around here."

"Your family lived in this house."

"That so?"

"How did you get here, Grayson?"

"I got up in the middle of the night—" Wendell began.

Sam held up a hand. "I want his version, if you don't mind."

"I've been having this dream. A woman on a bridge crying out for help. But nobody can tell me who she is or what happened."

"You a psychic or something?" Janie said.

"No, I'm Protestant," Grayson said. "That was a joke. But seriously, I'm pretty sure somebody killed her. And it's up to me now."

"Up to you to what?" Sam said.

"To find out the truth about her, because nobody else gives a hoot."

Janie squinted at Grayson. "You think somebody was killed out here?"

"You tell me. You know of any woman who's gone missing?"

Janie looked shaken and glanced at Wendell.

Sam nodded at Wendell, and the man followed him into the living room. Sam spoke quietly. "Did he drive here?"

"I didn't see or hear a vehicle. He showed up at the back door baptized."

"What do you mean?"

"Around four or so this morning I heard something out back, like a wounded animal. Saw something by the barn like a ghost in the moonlight. I got my flashlight and my gun and found him out there wrapped in a sheet he'd found on our clothesline. Otherwise, naked as the day he was born and wet as a muskrat. Said he fell into the river and didn't know where his clothes went. Says his name is Hayes. Is he your brother or something?"

Sam nodded, and the fireplace stirred memories of Christmas stockings and trees cut from the hillside. His father yelling at them for tracking in snow after sledding. Then, of Christmases more recent and the hospital bed in the dining room and the IV drip and the smell of alcohol and urine.

"He's not right in the head, is he?" the man said. "That story about the dead woman he's looking for. That can't be real."

"Your guess is as good as mine."

"Janie gets spooked at stories like that. What's wrong with him?"

"I don't know. It's been a long time since I've seen him."

Wendell looked away as if he were doing math in his head. "Isn't he the fellow who wrote those books?"

"Yeah."

"It'd be a shame for somebody with that kind of mind to lose it."

Sam nodded.

"I'll see if I can find him some clothes. Most of my things will be too big for him."

"You should have told me on the phone you thought you'd found my brother. I never would have come."

Sam headed toward the door.

"Wait," Wendell said. "Where are you going?"

"This is not my concern."

"How in the world do you figure that? You said he was your brother."

Sam let the screen door whack metal on metal.

"You can't just leave him here!" Janie called out from the kitchen. "What are we supposed to do with him?"

Sam threw up both hands. "Call the sheriff."

"That's how you treat family?" Janie said.

Sam sped away, cursing his brother, Wendell, and Janie. Cursing himself. His brother's face had sent a pulse through Sam like touching a nerve in his spine.

He had vowed never to see his brother again. And assuming Grayson died before he did, Sam vowed he would not go to any funeral or send flowers or visit any grave.

He hadn't prepared for what he'd do or say if Grayson returned. He had anticipated Grayson's scrawled handwriting on an envelope someday, maybe a birthday card or some tortured prose.

I'm sorry for what I did. I know I don't deserve it, but I want to ask you to forgive me.

Sam had been thankful that never came. And neither did a phone call. Grayson and his choices and his life were behind him, and Sam had no obligation to even think of his brother. So why did it seem Grayson still controlled him?

Grayson hadn't recognized him, and though he told Wendell he didn't know what was wrong, he had a strong suspicion.

When he passed the gas station and the road that led to the interstate and crossed the bridge over the river, his stomach still churned. He passed the grocery store, a family-owned business that had survived the encroachment of the national chains. Nearby sat a boxy establishment that had carried everything from hair coloring to macaroni and cheese to weed killer, all at the cheapest price in town. The current occupant rented furniture and everything from chainsaws to bush hogs to flat-screen televisions. Sam had rented a hospital bed here and set it up in the dining room, where he and his mother nursed his father.

A few years later, he rented the same bed from the same store for his mother and realized that with all the monthly charges, he could have bought three hospital beds. But that was one thing you couldn't know about life—how long the pain would last and whether you might save money paying month to month.

Grayson had skipped out on all of that, as well as both funerals. And people had asked Sam how his brother could live with himself after abandoning him and his parents.

As a kid, Sam idolized the way his older brother carried himself, the way he spoke, the confidence, the swagger. He wanted to be like Grayson, talk like him, tell stories like him, even dress like him. He'd worn ratty sweaters and T-shirts Grayson had cast away, and the clothes had actually made Sam feel like his brother. It seemed that with all of Grayson's natural abilities and then his education, there was nothing Grayson couldn't accomplish.

Except treating others like human beings, Sam thought.

CHAPTER 23

JOSH'S HEART SANK WHEN HE FOUND DUBOSE at the river, barking at something else caught in the debris. Josh fished out Gray's T-shirt, and Dubose jumped on him and sniffed at it, then ran back to the river. Had Gray fallen, or had he shed his clothes and jumped?

Would Charlotte want any mementos of her husband?

A sheriff's deputy took information from Josh and Pooch and Annie, then called for a body recovery team.

Annie and Pooch followed Dubose on a path downriver, while Josh went the other direction, hoping Gray's body hadn't been pulled as far as they feared. Soon they yelled for him and Josh ran, dreading to see what had alarmed them.

"Are those his?" Pooch said, pointing to boxer shorts wrapped around a rock.

"I think so," Josh said. "Why would he have taken those off?"

The deputy drew alongside. "You'd be surprised what fast-moving water can do. I'm not gonna lie. You may not want to be here when we find the body. Some things you can't unsee."

While the deputy turned away to take a call on his radio, Josh entertained the unthinkable. Would Charlotte bury Gray in Sycamore? Or Arizona or Colorado? With him gone, there was no need for her to move so far.

"I can't help thinking this is partly my fault," Pooch said. "I could have just lied and told him I'd help him."

"How do you think I feel?" Josh said. "I had one job—to look after him. How am I going to face his wife? I thought I could help him make a little sense of his life with this trip. Show him that no matter what, there are people who love him. Good intentions . . ."

Josh bent over, feeling sick. "I should have slept in the room with him. I'd have heard him get up."

Pooch put a hand on his shoulder. "It's not like there was anybody here who wasn't trying. Even Grayson, in his own way."

The deputy turned back. "You okay, Mr. Chambers?"

"Not really."

The man smiled, which unnerved Josh. How could he smile with a dead man in the river?

"I have news you'll want to hear."

"Somebody find him downriver?" Pooch said.

"No, upriver."

Josh retched in the grass, and Annie put a hand on his back until the feeling subsided.

The officer pointed. "Actually, across the river and through that field."

"What are you talking about?" Pooch said.

"Showed up at a house early this morning, naked and shivering."

Josh let out a whoop and bolted for Pooch's truck, calling Charlotte as he ran.

She picked up, her voice tight, and wept at the news. "Get on the road tonight, Josh," she said sternly. "I want him home."

"He might need to get checked out first."

"Just don't let him out of your sight again. And remember, he doesn't trust doctors."

"What if I can't convince him to leave?"

"That's your job, Josh."

They followed the sheriff in Pooch's truck, Dubose panting and pacing in the backseat.

When they pulled into the driveway, the deputy talked to a large man in a thin T-shirt and a woman with a hard face and eyes that seemed more sad than angry.

"There he is," Pooch said. "Pacing like a caged lion."

Gray stood inside the dilapidated barn behind the house. Dubose whined, and Josh let him out. The dog ran to Grayson, barking wildly. Josh and Pooch followed.

Gray wore a pair of blue jeans that ballooned around him, cinched by a belt that could have wrapped him twice. Tucked into the jeans was a long-sleeved plaid shirt. He also wore brown work boots, the shoelaces flopping like rabbit ears.

"You are a sight for sore eyes, Grayson," Pooch said. "But we're sure glad to see you in one piece."

Gray was on one knee petting Dubose, who wouldn't stop shaking and wagging his tail.

"What happened, Gray?" Josh said. "How did you get here?"

"What do you mean?"

"What are you doing on this side of the river in those clothes?"

"Somebody gave them to me, I guess. They're a little big."

"You think?" Pooch said.

Gray's eyes darted. "I lost my legal pad."

"It's in the truck," Pooch said. "I found it on the other side of the river. It looks like you might have been up on the bridge. Tell me you didn't go up there."

Gray waved him off. "I don't know what you're talking about. And what are the police doing here?"

"They were looking for you, numbskull," Pooch said.

"We called them," Josh said in a kind tone. "We thought you were dead."

Gray laughed. "That's a good one. I want my pad now." He pulled at his ear.

Josh called Charlotte and handed Gray the phone. "Somebody wants to talk to you."

"Me? Who is this?" His face brightened. "Lotty!"

Gray rushed through a rambling version of events that sounded implausible to Josh, but clearly not to Gray. Then he listened and clouded over.

"Not a chance in Charleston, Lotty. Come on. I've come all this way. I got something I need to do." A pause. "Who did you hear that from?" Gray shook his head. "Josh doesn't know what he's talking about. I wrote something . . . Hold on a minute." He fished in his pocket for a crumpled napkin. "Here it is. There was a fellow here earlier, and I wrote his name down. Sam. I know him from somewhere, but I can't place him. And, Lotty, you're not going to believe this, but he says the place where I'm standing is where I grew up. But for the life of me, I don't recognize the people here—except for Pooch and the other fellow. The Black one." A pause. "Right. Josh. So I'll let you know when I've found her—you know, that woman in my dream. I'm getting closer, Lotty."

"He's even more erratic," Pooch whispered.

"Needs his medication," Josh said.

"Here comes the officer, Lotty. I need to go." Gray handed the phone to Josh.

The deputy eyed Gray up and down. "Sounds like you had quite a night, sir."

"I'm okay now. Sorry to trouble you."

"You want to tell me what happened?"

"Nothing. I'm just visiting."

The deputy sighed. "Mr. Hayes, we need to get you checked out."

"No need for that. I feel fine."

"I understand. But the protocol is to take you—"

"Protocol? That's a ten-dollar word for an intellectual lightweight, isn't it?"

"Excuse me?"

"Gray," Josh said.

"Deputy," Pooch said, turning his back to Gray, "he's a friend of ours and kind of mixed up." Pooch tapped the side of his head.

The officer leaned to see Gray again. "I called out the search team because of you."

Gray lifted both palms. "Well, congratulations. You found me."

"Let's get you checked out," Josh said, "just in case."

"I told you I was fine, now drop it."

The deputy whispered to Josh, "He's broken no laws, and I can't force him. Just make sure he doesn't wander off again."

As the officer left, Gray said, "Pooch, we need to leave. I need my legal pad and—"

"Hold your horses, Grayson. Something came to me as I was thinking about that dream of yours, and—"

"The one with the woman?"

Pooch sat on a hay bale and patted the spot beside him. "Come on. Take a load off so we can talk."

"I don't want to talk; I want my pad."

Pooch soldiered on with Gray standing over him. "You kept him right here in this barn, snuggled between some fresh hay bales. Remember?"

"What are you talking about?"

"You lived in that house right there. We played together in this barn. Out in the field. Both sides of the river. Threw footballs and hit baseballs as far as we could."

"Right. So what's that got to do with anything?"

"I think there's a connection between what you've dreamed about and what you've lived. The woman who gets thrown in the water. You try to rescue her but you can't. Remember?"

Gray nodded.

"What do you think it means?"

"I think it's a sign," Gray said. "Somebody needed help, maybe still needs it."

"But what if the person who needs help is you?"

"Come again?"

"Something happened when you were a kid. You don't remember it like I do. And it happened on that bridge you were on last night."

Gray pulled at his ear again.

"You fell from that bridge last night, right?"

"I think so."

"Well, the mind is powerful. There's a lot stored up there that can get mixed together. Truth and fiction. So the mind can take something real and play a trick on you, make you think something happened one way and come to find out it didn't happen that way at all. That can happen to all of us."

Gray seemed to study Pooch. "If you're going to tell a story, get to it."

"All right. When my daddy found out you and I had met at elementary school and become fast friends, he told me to be careful. Said if you were anything like your father, it would be best not to associate with you."

"That's a mean thing for him to say," Gray said.

"Well, he knew your daddy, and he cared about me. He was right about him but wrong about you. And you know better than anybody that your daddy could be nice as you please one minute and then—"

"I know what kind of man my father was."

"Of course you do. You lived it, you and your brother and your mama. Your daddy would not have liked Josh much, am I right?"

Gray frowned.

"The worst day, when he was the meanest, was when you were about ten and your daddy took you out on that bridge. You remember that?"

"I don't know if I do or don't."

"The burlap sack?"

"I told you, I don't know—"

"Your daddy pulled you up on the bridge."

Gray shook his head. "I don't remember it."

Pooch pursed his lips. "Does the name *Fern* ring any bells for you?"

CHAPTER 24

GRAY FOLDED HIS ARMS, protecting himself against a stirring he couldn't explain, like being interrogated for a crime that might condemn him. "I don't think I want to hear any more of this story."

"I need you to, Grayson," Pooch said. "And sit down here. You're making me nervous." Pooch patted the bale again, and Gray sat.

Pooch's voice was subdued, and Gray had to lean close to hear. "You were reading a story about a boy who saved up his money and sent off for two hunting dogs. *Where the Red Fern Grows*. Remember that?"

"That was a sad one. The boy stumbled on the entrails of one of them. The dogs were defending him."

"That book stuck with you."

"Old Dan and Little Ann, right?" Gray said.

Pooch nodded. "So you were walking home from the bus stop one day after school, just after your brother was born, and the way you told it to me, you heard a sound in the weeds and found a pup underneath a fern. You carried him home, pulled the stickers from his coat, and of course wanted to keep him. You said it was a sign that the dog was under the fern, a cute little thing that latched onto you, his savior. You named him Fern.

"Just one problem. Your daddy didn't allow animals of any kind, strange because you had a barn behind your house. But in his mind, animals made a mess, cost money to feed. Too much trouble. End of story. So you did the logical thing—you hid that pup. Right here in this barn. But of course, eventually he found it. And that's what was inside the sack your daddy carried that day, yelping and squirming to beat forty."

Gray looked away. "I want you to stop."

"So you remember?"

Gray moved to stand, but Pooch touched his shoulder to hold him there. "Hear me out. This is important. I don't know why people remember or forget the things they do. But if you've got a friend to help you recall what you can't, you've been given a gift."

"You think you're God's gift to me? You've got another think coming."

Pooch paused. "Your daddy pushed you up the tree, made you climb ahead of him to the middle of that bridge. It was made for one and swayed with the weight." Pooch leaned forward, as if willing himself to tell the painful story. "Your daddy followed you with that squirming sack, and when you got to the middle, he handed it to you and told you to toss it into the water. You stood ramrod straight and shook your head. So he called you a vile name. Your daddy was not used to hearing no."

"I know what kind of man he was," Gray said, and his voice sounded childish to him.

"He cuffed you on the back of the head, and you started crying and begged him not to make you do it. You didn't beg him to stop hitting you or even to not make you do something you didn't want to—you were begging for the life of that little dog."

Gray closed his eyes and shook his head. "Why are you telling me this? That never happened."

"Yes, it did. But it won't make sense if you don't hear the worst. This might be the reason you're having that dream, Grayson. It's locked inside you, trying to come out. You and your daddy struggled on that bridge. And the struggle is still there."

"I don't want to hear any more!" Gray stood.

"Finally you turned away from him and cradled that little dog, keeping it safe. And that's when your daddy hit you harder in the back of the head and yelled awful things."

"Just stop it!" Gray moved stiff-legged to the door of the barn. His whole body was sore, and he couldn't remember why.

Pooch approached him. "When you didn't obey him, your daddy took off his belt."

The sun warmed Gray's face and he stood stock-still, hands balled into fists.

"He beat you, Grayson. Hit you on your back and buttocks. You reached back to try to keep him from hurting you, but you wouldn't let go of the sack. And then he hit you so hard you had to put the sack between your feet and bend over it, the bridge swinging like a pendulum. You protected that pup with your own body. But he was hitting you so hard—"

"Why are you telling me this?" Gray shouted.

"—that you couldn't take any more. You picked up the sack and ran. But you couldn't outrun your daddy. He grabbed your arm and hit you with the buckle." Pooch's voice caught. "You can say this isn't true all you want, but you have a scar behind your left ear."

Gray shadowboxed the memory, but he felt a long, jagged ridge behind his ear. And he felt pain there as he reached for the memory.

"The buckle opened the wound, Grayson. You went down on your knees, and the blood gushed through your fingers and down your arm onto your shirt. Your daddy cursed at you and said, 'See what you made me do?' He grabbed the sack and yanked you up and made you stand. He made you take the sack again and told you to throw it in the river, and it was clear he wasn't going to stop beating you until you did what he said."

Gray looked at the ground, then out at the clouds and the sunshine and the brightly colored leaves. This was all too much to take in.

"You told me later that you thought for sure he was going to kill you. And I believe he would have."

"Is that how you know this? Because I told you?" He ground his teeth. "You're the meanest man on the face of the earth to tell me that."

"No, I'm not, Grayson—not mean to tell you the truth about what your daddy did. And not mean to tell you what happened next."

"I'm not listening anymore."

"You dropped the sack over the side into the water. The dog whimpered and thrashed as the sack began to sink, the current dragging it downstream. And you cried and wanted to jump in, but you were scared. Your daddy left the bridge and climbed down and yelled for you to follow. He didn't take you to a doctor. Didn't do a thing for you."

"You're a liar. That never happened."

"Yes, it did. And deep inside you know I'm telling the truth."

Gray wiped at his face. "You're just repeating something I made up."

"I've read your stories, Grayson. What I just told you comes out in every one of them. Pain has a way of doing that."

Gray started for the truck, Dubose at his side. He muttered to himself, shaking his head.

Pooch called out, "I know this is not something you made up, because I was there! I saw the whole thing!"

Gray stopped and turned, venom rising. "If that's true, why didn't you help me? Why didn't you do something?"

"I was a kid, Grayson. Just like you. Scared to death he'd throw me off if I came up there."

"Some friend."

"But you have to hear all of it, Grayson, something only you and I knew."

"What are you talking about?"

"I told you what happened next, but you don't remember. So I want you to look at something."

Pooch reached Gray and pulled from his pocket a wrinkled black-and-white photo, worn and faded. It showed a hunting dog with a group of men with shotguns, and the dog looked eager, ready to hunt. "That's my uncle right there," Pooch said. "And that's Fern. This was a few years after what happened on the bridge."

"Wait. You said he drowned."

"No, I said you tossed him in."

"And he sank . . ."

"I was fishing a little downstream from the bridge that day. When you two climbed up there from the other side, I hid in the bushes and saw your daddy hitting you. It tore me up, Grayson. Does to this day.

When your daddy left, I used my fishing pole to snag that sack and pull it to the edge."

"You saved him?"

"I didn't think so at first. The little thing looked lifeless and water-logged, but I laid him on the bank and pushed on his tummy and begged God to let him live. I never prayed so hard before or since. It felt like a miracle when he coughed up a bunch of water.

"My uncle was over at the house that day and said he'd take him home, that he looked like he'd be a good hunting dog. Every time I'd go over to his farm way up in Emmaus, all the dogs would run out barking their heads off at us, except for Fern. I think he knew who I was. And that picture is worth a million dollars to me."

"He lived," Gray said.

"He sure did. So you don't have to let that bother you anymore. My uncle said he lived a good, long life. Best hunting dog he ever had."

Gray reached behind him for something, then a cloud came over his face. "So you think that's why I've been having that dream?"

"I wouldn't pretend to know for sure. But your daddy looked at that dog as something to be thrown away. My uncle saw something your daddy didn't. Follow me?"

"I think so."

Pooch drew near to Gray and lowered his voice. "You asked me to do you a favor and take your life when things got hard—to toss you off the bridge. I'm telling you, Grayson, if you have the breath of life, something good can come out of it. Let people grab that sack you're in and pull you to shore."

Gray looked his friend in the eyes. There was something there he hadn't noticed. And he judged it to be love.

CHAPTER 25

JOSH CALLED CHARLOTTE FROM THE FIELD next to Pooch's house, pacing in the tall grass by the rusted barbwire fence as her phone went to voicemail. He hated to leave a message with news this good, but he couldn't make her wait. "Gray's more than alive, Charlotte. He's fine, actually. I wish you could see him. I think he had a breakthrough that made the whole trip worthwhile. I'll tell you all about it when I hear from you, but I knew you'd want to know. Sorry about all the worry this has caused."

Josh headed toward the house at the sound of a commotion. Pooch met him on the front porch. "He couldn't find his favorite pen," he whispered, nodding at the window. Gray sat at the kitchen table, furiously writing. "I gave him one he could tolerate, but he sure is persnickety. Probably dropped it last night. I'll go back up and see if I can find it where I found his pad."

"No need," Josh said. "Charlotte sent me with a bunch of those pens because he loses them and feels he can't write. She orders them or drives to a store in Tucson."

"I can't imagine what she's been through," Pooch said. "There's no predicting what he'll do. I mean, he's happy as a clam with that pad in front of him—like he has a new lease on life."

"Maybe he's found a new story to tell." Josh sat on the top step. "That story about the dog. Was that true?"

"You think I'd make up something like that?"

"Just wondering if there was more to it than a story he can't remember."

"I actually held back, Josh. It was ten times worse than I could ever tell it. A man in Grayson's condition doesn't need every gory detail."

"It sure seemed to speak to him."

Pooch nodded. "In grade school, he had the wildest imagination, curious about everything, resourceful as all get-out, building forts in the woods—that bridge was his idea. He's the one who found the cables. And the teacher would have him come to the front and read his stories. Grayson would make you feel you were right there in the thick of it. It was just plain as day that he was different.

"But it also seemed there was always something hanging over him, like a cloud. And I couldn't figure it out until I walked into his house. Even when his daddy was gone, there was this presence. I don't think you can understand why somebody acts the way they do until you see what they've been through. And that day at the river, I saw it. So when Grayson would say or do something that ticked me off, I'd remember what he was living with. He could be a real pill. Had to have things his way or he'd get agitated, even playing baseball or basketball. Other guys would get mad and leave. Say they'd never play with him again. But I saw a kid trying to make sense of things, trying to control the pain in his own way."

"Why could you see it and others couldn't?"

Pooch shrugged. "I knew what they didn't."

"Maybe that's why he remembers you and not others here."

"Maybe. I mean, Grayson knew Annie. They even went out a couple of times. But it's like she's locked in some basement and he can't find the key. And I don't know if it's the dementia or he's just blocked it. It doesn't make sense, but then, it does. Just like Ezra."

"Who's Ezra?"

"Sorry. When I was younger, I worked at the glass factory. Ezra taught me how to blow glass—one of those things you can't learn from a book. It's an art, really. Blowing glass will be the last thing on earth to become automated, because they can't build a machine to do it justice.

"Anyway, everybody loved Ezra. And other than blow glass, he could pick a guitar. He could play anything. You could turn on the radio and he'd pick out the tune and all the chord changes, like he had some kind of tuning fork inside him.

"Well, Ezra started having problems remembering things. Everybody knew it but him, and people understood. One day at the glass factory, he set his torch down and forgot it, and we were lucky the whole place didn't burn to the ground. They gave him his retirement early, set him and his wife up pretty good. It wasn't long until he was just a shell. It was sad. He'd ask the same questions over and over.

"I'd go over of an evening and sit with him, give his wife a break and let her go to the store. Sunday mornings I'd stay with him while she went to church. It got to where he didn't speak at all. But I'd still talk to him and act like he was answering me, just to keep the conversation going."

"A one-man show."

Pooch smiled. "I reckon so. Eventually he couldn't feed himself or even get dressed. You had to help him do everything. But we were watching TV one Sunday morning, and this commercial came on for some CD with favorite bluegrass songs. Ezra's fingers were moving on both hands, like he was fretting chords and picking.

"I said, 'Ezra, want me to get your guitar?' And he looked at me like he recognized me, a flicker in his eyes I hadn't seen in a long time. I found his guitar, and would you believe he actually tuned it and began to play along with Roy Acuff's "Great Speckled Bird"? And in the same key! He just came alive with that guitar in his hands. Call it muscle memory or whatever you want, it was like watching a sunrise. And when he finished, he just sat there with a smile on his face."

Pooch sat back and seemed to bask in the memory. "I'm thinking Grayson is sort of letting go of things. That's why he came here, why he wanted me to take his life when it got hard. This trip is something you're never going to regret. It's like me handing Ezra that guitar and turning him loose—a gift that can't be repaid."

Josh studied the trees. Leaves fell, and he thought they looked like grains of sand in an hourglass. "I hope he can walk away now with some closure—at least as much as there can be in his condition."

"What's your plan, then?" Pooch said.

"Who knows how long he's been awake? I assume he'll crash at some point. Charlotte wants us to head back tonight, but I think I can talk her into letting us stay one more night before we head out. She wants us to meet her. We'd leave the tools with you, if you can use them."

"I'd be honored."

"I have a confession about that story you told Gray."

"I'm listening."

"I don't think it explains why Gray dreams about a woman on the bridge. I think two things are coming together in that dream. Maybe more."

"That's not a confession; that's an opinion."

"It's a confession because . . ."

A noisy muffler interrupted him as a rusted Buick pulled into the driveway and eased behind the van. A woman got out.

"Is that who I think it is?" Josh said.

"If you're thinking that's trouble, it is."

Gray wrote madly, unable to keep up with his swirling ideas. One story from his friend had sent him to the page like old times, his heart and mind connected and flowing in a stream he couldn't stanch. He'd gone through phases in life when the dam broke and there was no way to hold back the words. In fact, he'd always felt his stories would come out somehow, so writing was not something he *chose* to do but *had* to do.

Someone was quoted as saying writing was easy—you just open a vein. If that was true, he had burst an artery. One thought led to another, and he hoped that when he was spent, someone could decipher the disconnected ideas.

"All my life I've struggled to figure out who I really am," he wrote. "Maybe that is the destiny of every man—to finally find your true identity and step into it, like you would an elevator. I'm just beginning to realize this as my years are dwindling.

"I've believed that forgetting is a slow move away from my wife and myself, pushing off from the dock and letting the tide carry me. An involuntary reaction to a disease I cannot control. Yet perhaps forgetting does not push me away, but rather pulls me closer to the man I was all along.

"I write to explain my life, taking what's inside and making it something else so I can deal with truths too difficult to grasp. And in the process, I leave it as a legacy for those who might someday stumble upon it and find direction."

Gray wrote about the dream, the bridge, the fall—how it felt to shiver naked on the bank and walk through the field to the home of his youth. A man and his wife had found him, and another man had come along.

He jumped to the story Pooch had told of the pup and his father and the sack and the bridge, and much like the recurring dream, he found he was transcribing now instead of creating.

In the middle of white-hot images and emotions, he turned the legal pad over and began to write on the back a letter to Lotty. It became an unbidden and effortless revealing of his heart that spilled onto the page something he could never say aloud.

Deep into the process—no fatigue, hunger, or thirst touching him—a noise interrupted him. The rattle of a muffler, the slam of a car door, voices outside. He rose in frustration and moved to the living room.

A woman's voice. "Is he in there?"

"Please don't do this."

Gray moved the curtain and peeked out the window. A Black guy was talking with a woman about Gray's age, not homely but not beautiful. Her hair was mouse-colored, and her nose hooked at the end. Skin beneath her arms wobbled when she moved.

"We've tried hard not to upset him," the man said. "He's in a fragile state right now."

"He's in West Virginia, Joshua," the woman said. "I've been in a fragile state all my life, and that hasn't kept people from talking to me."

Josh—that's the man's name.

"You might set him off," Josh said.

The woman moved like a deer stepping into a new meadow. "You talk about him like he's a firecracker and I'm a match. You know me better than that. And I know him a lot better than you do."

Gray strained to hear.

"Alice, I need to explain," Josh said.

"Explain what? That he's seen the light? Changed his ways? I ought to be allowed to see for myself, don't you think?"

"Please, Alice. This is not about you. There might be a time down the road—"

"I don't want to wait. Is it true? Did you travel all this way with him?"

"Yes. And—"

"He doesn't know who you are?"

"Please, keep your voice down." Josh glanced back at the house, and Gray moved behind the curtain, not sure he'd been quick enough.

"So it's true, then," Alice said. "He really doesn't remember you, doesn't recall what he did."

Her voice hit Gray like a wrong turn off the main road he'd taken long ago. "When were you going to tell him?" she said. "Or were you going to hide it from him forever? A man has a right to know things like that, don't you think?"

Gray wanted to grab his legal pad and record the conversation, but the mystery of her words and how sure she was held him there.

"He can't hide from what he did to my daughter. You have to know it will come out eventually. If you think taking a trip all this way will cure him and remove his guilt—"

Gray opened the door and held the woman's gaze. "I'm not hiding. I'm right here. What is it you want to say to me?"

The woman's mouth dropped. "It is you."

Josh rushed up the steps. "Gray, let's get you back inside."

"Take your hands off me." He shook free and stepped around Josh and past Pooch, who sat in the porch swing. Gray focused on the woman. "Who are you? What's all this about you and your daughter?"

Josh lowered his voice and spoke as if he regretted it. "Gray, this is Alice."

"Good to meet you, Alice. What can I do for you?"

Alice stared. "You expect me to believe you really don't remember me?"

"Lady, I've never seen you in my life."

"That's what I'm trying to tell you, Alice," Josh said.

"Quiet!" Gray said. "I can speak for myself."

"Gray, you don't understand," Josh said.

"Let me refresh his memory," Alice said. "If this is not an act—"

"He has Alzheimer's," Josh said.

Suddenly something about her eyes seemed less angry and more hurt. Finally she said, "Grayson, do you remember all the studying you did to get your degree? And the teaching job that came after it?"

His eyes darted. "I remember my office in Old Main."

"Okay." She took another doe-like step into the meadow.

"Alice, please," Josh said. "This is not the time."

"Let her talk," Gray said.

"Do you remember how you got that degree, Grayson? How you paid for it?"

Gray looked at the ground and grabbed at his ear and felt the scar behind it. "Why don't you stop asking questions and tell me what you came to tell me?"

"All right. You didn't pay for it. I did. I used the little money I'd saved from what my parents left me and worked my tail off to make the rest, because you said you wouldn't go into debt. You used me, Grayson."

"I don't recall what you're saying, but I'm not going to argue with you. There's a lot I don't remember about my life."

"Do you recall leaving that job, why you got in the van and took off?"

"I left with Lotty. We headed out west together. That what you're talking about?"

Pain and determination lined her face. "When something better came along, something younger and prettier, you left without giving me a second thought. Any of that still swirling up there?"

Gray scratched the back of his head. "Look, if I did something wrong, I'll admit it and make good on it if I can. I've never said I was perfect. But I believe I'm forgiven."

"Oh, that's a great topic, Grayson. Let's talk about forgiveness." Her voice was sweet now, gentle as a summer rain. "I'm real happy you've found forgiveness. Sounds like you had a religious experience."

"It's not religion. Something that grabbed hold of me, uh . . ."

"Alice," she said.

"Right, sorry. I don't recall things as well as I used to."

"But you've been forgiven of everything you remember or don't remember, right?"

"I'm not sure, but I'm willing to deal with it."

"And you don't recall our time together. The vow you made. The wedding ring you put on my finger." There was moisture in her eyes now and a catch in her voice. "You don't recall the way you broke my heart. And all the years from then until now, wondering what I did or didn't do. Or if I was better off without you and should move on with my life."

Gray squinted, dumbfounded.

"I was never enough for you, Grayson. I could never make you as happy as you wanted to be. You had your head in the clouds, dreaming the big dreams you wanted to chase. I tried with everything in me to be what you wanted. I thought you hung the moon, thought I was so lucky to have fallen in love with somebody like you."

"Alice," Josh said. "This is not the way—"

She put up a hand. "You know the worst of it, Grayson? It's not the betrayal, not the broken promises. The worst is that I let you do that to me. I sat there and took it. And I let our daughter suffer because I wasn't strong enough to stand. I blamed myself. If only I had done something different."

Gray started to speak, but Alice continued. "I suppose you don't remember our daughter." A tear leaked all the way to her jaw. "You don't recall the promises you made to her."

"I don't know what to say, Alice. I don't remember any of that."

"Do you remember killing her—"

"Stop it," Josh said. "She wouldn't want this. Please, Alice. Don't destroy what we're doing."

Gray turned to him. "And what is it you're doing? Trying to keep me from the truth? That's not right."

"No, Gray. We're trying to help you. We're trying to bring people together, not tear them apart."

Pooch muttered, "This river gets muddier the farther downstream you go."

Alice said, "Why did you do that, Grayson? How could you do a thing like that to her?"

"What did I do? Tell me straight out."

Alice glanced at Josh and shook her head. "I guess it's not for me to say. It took me a long time to work through what you did, and I don't think I'm all the way through it. I can say I'm glad you got your life together and have some semblance of peace. I just wish it hadn't taken so long."

She walked to her car.

"Tell me what I did."

Alice opened the door, and the hinges screeched. "You'll find out soon enough."

PART 3

CHAPTER 26

THE EXPLODING COLORS ON THE HILLSIDE captivated Charlotte until the bumpy landing at Yeager Airport in Charleston, West Virginia, made her close her eyes and hold the armrest. She had never trusted planes landing on top of mountains.

The initial phone call from Josh had come before sunup, and she knew she had to get to Sycamore. She left a message for Doctor Barshaw and caught the next flight out of Tucson.

It had been a mistake to let Gray go. Her intentions were good, but good intentions often led to unintended results. She had hoped to sleep through the flight to Atlanta, then transfer to Charleston, find Gray, and leave. But sleep eluded her. Too many thoughts. Too much shame.

Josh had lobbied hard for the trip with Gray. His vision and passion had swayed her. Had it been her idea, she never would have approached him. But now here she was, doing the unthinkable, heading into a storm she had run from all her adult life—returning to the spot that held so much pain and regret.

Charlotte had enough of her own guilt to immobilize her, but she also carried Gray's, and that had bound them together through the years, actually drawn them closer. But because of Gray's condition, she now bore the guilt alone. Which brought Sam to mind. Loveable, stalwart, faithful, simple Sam.

Waiting in Atlanta for the final leg of her trip, Charlotte took the call from Josh that told her Gray was alive—and she actually got to speak with him. That made the flight to Charleston seem only that much longer.

Finally in a rental car, Charlotte knew the drive from the airport would take an hour. As badly as she wanted to see Gray, she was glad for the time to steel herself for her return to this world she had promised never to reenter. There was much more here than simply retrieving Gray.

Her phone rang. "Charlotte, I'm so sorry," Dr. Barshaw said. "Have you heard anything?"

"They found him. He's safe. It's the best we could hope for. I'm on my way to pick him up." She paused. "The trip with Josh was not such a good idea."

"It certainly has presented problems we didn't anticipate. This must be incredibly stressful for you."

You think? Why did you even let us go this route with Gray?

"I'll just be glad to get to him so I can keep an eye on him. I've hardly slept since he left."

"And the move? Have your plans changed?"

A heavy sigh. "No. I can't see another way. I had some things put into storage, and the rest is headed to Nashville. But I don't know how this will work. It feels like everything has fallen apart."

"I understand. But it'll be good having others to help carry the load."

Charlotte bit her tongue, wanting to curse the man for how wrong he'd been to help them get the plan together.

"Charlotte, I know this is painful, and what's ahead will be hard. But you've found the courage to go back, something you never wanted to do. This path could be good. For you, for Gray, for everyone."

"He fell in a river and nearly drowned, doctor."

"Yes, I don't mean to sound uncaring. I'm sorry. But this wasn't some plan we devised. This is what Grayson wanted. Even in his broken state of mind, you're allowing him the dignity of leading. You're loving him well. He may not be able to express his thanks or even understand it. But you're doing a good thing here. I want you to know that."

"It doesn't feel good. It feels like death."

"I understand. Please care for yourself in all of this. That's often the last thing caregivers think about. And call me. I can talk with Gray if he's struggling."

The conversation reminded her of something her pastor had said, that no matter how alone she felt, God was walking with her through her troubles. "There's a divine design to your life. This is not happenstance. Gray's diagnosis gives you an opportunity to trust God in the middle of not understanding what is happening or why. You're exercising your faith in a way you never could if you understood."

He had quoted verses that went over Charlotte's head, not because she didn't understand them or believe them, but because she just wasn't ready. The gist was that God was in control, and she needed to trust him and be open to learning lessons in the valley.

Charlotte vise-gripped the steering wheel and screamed, "If you have so much control, why don't you do something? At least say something!"

Five miles from her exit, Charlotte put a hand over her racing heart. One verse her pastor quoted said that everything works together for good. "Not because everything that happens is good, but God can use it all to work things together for good."

She wanted to believe that, but too much of life had left her feeling hollow. How could something like Alzheimer's work together for good? Was God so cruel that he would make her husband suffer for some greater purpose, dragging her through the pain of losing him this way?

Charlotte had asked this very thing of the pastor in a Bible study she and Gray attended, and she assumed others would judge her unspiritual. But they responded not in anger or even surprise, but with what felt like love. Even admiration.

"Your feelings are logical," the pastor said. "Many who say they believe in God really believe only in the God they've created."

"So what about all God allows? The cancer, the child who runs into the street, the tragedies. If he's all-powerful, why wouldn't he intervene?"

"We don't see the world through God's eyes. Faith means trusting not only when we understand, but also when we don't."

The pastor's wife listened to the story Charlotte had held close for years, one of regret and guilt and shame.

"Regrets are like seashells," the woman said. "Pick one up and you find another." She placed a hand on Charlotte's arm. "Life's tide puts us where we long to be whole. But we're drawn to where we hurt the most. That's not punishment. It's grace. It's God's way of helping us find our way back to becoming whole again."

CHAPTER 27

GRAY AWOKE WITH A START, trying to catch his breath, pain coursing through his body as he sat up. The dream had been clearer and more frightening than ever. The girl, the woman, was on the bridge, and the shadows had receded so he could see her face. The face of the man beside her had startled him awake.

He tried to shake the image, but as he shook the sleep away, he felt closer to finding her, closer to understanding what had happened.

The face of the man on the bridge was his own. What had he done?

Gray stood and paced. Dim light through the window made him wonder whether it was morning or evening. He shook his head, clenched his fists, and gritted his teeth.

I need to get the van started. I need to get back home. I need to find Pooch and ask if he'll do what I need him to do. I need to find out about that woman. What did I do?

He sat on the bed and leafed through the legal pad. Was it his penmanship or his eyes that were failing? His latest scribblings showed a woman had said he did awful things. He didn't get her name. There was also a man who looked familiar at an old house that also seemed familiar.

How was it he had fallen asleep in what looked like rodeo clown clothes—jeans way too big and a plaid shirt he could swim in?

He stood and took them off, yanking the shirt over his head, a button popping and rolling across the floor. He found his gym bag and put on a shirt and pants, but he couldn't find his belt, so he wrapped around his waist the one from the oversize jeans.

Strange. Metal cans hung from the door and the window. He caught a muggy, fecund aroma of wet earth and honeysuckle and rosebushes—the unmistakable scent of fall in the hills. The van sat in the driveway. Gray realized he didn't need to get it started after all. He was home.

Insects sang and bugs rose and lit as he quietly removed the cans and opened the window. His mind filled with the rivers he'd crossed in his life and all the roads taken and not taken, and the faces of the people he knew and now didn't know all rose inside like a great cloud of witnesses.

Voices outside the door made him tiptoe over and press his ear close. They would want him to do what they wanted him to do, and he couldn't do any of that right now.

I have to get to the river.

He tucked his legal pad behind him at his waist and climbed out the window, barely missing a dog who sniffed at him and followed to the end of its chain. Gray came to Pooch's truck and the van and another car behind it.

He hurried down the driveway barefoot, walking like a scarecrow, gravel biting his feet until he reached pavement. He walked by moonlight near the double yellow lines on the asphalt, unsure how to get to the river but sensing he was close.

So much slipped through his mind now, like sand through his fingers. He focused on the face of the woman on the bridge and her call for help. In his dreams he had always been in the water. How could he also be the man on the bridge?

Pooch had said something about that bridge, something that made him happy. He had told him a story and shown him something. The more Gray tried to remember, the more frustrated he became. He pulled out his pad but couldn't see the words. Agitated, he walked faster, sensing a time coming when he wouldn't remember how to fight this hard to recall things. He would need to let go, and that scared him. He'd always been able to accomplish things in his own strength.

But maybe letting go would be best. Faith was about letting go, allowing himself to be plunged into the river where he could rest, buoyed by grace and mercy.

Gray wanted to write these thoughts that seemed good and true, but like all his thoughts lately, they faded and hid.

The Black fellow. He had been in the van with Dubose. Was he a friend of Pooch's? No, he was Lotty's friend; she trusted him. He searched for the man's name. Gray stopped on the yellow line. What if that fellow was having an affair with Lotty? He needed to confront him. Take a swing. How could Lotty cheat like that?

He shook his head like a wet dog climbing out of a river. "Lord, help me keep things straight. Help me unjumble my life."

Keep moving, he thought.

He loped along, an idea forming. Pooch. His best friend would understand. He needed to take Pooch to that fish restaurant he loved. Lay out the situation before him. Pooch would help.

He smiled. That was a good plan. The road curved ahead, and Gray remembered the land and feeling fully alive in this place.

He froze at headlights.

A vehicle careened around the corner and came straight for him.

He closed his eyes and braced himself.

CHAPTER 28

WIND BLEW THROUGH THE CAB of his truck as Sam sped toward Pooch's house, arm out the window, head clouded by alcohol from the day before. His years of sobriety had ended. Now he was on day one, starting over.

He sped up an incline where a white mist rose. He slowed as he neared it. When he was a kid, Grayson had terrified him by telling him these were road ghosts and that he should never walk through them because they would follow him home.

Pooch had called him out of the blue and asked him to come to the house to discuss Grayson. Sam tried to tell him Grayson was not his problem, that he was done with his brother. But there was something in Pooch's voice.

"Is he staying with you?" Sam had said.

"He is."

"Then do what you want, but I'm not coming."

"Sam, wait," Pooch said. "You did a lot for your mother and father. And that dad of yours was no saint."

"What's your point?"

"If you won't come over here for your brother, do it for them."

"Grayson never did anything for them. Didn't even come for their funerals."

"I know you have plenty of reason to feel the way you do. But I also know you well enough to believe you're going to want to hear what . . . what all of us have to say."

"Us?"

"Sam, Grayson asked me to take his life because he knows what it's going to be like for his wife soon."

"So do it, then. Or do you want me to? Is that why you called?"

"I'm just asking you to join us. It would mean a lot."

Sam hadn't said another word, and he liked that Pooch didn't know if he would come or not. He spent twenty minutes pacing before getting in his truck to go pick up a twenty-four pack of tallboys. But when he got to the corner store he kept driving, cursing his curiosity.

The crisp, fall air blowing through the cab, Sam was rounding a sharp corner on the narrow, two-lane road when he glanced down at a ding on his phone. When he looked up, he had drifted to where a man stood frozen on the double yellow lines.

Sam cursed and jerked the wheel to the right as he slammed on his brakes, turning his head so he wouldn't see the inevitable. But by some miracle, the truck fishtailed into a ditch. Sam's airbag exploded, catching him full in the face.

White dust wafted through the cab, and Sam coughed and sputtered and grabbed his bleeding nose. The right side of the truck was buried in the soft earth, and the back left tire was off the ground.

"You all right, mister?" the man said, approaching his window. Sam couldn't imagine how he had not hit him.

But that voice. It was the one that haunted him, that sounded so much like his father's.

"You ought to slow down," Grayson said. "You're going to kill somebody one day. Let me help you out of there."

"Stand back. I don't need your help."

Sam opened his door, but it was too heavy to hold. He let it shut again and struggled through the window, blood dripping. When he dropped to the ground, his head felt as if it would explode. Woozy, he surveyed the damage. He'd definitely need a tow.

The high-intensity headlights cast an eerie glow as he came

face-to-face with his brother. He spoke with a hand over his nose. "That's rich, Grayson. You cause the accident and then scold me."

"You wouldn't be in the ditch if you'd been going the speed limit. And paying attention. Probably staring at your phone, am I right? I swear, the world has gone screen crazy."

Sam grabbed Grayson's arm with his free hand, blood dripping through the fingers of his other. "You know how long and hard I worked to buy that truck? Now look at it!"

Grayson jerked away. "Settle down, pal."

"I'm not your pal!"

"I'm sorry about your truck, mister. But I'm the one who ought to be upset. You almost killed me."

Sam knew there was really no point in talking with Grayson if he was off in the head.

"You're the one who was driving, not me," Grayson said, sniffing the air like a bloodhound. "Have you been drinking?"

Sam rolled his eyes. "What are you doing out here, Grayson?"

"Is this not a free country? Have they made it a crime to walk on a road at night?"

"I can't do this," Sam said. He put his hands on his knees and felt sick.

Grayson moved closer, and his voice was softer. He handed Sam a handkerchief. "A gentleman always carries a handkerchief. That's what Lotty says."

"Hold it tight on your nose, and tilt your head back," Gray said. "There you go. Hey, I'll bet you Pooch could pull you out. You know him? I think he's got a winch."

"I need more than to be pulled out," Sam said sharply. "Something broke. I think it might be the front axle."

"Well, that's a shame. That'll cost a pretty penny."

"It might be totaled, Grayson. And that's on you."

"Hey, don't blame me. I didn't jump out at you. Say, how is it that you know my name?"

"Everybody knows the great Grayson Hayes. The mystery writer from the small town who went off to seek fame and fortune. And look at him now."

"That's hogwash. I didn't find any fame, and I found less fortune."

"But here you are, making your triumphal reentry. Back where you started. The town that made you who you are. The people you left behind and never thought of again, except to put them in your stories."

Grayson narrowed his gaze. "I don't know why you have such a chip on your shoulder. You've got no reason to be mad at me." He nodded to the truck. "You did this to yourself."

"And there he goes, ladies and gentlemen, blaming everybody else for the things he did." Sam edged closer. "Maybe you wanted to get hit. Is that why you wandered out here?"

"I wanted to get to the river."

Sam turned away. It was sad that his own flesh and blood hadn't recognized him the day before either, but there were positives to that. It struck Sam that he saw his brother through the prism of pain Grayson had caused. Though Sam had long tried to bury the past, his brother's return had resurrected pain that now stood barefoot before him. Grayson had cracked at some primal place, with no hope of stopping the leak.

Sam had long considered driving west and confronting him, imagined delivering the meager inheritance his parents left. But all the imaginings had left him bitter.

Sam had also entertained leaving Sycamore. But he had stayed to care for his parents. That made him feel superior to his brother, securing the moral high ground in their uncivil war. But now he wondered if a person could stay and run at the same time.

Sam had even imagined one day standing over Grayson's grave and not even expending the energy to spit in the dirt. But now, in the moonlight next to his wounded truck, he saw the light inside his brother dimming like an abandoned campfire.

Yet even now, Sam detected that Grayson's memory was an archipelago, much of both past and present submerged, with only a bit of land visible above the flood. But what remained was the same ornery, opinionated, flexible-as-a-tire-iron Grayson he had always been. A man with a plan and the guts to follow it, whether he succeeded or failed.

Sam had hated Grayson so much that after their parents died, he took the family albums and stuffed in a paper bag every picture with Grayson in it and tossed it in the attic.

Now everything in him wanted to leave, let Grayson find his own way. Or lead him to the river and show him the widest, deepest part and let him wade in and end the pain for them all.

"They'll be looking for you back at Pooch's house."

"I'm not headed that way," Grayson said. "If you're okay, I'll move down the road to the river."

"In the dark? What do you think you're going to see?"

Grayson's eyes darted. "I need to get over there. It's my destiny. I keep having this dream. She's calling to me."

"Who?"

"A woman. I'm going to find her."

"You don't even have shoes on, Grayson. What are you thinking?"

Grayson looked down and sounded like a child. "I think I did something wrong. I might have taken somebody's life."

Sam swallowed hard. "You think you killed somebody?"

"Pretty sure. Why else would somebody have a dream like that over and over again?"

"Well, you're not going to find anything this time of night. Too dark. You're liable to step on a copperhead. Let's go to Pooch's house."

Gray waved and started walking again. "No can do."

It was like talking to a stone. "There are probably people there who are worried about you."

"That's on them, not me."

"Hold up, Grayson. Just stop, okay? Let me grab something from the truck. And move to the side of the road. I'd rather not have to scrape you off the pavement."

Sam painfully climbed up the side of the truck and through the window. He turned off the headlights and hit the emergency flashers, then fumbled in the dark on the floorboard and found his phone. He wriggled his way back out and blew the powder off the screen. The message he'd received was from a 520 area code. A number he didn't recognize.

Sam, it's Charlotte. Please come to Pooch's.

What in the world?

Sam used his phone to light the way and turned his brother around. "The river's this way," he lied.

Grayson walked with his head down, as if deep in thought. "Did you hear it when you drove up on me? Fluttering. Angel wings. Plain as day. Rustling and flapping as you nearly hit me. Felt the wind on my face. They were there, all right. Ministering spirits."

"Sure it wasn't my Hemi? I was right on top of you."

"They guided you away; I know it. It was a miracle, that's what it was."

"So you're religious now, Grayson? Is that it?"

"No, sir. Religion is people trying to make their own way to heaven. I don't want anything to do with religion."

Sam rubbed his day-old beard and felt crusted blood. "You could have been killed."

"That's my point. I was protected. I wish I hadn't been, but I was."

"Why do you say that, Grayson?"

"You keep calling me by my name. Do I know you?"

"I told you. A lot of people around here remember you."

"Well, some of them seem mad I came back."

"Why didn't those angels keep my truck from going in the ditch?"

Grayson shrugged. "They were here for me, not you."

"Tell me again, what's at the river that's so important? What kind of answers are you looking for?"

"Can I trust you?"

"Try me."

"All right. I can't do one productive thing. I can't provide for my wife. And I think the best thing I could do would be to slip the surly bonds of earth. Let the life insurance kick in."

"Grayson, you're not thinking straight."

"God will understand. I think he'll forgive me."

"For taking your life?"

"Not taking it, giving it up."

Sam stepped in front of Grayson, blocking his way. "You're wrong. Think about it. If those were angels back there, they saved you. And if they did that, there had to be a reason."

"Did you hear them?"

Sam tasted copper in the back of his throat. "Yeah, I heard them."

Grayson's voice trembled. "I've made lots of mistakes. Too many to count. Do you think God can forgive the things you can't remember?"

Sam tried to come up with something he could honestly say and that Grayson would hear. But he was still too angry.

"Grayson, if God sent angels to keep you from harm, he must be able to forgive what you can't remember."

His brother looked like a child now, innocence and wonder in eyes that searched in the darkness. His slack-jawed look turned to a smile.

Sam touched Grayson's shoulder and pointed him in the right direction.

"Why are you doing this?" Grayson said.

The question was like the brush of an angel's wing, and with it came a realization that more was going on than Sam could understand. Something primal had brought Grayson back to his childhood, to something he couldn't escape. Something deep was bringing everybody together. And instead of feeling haphazard, it felt ordered.

A divide had been crossed, and the brothers walked shoulder to shoulder now. From childhood, Grayson had always been taller. But the years and Grayson's stooping shoulders had brought them level.

Grayson said again, "Why are you doing this? You don't even know me."

"Just because you don't know me doesn't mean I don't know you."

Grayson shook his head, and the two moved on in silence until Sam said, "Why didn't you ever come back here? To your home."

Grayson chuckled. "That's a stupid question. I'm here. I did come back."

"I mean years ago. To see your family. Your mother and father wondered about you."

"They did? You knew them?"

"Everybody here knew them."

"You can't go home again. Somebody said that. A writer, I think. Tom Wolfe. That was his name."

"See, that's what gets me. How can you remember something like that and not other things?"

"There's stuff on the surface I can grab sometimes. But everything else is covered like a flood." Grayson seemed lost in thought. "Do you know my brother?"

"Why do you ask?"

"Somebody said he still lives around here."

"Yeah, I know him."

Grayson stopped. "How's he doing? Is he all right?"

"I hear he's okay. Let's keep moving."

"Good. What's he do for a living?"

"He's in construction."

"You don't say. You know, I brought some tools. What's he build?"

"Offices and apartments. Sometimes houses. He built his own."

"Really?" Grayson laughed. "My brother built his own house. Building a home where people can raise a family is an honorable thing. Life-giving. Something that lasts. To build a home with your own two hands, that's something else."

"What do you do now, Grayson? You used to teach, didn't you?"

"I take up space." He paused. "Tell me this: What kind of man is he? Somebody you can trust?"

"I suppose."

"What's that mean?"

"He's a good guy but has his demons, like all of us."

"What kind of demons?"

"The kind that live in bottles. It's a struggle."

Grayson's voice trembled. "Is he like me?"

Sam had to weigh his answer. "He doesn't go looking for the river after dark, if that's what you mean."

"You know what I mean." Grayson pointed to his head. "Is his mind mixed up?"

Sam studied his brother. "We're all mixed up, Grayson."

"Maybe. Some more than others, though. I wish I could remember. Or talk to him. If you were to see him . . ."

They reached Pooch's mailbox. Pooch's truck sat at the front of the driveway next to the house. Behind it was the VW van, and behind that what looked like a rental car.

Grayson's words hung between them like ripe persimmons just out of reach. "What would you say to him if you saw him?" Sam said.

Grayson stopped at the edge of the gravel. "Say to who?"

A tightness in his chest now. Sam put a hand on Grayson's shoulder.

"What's wrong?" Gray said.

"I need to know something. Why did you do that to your brother?"

A quizzical look. Fear rose in his voice, as if the answer might be something he didn't want to hear. "What did I do?"

Sam stuffed the bloody handkerchief in his pocket. His brother could remember a childhood friend, but not his own flesh and blood? Did he really forget, or was he just afraid to remember?

Sam's own voice quavered. "He loved her. With everything in him. When you took her away, it was like a knife through his heart."

"Took who away? I never stabbed anybody."

"I know you didn't." Sam tried to smile. "Come on."

Grayson yelped, then hopped in the gravel and sat rubbing his foot with both hands.

Sam suddenly took off his shoes and slid them onto Grayson's feet, helped him up, and pointed him toward the house. Gray mounted the porch alone.

CHAPTER 29

GRAY RECOGNIZED POOCH'S PLACE as soon as he walked through the front door. He headed straight for his room. There was so much to write. The question was whether he could hang on to all that had stirred his soul.

Dubose wagged his tail and nuzzled his hand, and Gray bent to pet him. "Hey, boy. How're you doing?" The dog sniffed Gray's shoes.

"Grayson," Pooch said with a furrowed brow. "Where have you been?"

Gray waved and stood. "I have to find my legal pad."

A red-headed woman approached and pushed past him down the hall. How had he walked past these people in the living room without noticing?

"I'll find it for you," she said, but stopped suddenly. "It's tucked in the back of your pants."

"Gray, don't you see who's here?"

The man who spoke was a Black fellow he knew from somewhere.

Then a woman said, "Gray?"

The voice was otherworldly—the sweetest he'd ever heard—and made his heart flutter.

"Lotty! When did you get here?"

She opened her arms, and he rushed to her and a warmth spread through him. He couldn't contain his smile as he pulled back to look at her and realized the power the woman had and what he'd been without for . . . how long?

"Boy, am I glad to see you," Gray said.

"We thought you were sleeping," she said. "What were you doing outside?"

Gray felt something strange and noticed his shoes. They weren't the kind he liked and were tight. His ear itched all of a sudden, and he grabbed at it.

"It's okay, Gray," she said. "You're safe now."

"What's wrong?" he said, looking from her to the Black man and back again. "What did I do? You're not smiling."

"I'm just tired." She appeared to try to smile. "I traveled a long way today."

"But you're here, aren't you? This place you said you could never come back to."

"Here I am."

"I had the dream again, Lotty, and knew what I had to do. I've told you about the dream, haven't I?"

"The woman on the bridge."

"She's still there. Crying out to me in the white dress. And there were angel wings."

Lotty squinted at him.

"The fellow who was with me—he can tell you." Gray retreated to the front door and saw the barefoot man walking down the driveway. "Hey, come back here! Angel man!"

Sam turned and froze as Charlotte—dark-haired with a milky-white complexion—joined Grayson at the door. He whispered her name and felt his face flush as she stepped out under the porch light. Her hair was long and silky, like he remembered, but with some gray. The requisite lines showed a woman who had aged with kindness, it seemed.

"Sam," she said.

That voice nearly brought him to his knees.

"What happened to your nose?" she said, descending the steps.

"Had a problem with my truck on the way."

"Smashed it big-time," Grayson said. "A miracle he didn't flip over. Nearly ran me down."

"I need to go take care of it," Sam said as Pooch emerged.

"Nonsense," Pooch said. "Get in here. What happened to your shoes?"

Pooch ushered Sam inside and sat him in a rocking chair. Annie got him a glass of water, some ibuprofen, and a frozen bag of peas.

"Gray," Charlotte said, "why don't you take your pad to the kitchen and write."

"Great idea," he said. "I've got a lot to get down."

Pooch whispered, "Let's move to the porch. Annie, would you keep an eye on him for us?"

Sam followed them out, peeking over the frozen peas.

The Black man introduced himself. "I drove with Gray from Arizona."

Sam shook his hand, surprised. Grayson had always shared their father's prejudice. "How'd you get along with him?"

"It's been interesting."

Sam nodded. "Bet you could write a book of your own."

"What happened, Sam?" Charlotte said. "How did you find him?"

Sam told them about nearly hitting Grayson and how he had surreptitiously led him back to Pooch's house. "He was dead set on going to the river. He talked about some dream calling him there and said he thought he took somebody's life."

Charlotte and Josh seemed to exchange knowing glances. How did they know each other?

Sam continued. "He said he wanted to slip the surly bonds. That's Grayson. Poetic to a fault. I assume he meant he was going to jump in the river. He said he wanted to provide for you, Charlotte. Life insurance. He said he thought God would forgive him."

The news didn't seem to surprise Charlotte. She said, "Did he recognize you?"

"Had no idea. But he asked if I knew his brother. Something about me stuck, I guess."

"What did he mean about angel wings?" Pooch said. "That's a new one."

"He thought I missed hitting him because an angel intervened. I half believe him."

Charlotte put a hand to her forehead. "I should never have let him go."

"I should have watched him closer," Josh said. "I had no idea he could be so . . . resourceful."

"He's a force of nature," Pooch said. "How do you corral a hurricane?"

"Don't beat yourself up for it, Josh," Sam said. "I'm sure you were trying to do something good."

Pooch stood and peeked in the window. "While he's occupied, I'm going to go take a look at your truck. You stay here and take care of that schnoz."

Josh stood. "I'll go with you."

Suddenly alone with Charlotte, Sam held the frozen bag to the bridge of his nose, glad he didn't have to look at her. Crickets and frogs and a train whistle punctuated the night.

Finally, Charlotte said, "We should talk about it."

"I've told you all that happened."

"Not about Gray. About us."

Sam tilted his head back. "There's not a lot to say, Charlotte." Her name caught on his tongue.

"It would help me," she said.

"All right."

Charlotte felt she was walking a tightrope blindfolded over the Grand Canyon and tried to muster the courage to say things she'd held in for years. She sounded like a little girl pleading for something she couldn't name. "I've wanted to call. Gray and I both have. Especially when your parents passed."

Her words felt hollow—the weight of the years too heavy for this. But somehow she gained momentum. "I sent you a note."

"I never read it."

Her heart fell. "I wrote a long letter years later. After Gray and I experienced a big change. But I couldn't send it."

"That makes me feel a lot better."

"Sam, I'm sorry. That's something I should have said a long time ago."

"Well, we've found something we agree on, haven't we?" He kept his head back, his eyes covered. "I've wondered what I'd say if I ever saw you again. I never thought you'd come back. And if he wouldn't even come back for their funerals—"

"We wanted to, Sam."

He took the peas away and leaned forward. "My brother had to lose his memory to come back here. That's rich, isn't it? Did you two ever talk about me? You know, 'Wonder how little brother is doing'?"

She studied his face, and it appeared he had carried the pain while she and Gray had distanced themselves from it. She saw something in his eyes she couldn't decipher.

"I imagined what I would do if he ever called," Sam said. "I would just hang up at the sound of his voice, because there's nothing to say but, 'Goodbye. Have a nice life.' I grew up with him, so I could understand why he would leave and turn his back. I never understood how you could do that."

Charlotte had always believed listening was a gift, but she hadn't realized how much the gift might cost. "We didn't talk about the pain we caused you. And the longer we spent away, the easier it was to just move on. I didn't mean to hurt you. I didn't want to."

"You know the worst part? If you had come to me and said you'd fallen for him—even if you'd blamed me for suggesting you take a class from him—I might have been able to handle that. It would have at least felt like I existed. But apparently I didn't matter."

"I'm sorry for all of it, Sam. Sorry he doesn't remember. Sorry for what I did. You deserved better." She ran a hand through her hair. "None of this is coming out right."

Sam pressed the peas to his nose again. "What's your plan? What are you going to do with him?"

She looked through the window at Gray in the kitchen, his face a few inches from his legal pad, writing furiously. "Josh is helping. We're trying to let Gray lead us. In a way, seeing you and Gray together is a great gift. Even if he doesn't understand it." She put a hand on his arm. "I'm not going to ask you to forgive me. I just need you to know that I'm really sorry."

CHAPTER 30

SAM SPENT A FITFUL NIGHT, even with a handful of pain medicine. Pooch and Josh had pulled his truck from the ditch and got it to the barn behind Pooch's house. Josh suggested Sam take Grayson's van and showed him the kill switch Charlotte had installed.

Seeing his brother and Charlotte made Sam want a drink, but he knew if he started he wouldn't stop.

As a young man, Sam had believed Charlotte was the one, the perfect match who could make him happy. Everything would fall into place, and life would be grand. Every woman he'd met since, even the ones who interested him, could never live up to what he would have had with her.

All night he replayed significant moments of his life. Many men have no idea the moment they gave up on life and settled into merely existing. Sam knew it down to the second and replayed it like an umpire's bad call.

Sam had used Charlotte and Gray's betrayal to become a fiercely loyal son. He never received much thanks from his parents, but somehow doing the job was enough.

The only time he had spoken about Charlotte and Grayson had been one night after supper when his father had turned on *Wheel of Fortune* in the living room and his mother stayed behind, running a hand over the plastic tablecloth. She lifted her plate and revealed an envelope. "This came for you today."

Sam recognized the flowery script as Charlotte's. She had sent a letter to him through his mother, yet another indignity. His mother pushed the unopened envelope across the table, and when he didn't reach for it, she stood and put it in front of him. With sad eyes sagging from the weight of her own life, he supposed, she said of the life-altering "What-thou-doest-do-quickly" experience that had befallen him, "I'm so sorry about this, honey."

She cleared the table and wrapped the leftovers, then briefly touched his shoulder before joining his father in the living room. Sam gazed at the effortless penmanship, stood, and moved to the trash can. But he thought better of throwing it away. He slid it between the onion-skin pages of a King James Bible on a kitchen bookshelf, then walked outside and sat thinking that you only got one shot at a lifelong true love.

Eventually a stroke took his father's speech. Sam rented a hospital bed, and his mother fed and bathed him and did everything to keep him out of a nursing home, doing for him what she would want others to do for her.

Sam suggested moving him to assisted living, where she could visit as often as she wanted. "Let others do the hard things. You just love him."

"He's lived here his whole life, and he's going to die here," she said. "Whether you help or not, this is where he'll take his last breath."

Years later, after her own hospitalizations, she said, "I helped your daddy die where he wanted. Now you need to do the same for me."

The obligation became an act of love, as close to hell on earth as he ever wanted to get. At the funeral, several women from his parents' church told him what a good son he was, and he had tried to smile and thank them, but the words didn't come.

He sold some of the property to finance building his own house and sent half the money to Grayson. He fixed up the old place for rental income, and that was that. He donated his parents' clothes and burned some of the furniture. A rummage sale would have made sense, but Sam didn't want to field questions about why Grayson hadn't come to the funeral or what happened to him and that black-haired beauty Sam had dated.

He stored in the attic of the old house memorabilia and photo albums. His mother had gone through several phases of collecting, everything from Precious Moments figurines to life-like dolls in cribs that gave Sam the willies.

Above all, his mother had a penchant for owls—pewter owls, wooden owls, owl paintings, and serving plates with owls pictured in the middle. She had owl salt and pepper shakers, an owl on the mailbox, and a mother owl with six owlets trailing her secured to the porch railing. She even had a cuckoo clock with an owl that popped out each hour and whooed.

"Why owls?" he'd asked one day when she brought home a concrete owl for the porch.

"They're just beautiful creatures. Stately. Wise. You ever see one fly?"

"A time or two."

"Most of the time they're hidden but right in front of you on the corner of a roof or a high limb. There's a presence to them."

"They're creepy, Mama."

"To some, I suppose, but not to me. When I see one, I feel like God is watching out for me. Silent but present."

His back had hurt for a week after lifting the owl, but he didn't hold it against her. Why he never donated those owls was a mystery, even to him. But for some reason, he couldn't part with the menagerie or all the other stuff she had collected—including Bible commentaries and a dictionary bigger than a gun safe.

He had framed one piece of her embroidery for her—using wood he had salvaged from her father's collapsed barn—and given it to her one Christmas. Her mouth dropped. "I've been looking all over for this. And you had it all this time."

She asked him to hang it underneath the cuckoo owl, where the sun shone brightly each morning. Over the years, the words had faded.

Only one life—'twill soon be past.

Only what's done for Christ will last.

Sam realized there were things a man can see that even the sun cannot fade.

The wound of his life had been the talk of the town, and the talk turned into rumors that projected onto Sam what was in their own hearts about jilted lovers and revenge. As much as Sam thought it might be nice to have a relationship, every time he came close, he retreated.

Mary Beth, the daughter of his parents' friends from church, was sweet with a gorgeous smile, but a bit on the religious side. In the end he had made her cry, telling her it was best they go no further. He felt the truth was better, even if it hurt.

Sandra was also pleasing to the eye and sang like an angel. But he never felt the same about her as she did about him.

Roxane wanted a child but not a husband. When he had gathered the courage to tell her he wasn't in the market for more than friendship, she sighed in relief. "I was afraid you were stuck on me. But I want a child. And my biological clock keeps me awake at night."

"Why don't you get a dog?"

"Funny, Sam. I don't want a dog; I want a human being who carries my DNA. And I think yours would produce a handsome son or a beautiful daughter."

"So, you get a child. What do I get?"

She raised her eyebrows. "You get the process."

He thought about it for two seconds, and that was the end of Roxane.

Once, in the middle of the night, Sam heard a flap of wings outside, then the soft, feathery voice of an owl. Calling for its mate? Or perhaps trying to communicate to Sam some truth of the universe.

Sam was no expert, but from what he had ever seen of it, love was a fickle thing. And you can no more control it or understand it than you can hold a cloud or a sunbeam. The best you can hope for is to let it pass in front of you for as long as it will stay. When love shines on your heart, you give thanks and welcome it. But with love, of course, comes the risk of betrayal and deep wounds.

He didn't know if the owl was saying all that, but it seemed more than chance that he had heard it. And he truly thought that all the pain he'd carried no longer held him. He would get busy living.

Sam pulled up to the house of his youth, knowing he should have called ahead but not sure he would go through with his plan. He owed it to Grayson to do this. And Charlotte.

Wendell lumbered out carrying a full trash bag that he stuffed into an overflowing bin by the garage. "Your brother get away from you again, Sam?"

"I was wondering if I could come in for a few minutes."

Wendell cocked his head as Sam approached with a flashlight. "What in the world happened to you?"

"Long story. Ran into a ditch last night. I wonder if you'd let me crawl up in the attic. Something up there I want to give to my brother and his wife. Won't take long."

"It's your house."

Sam climbed the stairs he'd climbed as a child. When Sam was four or so, Grayson had once dragged his mattress to the top and challenged him to ride it down like a bucking bronc. Everything went fine until right at the end, when the mattress kicked left and the bronc threw him. He'd lost a couple of baby teeth and gained a fat lip. Their father had taken Grayson to the barn when he pieced together what had happened. They never rode the mattress again.

In the attic, the flashlight revealed cobwebs and thick dust. Something skittered in a corner. An ancient Christmas tree, maybe five feet tall, stood in a corner with a few ornaments on its limbs and an ample supply of limp tinsel.

The tree brought back memories of Grayson and him bounding down the stairs on Christmas mornings. His brother had brought the magic to those celebrations, because his parents had mostly been disengaged. Grayson was the one who told him about sleigh bells and made sure the fireplace was clear of obstructions for the jolly old elf.

Sam stepped between boxes and scattered furniture and owls. In a box in the corner, he found what he was looking for. It was a paper bag—his grandmother had called it a poke—and when he lifted it, the bag tore and pictures spilled out.

As he gathered photos, he noticed a stack of books. A thick *Southern Living* cookbook his mother had pored over was there, along with biographies of entertainers and political figures long gone and a leather-bound King James Bible.

He picked up the Bible and found a laminated bookmark with the famous footprints poem, complete with the image of the two sets of footprints that become one. His mother loved the thought of being carried when she was too weak to walk.

The onionskin pages crackled as he leafed through the Bible, which had always seemed more of an ornament to their home, like an owl that sat on the kitchen bookshelf. He found a thick sheaf of folded notebook paper. His mother had saved the fledgling attempt of a boy to make sense of his life by writing it. It was about a boy who discovered a child hiding in a nearby barn. The boy brought the child food, but the malevolent owner discovered the squatter. The story ended with the hero defeating the villain and escaping with the child.

What struck Sam was that the boy in the story was alone in his struggle to defeat the enemy and save the child.

Sam flipped through the rest of the Bible and found the unopened envelope with Charlotte's handwriting. He put that with the pictures and stuffed everything into his pockets.

"Find what you were looking for?" Wendell said.

"I think so. Thanks."

Janie grabbed from under the sink a plastic bag, into which Sam deposited his treasures.

CHAPTER 31

GRAY AWOKE, comforted by the sight of his legal pad on the bedside table in the early morning light. But there was something he needed to do. What was it? He sat up and swung his feet to the floor, but something stirred behind him and made him jump from the bed. A woman lay facedown on the pillow next to his, black hair around her shoulders like a shawl.

"Hey," he said, crawling back onto the bed and nudging her. "Wake up. You need to get out of here."

She moaned and turned to peek at him through one green eye. "Gray," she rasped, "what are you talking about?"

"How do you know my name?"

She pushed herself up and stretched. "Gray, it's me."

"Lotty?"

She pulled her hair back like some actress in a movie. "Who did you think I was?" she said, a tease in her voice. "Have you been seeing other women while you've been gone?"

"Of course not," he said. "I thought maybe you'd snuck in here. You never know these days." He ran a hand through his hair. "It's good to see you, Lotty." He kissed her on the forehead. "When did you get here?"

"Last night. Remember?"

"Oh, yeah. Sure."

Lotty propped a pillow and pressed her back to the headboard. "Gray, Josh and I were talking last night."

"Who?"

"The fellow who drove with you."

"The Black guy. Right. Something I need to know?"

"We're ready to go to the new place."

He gave her a pained look. "What's wrong with the old one?"

"We sold it, Gray."

He jumped from the bed again, standing ramrod straight. "Sold it?"

She put a finger to her lips and glanced at the door.

"Nobody asked me about selling it. Why'd you go and do that?"

"Gray."

Her voice calmed him, and he tried to quell the rising tide. "I don't want to move. How am I supposed to write without a desk, without a place to gather my thoughts? What were you thinking?"

She spoke calmly. "Gray, the desk is on its way to our new place. I made sure you'd have it and your books and everything you need to make you feel at home."

Gray pulled at his ear and walked in a circle. "The way to feel at home is to go home. Why would you—?"

Lotty patted the bed. "Come and sit down."

"I don't want to sit down." He rubbed his chest, feeling his ribs.

"Please, Gray. Sit down."

Lotty was here. He let that sink in as he sat. She rubbed his back and shoulders, and some of the tightness left. But the questions lingered.

"Did you sleep okay?" she said.

"I slept fine. But I don't . . . It's like everything is . . . They're taking things away, and I don't like it. I don't want this." He reached for his legal pad.

"It's okay, Gray. I'm here. You've been away from me on this trip, and it's been a long one. You're just confused."

Gray furrowed his brow.

"You and Josh took the van, remember?"

"That's it!" He snapped his fingers and stood. "I need to get the van started. I think it's the electrical system. Maybe the battery."

"Gray, you got it started," she said, taking his hand and pulling him back onto the bed. "You and Josh drove all the way across the country."

"We did?"

"Thousands of miles. And you made it to Sycamore. You're here."

Gray looked out the window. "Would you look at that! Almost heaven. Aren't the trees pretty, Lotty? Like a rainbow. It's just like I remember it."

"They're gorgeous," she said.

"We drove all the way across the country?"

"You did."

He smiled. "And you came with us."

"No. You brought Dubose, though."

"He's a good dog."

"I flew here, and you and I are going someplace special now."

"What do you mean? Where?"

"You'll have a room with your desk and your books and a big supply of yellow legal pads. Stacks of them. And plenty of pens, too. And you're going to write such a good story, Gray. I can tell."

"I've been trying, Lotty. But everything gets mixed up. It's not like it used to be." He opened the pad. "It used to be a river I couldn't stop. Now it's not even a creek. Just a trickle. It's like somebody put a dam upriver."

"Let me see."

He clutched the pad tightly. "No, no, no. I couldn't stand you seeing it like this. I have to get it together, make sense of it."

"But maybe I can help."

"No, you have to let me do it. I can make sense of it if I write it out. Will you let me do that?"

"Sure, Gray. You can do that. Take your time. Make it the best story ever, okay?"

A warm feeling flooded, and he smiled. "That's what I want to do. And I'm going to go back there, as soon as I get the van started. There's an old boy back home I need to see."

"Gray, do you know where you are?"

"I'm in bed with you."

"We're in Pooch's house, Gray. We're here."

"We are?"

"You made it. And he and Annie were glad to see you."

"Annie?"

"His wife."

"I smell breakfast," he said. "Coffee and maybe sausage? Biscuits? Maybe those big catheads my mother used to make."

"I think you're right."

"But you don't let me have those because of the grease. And the flour probably isn't the kind you want me to eat."

"It's okay today, Gray. I can tell you're looking forward to them. That's all that matters."

"Would you have some with me? At least a bite? Just this once?"

"Sure, Gray. I'll try them."

"Now you're talking!" He clapped his hands on his legs.

"Gray, I was thinking we'd leave later today."

"That soon? I don't know that I'm ready."

"Why don't you think about it?"

He pulled at his ear. "There's something I need to do. But I'm not sure what it is." He patted his legal pad. "Let me see if I wrote it down— spend some time with my old friend here."

"Okay, Gray. I'll take Dubose out."

Dubose eagerly took in all the colors and smells and four-footed companions on Pooch's property. Charlotte walked with her arms folded against the chill and could see her breath. She felt the shift with Gray like a cold front moving in. They were on the cusp of something new and good, but also scary and uncontrollable. Life had become a series of choices she didn't want to make.

She had agreed with Dr. Barshaw that allowing Gray this trip could be life-giving. And she had mapped it out from the moment Josh showed up in Arizona to the day they would arrive at their new home.

Though Gray pushed back and had to have his way, she believed things would eventually settle and begin to work. Now here she was, having allowed Gray to lead, to write his own story as it were, even if he couldn't keep his thoughts together.

How could she have forgotten the beauty of these hills, the explosion of color? It reminded her that life could not be manipulated any more than the weather or the seasons, and that Gray had always been unpredictable too. He had deteriorated so quickly. How long before he would forget her name? How long until he forgot his own? How long before she would be alone with the painful memories?

The weight of it pressed on her, and she knew she couldn't live in anticipation of the loss right now. She had to live for today, to be all here, to see things and hold on to them instead of letting what was to come steal glimpses of Gray.

She could not help him see what he had missed. And she realized God was allowing her to see things she had missed. As she stepped through the dew-laden grass, she wondered if all of this was simply opening her own heart. What if she was the one who was becoming? What if God was using Gray in ways she hadn't expected or believed he could?

She leaned against a crooked fence post near the barn, Dubose a blur in the field beyond, Pooch's dog trotting beside him.

"Wish I could tell you it's going to get better."

Startled, she turned to find Pooch, his hands greasy and his smile sad. The man had aged in ways Gray hadn't, with deep creases in his face.

"I was just giving Sam's truck a once-over. Things can be a little clearer in the morning light."

"How much damage?"

"He'll need new airbags and a windshield, but I don't think . . ."

She didn't hear the rest about axles and control arms and bushings. Pooch seemed to read it on her face and stopped. He looked at her with a kindness that nearly folded her heart in two. "When he showed up the other day, I wanted to close the door. I could tell something was different, but I didn't know what. Annie had a hard time even looking at him."

"Thank you for letting him and Josh stay here."

"There's something about people in trouble that makes you want to move past your own hurt. I wouldn't wish what you're going through on anybody. I know you're trying to love him as well as you can, Charlotte. I see that."

She felt the tremble in her chin. "I don't know how to do this."

He wiped his hands on a rag. She would have hugged him and cried on his shoulder, but she knew he wouldn't know what to do. When she'd left the hills, she had stored the people in a box and moved on, believing the stereotypes. The people were unsophisticated and poorly educated and had a lack of vision. But standing here with Gray's childhood friend, the stereotypes gave way to a humanity and a compassion that moved her.

She turned to the field again, where Dubose chased a rabbit. Something about seeing a dog run free gave her a little hope.

"You need to know what he asked me when he first got here."

"He wanted you to take his life."

Pooch's face fell. "You knew that?"

"He told his doctor. Made him promise not to say anything. I've seen some of his scribblings. He wants to provide for me, and he feels he can't—that he's somehow failed."

"All his success didn't set you up?"

She smiled. "He did okay, but Gray's career never took off like he hoped. Now it never will. Sad, because I think he has more stories. But I'm grateful he got to do what he loved. That was enough."

"I wish they had some kind of a cure."

"That makes two of us." A yellow leaf floated to the ground nearby.

Pooch whistled for his dog, who had angled toward the road. Pooch's dog came, but Dubose continued.

"Pooch, I don't know what it was, but there was something about you he never forgot. Everything else, even Sam, got washed away. He trusted you."

Pooch pawed at the ground with the toe of his boot. "I don't think that's why he came back."

"What do you mean?"

"I think you're right about him trusting me. Or maybe he thought I was somebody safe. But I laid awake last night thinking about something Annie said. She thought he came here because he needed something he didn't have. He wanted to earn some kind of forgiveness from the people he hurt. I'm not saying he knew that up here." He pointed to his head. "I'm saying he felt it in here." He placed his dirty hand on his heart.

"It's always been hard for him to receive," Charlotte said. "He's always tried to earn everything. He even felt he had to do something to earn the friends he made through the years. And with God . . ."

Pooch chuckled. "That's the most surprising thing—Grayson and religion."

"Maybe that's part of what you're talking about him feeling in his heart. He's being led by something bigger."

A vehicle approached, and she yelled for Dubose.

"What are you being led by, Charlotte?"

The van pulled in, and Sam got out. As he approached them, Dubose ran to him and licked his hand, tail wagging.

"I'm not sure if I'm being led or being pushed, Pooch."

Pooch gave Sam the news about his truck. Sam thanked him and handed Charlotte a plastic bag. "Just some stuff from the old house you may want to show Grayson or keep for yourself."

She pulled out one of the pictures. "I've never seen any of these. We don't have any photos of Gray growing up."

Pooch pulled a weathered photo from his pocket, a faded black-and-white that showed men she had never seen and a dog in the foreground. "Add that to the pile," he said. "Sam can tell you the story."

Pooch went back to the barn. Sam shifted from one foot to the other and rubbed the back of his neck. "It's a long story. Pooch could tell it better."

She nodded. "I'd better get back inside and check on Gray."

"Hold on," Sam said, wincing as if he had a thorn in his foot. "I have an idea that might help you with Grayson. We'd need some help, though. And a little time."

"I was hoping to leave today."

"I think I could get it done in a day."

"I need all the help I can get."

"There's something else. I found those pictures in the attic, but I also found the letter you sent that I never read."

"After all these years."

"I blamed you and Grayson for a lot of bad choices I made. I won't lie, I still think what you did was awful. You hurt me a lot worse than this." He pointed to his nose. "But thank you for what you wrote."

What had she written so long ago, partly to unload some guilt?

"I always thought each person had one soul mate, and otherwise you were destined for a second-class life," he said. "I see now that I idealized you."

"Sam, I'm sorry. And I know Gray would say the same if he could."

Sam nodded. "I believe you're right. Now let me tell you my idea."

CHAPTER 32

GRAY SAT AT THE ROLLTOP DESK IN THE BEDROOM and wrote as much as he could as fast as he could, words flowing from some untapped spring. He wrote until he got so hungry he couldn't stand it. He took his legal pad to the kitchen and found Charlotte and the Black fellow and Pooch's wife. They were all eating and passing around pictures.

Another man was there too. "You look like you've been in a fight," Gray said, joining them.

Pooch's wife set next to his pad a plate with three biscuits and enough sausage and eggs to feed an army.

"Gray, take a look at these," Charlotte said. "Sam found them and brought them for you."

One photo was black-and-white, the other sepia tone. "Who is this?"

"That's you, Gray," Charlotte said. "When you were younger."

"Look at all those fish, Gray," the Black man said. "How did you lift all of those? That looks like it's just down by the river."

"It does, doesn't it? I don't remember this, but it sure looks like me, doesn't it?"

Pooch said, "We were Huck Finn and Tom Sawyer, having a fishing tournament. And you won going away."

"Is that right?" Gray said.

"We ought to do that again," Pooch said. "Would you like that, Grayson?"

"You bring the bait, and I'll catch a stringer full!"

"Well, the movers are arriving today," Charlotte said. "I need to be there this afternoon to—"

"Oh, Lotty, come on," Gray said. "It'll be a great time. I'll catch enough for a cookout tonight."

"You can get on the road tomorrow morning," Pooch said.

Charlotte appeared to consider this. Finally she shrugged and nodded. "All right, then."

Gray couldn't contain his smile. He fixated on the photos, and when he was finished eating, the fellow with the injured nose had left.

Sam unwrapped a new legal pad and placed it on the desk next to Grayson's, which he had taken from the table while his brother concentrated on the photos and the food and begging Charlotte to stay. The first page was ragged and the words smudged. But the writing was way more legible than what Grayson had written that morning: *I'm fighting a monster who wants to steal my memory. I will not let the monster win. I cannot let him win.*

Sam flipped back to the first page, a list:

* Your name is Grayson Hayes.
* Your wife's name is Charlotte. You call her Lotty. You love her and she loves you. Don't mess things up.
* You have Alzheimer's, and they say you will not get any better.
* You need to take care of Charlotte. There is a plan to make that happen. First get the van started. Then see page 34.
* Somebody killed a woman on a bridge. It's up to you to find who's responsible and bring them to justice. More on page 34.
* Don't let anybody see this notebook. This is for your eyes only.
* You are a Christian. God is taking care of you. Even when you get confused and think he's not there, he is. Trust him.
* This notebook is your lifeline. Do not lose it. Keep it with you at all times, and write down anything you think you need to remember. Don't worry about repeating yourself.

* Pooch Parsons will help you find the woman's killer. He lives in the town where you grew up. You can trust him. Start the van and drive it to West Virginia and find Pooch.
* Tell Pooch the dream you had. Then ask his help with the plan to end your life. See page 34.

Sam sighed heavily. This was from the mind of a man losing his way, and if this was the first page, what lay ahead? He flipped through and noticed ideas for stories, snippets of dialogue, random thoughts. Page thirty-four fell a third of the way into the legal pad.

A man shouldn't take his own life, but you have a friend who will help. His name is Pooch, and you grew up with him. He lived across the river. When you get the van running, find him. Don't use your credit card or Charlotte will figure out where you are. Ask Pooch to take your life when things get bad. Don't let Charlotte suffer.

The decline from the first page was dramatic. Grayson now had trouble staying between the lines, and his penmanship slanted to the right.

Charlotte says both my parents have died. And I have a brother. I don't remember him, but I think I hurt him somehow. I asked Charlotte what I did and why he doesn't call me. She said not to think about it, that everything was going to be okay and not to worry. But something tells me I need to make up for it. But how can I do that when I don't remember what I did?

Can God forgive what a man can't remember? Can a man atone for the mistakes that haunt him when his memory is in ruins? If I could go back and relive a moment or an action, I don't know where I'd go or what I'd do to make up for my failures.

Sam remembered Grayson at the top of the stairs, clapping for his ride on the mattress. Grayson pushing his bicycle along the road until Sam caught his balance and pedaled away. Grayson at the river, telling Sam to move back from the edge.

Then came the images of Grayson's betrayal. The arduous task of caring for his parents alone. He had tried to shove all that into some unfinished room and leave it there, but here it was again, sparked by the words in front of him.

Talk of forgiveness galled Sam. People spoke of it like candy you tossed in anyone's pillowcase who rang the bell. To Sam it was like giving a million dollars you didn't have to someone who didn't even ask.

If he were in his brother's shoes, would Sam plan the same horrific ending?

It seemed all of Grayson's machinations were nothing without his legal pad. Eventually, his mind would slip away, and he would remember nothing of these words or the passion that spurred them.

Charlotte was not dressed for fishing, but then neither was Pooch. He was an earthy man who seemed to wear his clothes as many days in a row as he could. Only Gray wore the hip waders and the hat with the ties attached and carried the fly rod as they walked a narrow path down toward the water.

Charlotte imagined Gray here as a young boy, heading toward the fishing hole—a quaint term. Now she saw why he called it that.

As they neared the river, the water sang over rocks and looked beautiful, even if mostly brown. She had once accompanied Gray on a fishing excursion in Colorado, where the water was clear and ran white over the rocks. He was writing a story about a man who had met with tragedy and retreated to the mountains for solace. And like all of Gray's stories, there was a mystery and something unexpected at the end. Some said it was his best story because of the depth of the main character's loss and confusion with life.

Gray had received a letter that began, *I want you to know your story saved my life.* Charlotte wept as she read it, because only she knew how hard it was for him to transform images and thoughts into a story that moved those who read it.

Now, as he stepped onto a fallen tree, she held her breath and kept from calling out to him to be careful.

Gray had always been smooth, like an athlete sure of each step. But now he walked with a stutter, tipping from one side to the other, as if one leg had become shorter than the other.

She found a stump just off the path and sat, watching as Pooch helped Gray find his spot, then pat his back. "Go get 'em, Tiger."

Gray stepped into the water and began the back-and-forth motion of the rod, pulling the line so the fly reached farther and farther until it lit on the surface. He left it there momentarily, as if tantalizing some hungry fish, then pulled it off again and repeated the process.

Gray had told Charlotte that fishing was the closest he could get to writing, because it slowed everything and left you alone with your heartbeat and thoughts. After he became a Christian, he had compared fishing with praying.

A quotation by Norman Maclean hung in Gray's office, and he had a signed copy of Maclean's book *A River Runs through It* that proved you didn't have to write a thousand pages to leave a legacy. Maclean had written eloquently about fishing and fire and the love of fathers and sons and brother for brother. The quotation read, *Stories of life are often more like rivers than books.*

Charlotte scooted over so Pooch could sit beside her. "Doesn't seem fair, does it?" he growled. "That poetry in motion coming to an end. I guess God knows what he's doing, but I sure don't understand it." He picked up a rock and tossed it away. "Grayson and I used to live down here in the summer. Build forts, create our own little world, campfires and sleeping beneath the stars. All you needed was a hook and a worm and a little hope."

"Looking at him, it doesn't seem like it's changed much."

Gray suddenly stopped and felt behind him. He turned, his face contorted.

"What's wrong?" Charlotte shouted.

"My legal pad! I left it in the kitchen!"

"It's safe, Gray! Don't worry!"

Pooch cupped his hands around his mouth. "Just catch something big, will you?"

Gray seemed to calm and waded farther into the river, casting and making the line sing. Sunlight leaked through the trees and rippled golden on the water, and Charlotte wanted to remember this moment forever.

"I thought Josh was coming," Pooch said.

"He needed to work out some things with his wife."

"That doesn't sound good."

"They're dealing with a lot right now."

"Nice of him to make time for Grayson's trip."

"Wouldn't have happened without Josh," she said.

Pooch watched Gray, seeming transfixed. "There was never any waste of motion to Grayson. That applied to everything from fishing to girlfriends, mind you."

"Really?"

"You've settled him down. He left a lot of broken hearts in his wake."

"Why do you think Sam never married?"

Pooch kept watching Gray but got a quizzical look. "You probably know more about that than I do. That's not an accusation—just an observation. Who can know why a man does the things he does? Maybe he never found a woman he could trust. Or one who could truly trust in him."

"It's a shame he didn't give anybody a chance."

"Maybe. Maybe he just hasn't been ready."

The rod bent, and Gray reeled in a fish.

"Would you look at that?" Pooch said. "Just like when we were kids. Feels like a dream, him being here in Sycamore. At least for me. For some it's not. Annie's brother came by, and things got a little dicey."

"What happened?"

"Del had too much Budweiser and not enough gumption." He explained about Del's older brother's death and the circumstances. "But I hear he's settled down now. I think Gray is safe as long as Annie's looking out for him."

Charlotte took a deep breath. "He's not the only one harboring a grudge. Does *she* know he's here?"

Pooch pulled a stringer from his pocket. "If you mean Alice, yes. She showed up too. Grayson had no idea who she was. Excuse me a minute."

As Pooch went to retrieve Gray's fish, Charlotte closed her eyes and sat with the tension inside. When Pooch returned, she asked if he would stay with Gray for a while. "I have something I need to do."

CHAPTER 33

THE MAILBOXES IN THE DEVELOPMENT all looked the same, reminding Charlotte of Gray's aversion to homeowners' associations. An older car sat in the driveway, rust on its side.

Her gorge rose, and she rolled down her window to take a deep breath. In the rearview mirror, she saw no makeup and her hair a frazzle. She wondered why she cared.

Charlotte had dreaded Gray's coming home would open old wounds, which always hurt more the second time they bleed. And now here she was too, stepping out of the car.

The tiny yard was well mowed, and a flower bed by the front porch looked ready for winter. The house was part brick and part aluminum siding that had been painted an inviting light blue.

"You going to stand out there or come to the door?" a sharp-edged voice said through the window.

Charlotte approached, and Alice emerged with sagging eyes. "Didn't think you'd have the courage."

Charlotte wanted to turn and run. What was she thinking? Why put herself through this? What good could come from rehearsing all the pain she had caused?

"You could have called, you know."

"I didn't want to call and then back out. Can we sit?"

"Not out here. I've got nosy neighbors."

Charlotte followed the woman across the carpeted living room and sat on a couch, Alice taking the loveseat—a chasm between them even here. "Tea? Coffee?" Alice nodded toward her kitchen. "Something stronger?"

"Thanks, I'm fine."

Alice plopped her hands in her lap. "I'm not going to make this easy for you, if that's what you're looking for."

"Make it as hard as you like. You deserve that, I think."

Raised eyebrows. "Is that what I deserve?"

"I mean, I understand your anger. What we did was awful."

"Well, we agree on that."

"Pooch said you saw Gray."

Alice stared at her fingernails. "I wanted my pound of flesh. I've waited long enough. I'm owed two pounds."

"And?"

She shook her head. "Seeing him, like a hollowed-out pumpkin, hurt like the dickens. He looked as innocent as a child. Didn't have a clue who I was. Doesn't take away the pain or the anger, but it kind of puts it in perspective. I feel sorry for him."

Charlotte swallowed hard.

"When you've hated somebody as long as I have," Alice continued, "you embrace it like a friend to give you comfort. Betrayal is a powerful force. And you two—here one day, gone the next . . . I never had a chance. I would have done whatever it took to keep him. But there was no way I could compete." She lifted a hand. "A face like that. A younger woman with all your charms . . ."

Charlotte lowered her head. *Just stay quiet.*

"So I hated you for stealing him. And I hated him for abandoning us. And I stewed on that a few years while I tried to keep going. And then I started hating myself for letting him walk over me and leave. And every time I'd look into Sarah's baby blues, I'd see him. And every time she'd ask me where her daddy was and when he was going to come back, it was like a knife. All that to say, I'm not jumping for joy to see either of you."

"I understand," Charlotte said.

Alice leaned forward, elbows on her knees. "No. You don't. Or you wouldn't have tried to turn her against me, to twist her and use her to make yourself feel better, to make everything turn out like some fairy tale. That's a double wound. You've put a wedge between my daughter and me."

"I know it looks that way, but—"

"How could you love a man who would do that to his daughter? Not even make a phone call."

"I wanted him to be in her life." Charlotte paused. "No, I should say I *wanted* to want him to be in her life. But if she got attached, what were we going to do? It was just so complicated, and I was young and didn't know how deep the scars would be."

"You were in love!" Alice said. "And when you're in love, you don't care who you hurt, even a little girl crying for her daddy."

Alice seemed to gather herself. "Somehow we moved on from that, and I felt she adjusted to it all. And then she falls in love and she reaches out, and Grayson makes his big overtures about how he can't wait to see her and meet the most important man in her life. She was on cloud nine. She'd found the man of her dreams, and her daddy was going to be there."

Charlotte wished she'd accepted the drink just then. Anything to focus on besides Alice's venom.

"How could you let him do that—promise he'd walk her down the aisle and somehow make up for all the years he'd lost? One look at the man she loves, and that was that. He couldn't get past his skin color."

"He isn't like that now. Believe me."

"A leopard doesn't change his spots." Alice set her jaw. "That whole weekend was more like a funeral than what should have been the best days of their lives."

"I know. I'm sorry."

Alice pressed her lips together. "I admit I didn't do cartwheels when she first brought him home—those old tapes in my head from my own family. You know, all the 'It won't be fair to the children. People will look at them funny. Stay with your own kind.' That was deep inside me."

"What changed you?"

"I got to know him. We talked for hours about family, about his work, about what happened to his daddy when he was young. Mostly I heard his heart for my daughter. I don't think there's anybody on the face of the earth who could hold a candle to him—red, yellow, chartreuse, I don't care. He's the one."

"He is special."

"But all of that is being tossed away with this plan of yours."

"That's not fair. It's not my plan."

"I don't believe that for a second."

"It's the truth. You can choose to believe it or not."

"So Sarah came to you?"

"Josh had the idea months ago. It started with me writing Sarah the same letter I sent you. You both deserved to know what was happening with Gray. Josh called because they were looking at different properties, and one of them had the small guest house near a lake. That started a conversation that led to me selling our home."

"So you told them the sob story, how bad he was doing, this is the last chance, and you got her to change her mind."

"It wasn't that way. Ask Josh. He's the one who had the vision for this, including the trip. I think he really believes this will help Sarah in the long run. And with the trouble she's had with her pregnancy—"

"That's where we butted heads. She hasn't talked to me in months. She doesn't need more stress. And having you two live next to them, that's disrespectful to me after all I've been through, the sacrifices I made. It takes the pain I've suffered and calls it nothing."

Alice stood and trudged into the kitchen, and Charlotte heard water running and a flame start and metal clunking on the stove. Then the soft sounds of a woman coming undone.

She found Alice leaning over the sink, shoulders shaking. "I hate this!" she said. "Hate bringing it all up. Hate the feelings I can't get rid of. Hate lying in bed at night and begging God to take it. And now having more heaped on top."

Charlotte forced herself to place a hand on Alice's shoulder. The woman jumped and pulled away, turning with red, puffy eyes. "I don't want to lose my daughter. I don't want to lose my grandchildren."

"You're not going to lose them," Charlotte said. "Sarah loves you. Josh thinks the world of you."

"But I can't be there if the two of you are right next door."

The kettle rocked as the water boiled. Then they sat at the kitchen table with mugs of herbal tea.

"Have you been there?" Alice said. "Nashville?"

"No. But Josh sent me pictures."

"Hope you don't have allergies. I've been down there in the spring and the fall, and I sneeze my head off. But Grayson will like the lake, even if he doesn't remember his own name."

"And the guest house?"

Alice shrugged. "It's not the Taj Mahal, but it has all you need. One bedroom and a loft that looks out over the lake. You'll just have to keep an eye on Grayson is all. But you already have to."

"It's getting harder. Little things agitate him. I tell myself not to let it get to me, that I have only a little time left."

Alice took a deep breath and let her hand hover over Charlotte's. Then she brought it back. "Boy, I never thought I'd be having tea with my archenemy. The way I had it worked out, if you ever came to the door, I was going to find a two-by-four and chase you down the street."

Charlotte laughed and cried at the same time.

Alice sighed. "I'm glad you had the courage to come. And I'm going to hold you to what you said about me not losing my grandkids."

CHAPTER 34

SAM FINISHED HIS WORK ON THE NEW LEGAL PAD at three in the morning, stiff as a board, his neck in spasms. How in the world did Grayson do that all these years?

He compared the new and old pads, then slipped the old into a zippered plastic bag and drove the van to Pooch's place, pulling off near the house, not wanting to awaken anyone with the whistling engine.

Sam found Charlotte sleeping on the porch swing. Pooch's dog growled, and Sam tried to calm him, but his bark made Charlotte sit straight up, looking alarmed.

"Sorry to wake you," he whispered.

She took the legal pads and made room for him on the swing.

"I'm no writer," he said, "but our chicken scratch is similar. I don't think he'll be able to tell the difference."

"That was sweet of you to do, Sam," she said.

"I kept a lot the same but massaged the parts where he feels like he needs to die in order to provide for you. From what I read, you sure have your hands full."

She nodded. "Hey, Josh and I will drive the rental to Nashville. You can use the van until your truck is fixed."

"Are you sure? The three of you and Dubose in that car?"

"I don't think taking Dubose is a good idea. I asked Pooch if he could stay here for a while."

"When I get my truck back, I could drive the van down to you and bring Dubose."

"Perfect. I left our other car at the airport in Tucson. We'll figure a way to get it."

"I've been thinking about taking some time off. I could fly out and drive it back for you."

"That's a long trip."

"Might do me some good."

"Talk to Josh about it," she said.

"How did Grayson do without his legal pad?"

"He was agitated. I assured him it would be right next to him when he woke up."

"The work was worth it. To see how his mind works and doesn't work at the same time . . . Painful in places. Kind of poignant in others."

"How so?"

"When he writes about you, it's like another Grayson comes out. He's just crazy about you. One part I didn't transcribe is a letter he wrote you on the back of a couple of pages. I dog-eared it for you."

"Thank you. Sam, you didn't have to do any of this. Nobody would have blamed you if you hadn't even spoken to us."

"I feel bad that I left him at the house after Wendell called me."

"It's understandable."

"Still, I regret it."

"You didn't have to talk to me at all. But I'm glad you did."

Sam rose, and with his back to Charlotte he said, "What you said about not asking me to forgive you? I don't even know what the word means after all this time."

"It means the world to me that you cared enough for Gray to do this. That's all I could ever ask."

After Sam left, Charlotte went to the kitchen and read through all Sam had written. She found it ingenious. Then she pulled the old legal pad from the plastic bag and found the dog-ear.

Dear Lotty,

I write this in my own hand in hopes that you will find it, whether I am still here or am gone. There are moments in every man's life when he is unable to see a clear path toward those he loves instead of away from them. I admit I have lived in a fog of my own making. A lot of my life has been focused on me and all I wanted to accomplish. I regret that. No man sets out to live in that cloud, but I have blamed my art, my stories, when I was really just being selfish. I know deep inside I have not loved you as you deserved, and that pains me.

I write this on the outskirts of my hometown, on the outskirts of my own life, and as I travel to my roots, a stirring in the mists of time has brought a moment of clarity where the haze has lifted and I am finally able to see myself with all my blemishes and faults. It is ugly and humiliating, Lotty, but also beautiful in its own way. And so I set my hand to say things I fear have eluded me, except for how they have leaked into my stories. Now I write a truth not couched in fiction.

I know I am going away from you, Lotty. And this trip across the country has allowed me to also feel the growing distance inside. This pains me more than you can know and more than I can express even here on the page, which usually allows me to say things from my heart that I can't get to in any other way.

I pray you will take comfort in this: that I have struggled well with the leaving, as a man might resist something inevitable, like drifting on a river headed for a waterfall. I have paddled hard for the shore, and I am getting tired, and I know you feel it with me. I would give anything to stay. And that breaks my heart.

I hear songbirds, Lotty. Here in the morning when my imagination stirs and the cool wind blows through the window, roosters rustle and call to the first light. And instead of creating some other world as a parable of my life, I am reaching for what is true, what I have known and yet not known. I am trying to find the pieces of my life and fit them into the whole. And as I get closer to leaving you and even myself, I believe I've had a breakthrough.

Since I have come to know God personally instead of thinking he's way out there in the Great Somewhere, I have struggled to see how the pieces fit. But that verse we studied doesn't say we get to see how everything fits. It says each piece is used by God for something he wants to do. I believe God gave us these days and the love we have shared and all the mistakes I've made for something bigger than we know.

Each day has been a grain of sand that slips through an hourglass, and I know I cannot remember them. But I also know the love you have shown me causes me to trust you will recall all of this for both of us.

Lotty, I release you to the world like I release my words, and I give you permission to turn that hourglass over, to live and love, whatever that means for you. I pray you will hear the birds singing in the morning. I pray you will hear my heart even when I cannot say the things trapped inside.

All my love,

Gray

Overcome, Charlotte slipped into their room, where Gray slept soundly. She placed the new legal pad on his nightstand and the other into her suitcase.

CHAPTER 35

GRAY HUGGED POOCH AND ANNIE for the second time and patted his leg to get Dubose in the car. Charlotte had explained twice that he wasn't coming with them.

Pooch distracted Gray with his legal pad, and Charlotte offered him the whole backseat. But he said, "I want to ride shotgun with the Black guy."

Fog hung low and the air felt heavy as Josh approached the interstate. Charlotte watched Gray from the backseat. He had his nose in the notebook, oblivious to the trees and traffic. Josh turned on the radio, but Gray put his hands over his ears. "I can't concentrate with that music."

Josh glanced in the rearview. "No problem, Gray."

They were almost to Kentucky when Gray looked up. "We forgot Dubose."

"No, we didn't, Gray," Charlotte said without emotion. "He's going to spend some time with Pooch, and then Sam's going to bring him to our new house."

"Sam?"

"Your brother. The one whose truck got in the accident."

"Right. And we've got a new house? What's wrong with the old one?"

"We sold it, Gray. We're moving to Tennessee."

"How far away is it?"

Josh took over. "We should be there by this afternoon. I can't wait for you to see it. There's a lake right next to the property. You'll be able to—"

"Enough talking. I'm going to read this now. I think I've got something good here, Lotty."

Gray read his first page list again and again. He turned the page but kept coming back to the first. He flipped the pad over. *100 sheets wide ruled*, it said. *Made in Mexico.* It was his. Had to be. But something was different about it.

He turned to the first page again.

* Your name is Grayson Hayes.
* This notebook is to help you remember what you can't on your own. Write down anything new you want to remember. Write your story ideas too.
* Your wife's name is Charlotte. You call her Lotty. She loves you deeply. She always will. And you will always love her. If she asks you to do something, do it. She cares more than anyone.
* You have Alzheimer's, and you can't remember things. That's okay. Don't worry. The people who care about you will remember for you.
* If anybody wants to see this notebook, let them. It will be good for them to see what you're thinking. Don't be afraid to show them what you've written.
* You are a Christian. God is taking care of you. Even when you get confused and think he's not there, he is. Trust him. And trust the people he's given to help you. He is going to fulfill his purpose for your life. Hang on to that truth.
* Your main job is as follows: Let people love you. Don't push them away. Allow God to love you through those he's put in your life. Live knowing you are loved. You don't earn that kind of love. You just receive it every day.
* You have a brother named Sam. He is your friend, and he is rooting for you as you write. Your brother loves you."

Gray turned to Charlotte, but she had fallen asleep in the backseat, a portrait of beauty and contentment.

The man driving turned to him. "Is something wrong?"

"No, sir. I'm just so glad I wrote all this down. Did you know I have a brother?"

"I did know that. Sam."

"That's his name. I don't know what I did to deserve all the people who care about me. And look at all the pages I have to read." He held up the legal pad.

Gray noticed something made the pad bulge. At the end, a clear, zippered plastic bag was taped to the cardboard backing. He carefully opened it and pulled out photographs he was sure he'd seen somewhere before, and he wondered who that was holding all the fish. A black-and-white picture of several men and a dog had *Fern* written on the back.

One last picture shocked Gray to his core. "It's her!" he yelled. "She's real! Lotty!"

Charlotte stirred in the back, and he thrust the picture over the seat. "This is her, the woman I see in this dream I keep having about a bridge over the river—"

"You've told me, Gray."

"I don't know where this picture came from, but I must have found her in Sycamore. This proves she's as real as real can be."

Lotty took the picture and smiled.

"I'm not crazy then, am I?"

"Not at all, Gray," Lotty said. "You're just fine."

"Do you know who she is? Did she get hurt by somebody?" He paused, an overwhelming feeling washing over him. "Did I kill her?"

"Why don't you tell him, Josh?" Lotty said, handing him the picture.

Josh peeked at it. "Gray, that's your daughter. And we're going to see her this afternoon."

"We are? And she's alive. Where does she live?"

"Near Nashville. There's a guest house where you and Charlotte will live. It has a writing loft that looks out over a lake. You can go fishing anytime you want."

Gray put a hand to his face. "She's real, Lotty."

Lotty patted his shoulder.

Gray wheeled around and searched the backseat. "Whoa! We have to turn around! Now! We left Dubose back there!"

Gray wrenched back and grabbed the steering wheel, yanking it left. The Black man struggled to stay in their lane as an eighteen-wheeler hauling cattle blew past them, horn blaring.

Charlotte had Josh pull over and insisted Gray trade seats with her, telling him again that they had left Dubose with Pooch, but that he would be coming later. When he balked, she promised they would stop so he could buy roses for his daughter, as well as more legal pads and pens—though she had stocked up on these for the new place.

Half an hour later, with a bouquet of roses in his lap, Gray said, "If I'm going to see her, I shouldn't be dressed like this."

"You look fine," Charlotte said.

"I need to get her something. A toy or something."

"Gray, she's a grown woman now. And you're giving her flowers."

Josh made it through backups and construction and finally pulled into his driveway, exhausted.

"What town are we in?" Gray said.

"Thompson's Station," Josh said.

"Is this your house?"

"Sure is. And right down there is where you'll stay."

"Kind of small, isn't it?" Gray said, squinting. "Looks like a train car."

"That's the storage unit with our furniture, Gray," Charlotte said. "See the house just beyond it?"

"And there's the lake," Josh said.

"That's huge. Does it have fish in it?"

Josh nodded. "It's deep on this side, so we need to be careful. The boat launch is—"

"Could I go down and put a line in the water?" Gray said.

Josh glanced at Charlotte. "Sure. We have your gear in the trunk."

"Don't you want to see the house?" Lotty said. "Meet your—"

"Let me catch us something for dinner." He left the roses in the front seat and headed toward the water. A few yards away, he turned. "Come, Dubose! Here, boy!"

"Pooch has him," Charlotte said. "And Sam is going to bring him after he gets his truck fixed."

"Lake sure looks pretty, doesn't it?"

Josh opened the trunk and told Charlotte. "Make sure he's okay. I'll bring his gear."

The front door opened and a little voice yelled, "Daddy!"

Josh ran to pick up his four-year-old daughter and twirled, hugging her tightly.

Sarah walked slowly down the front steps, one hand on the railing, the other on the small of her back. Her belly had grown while Josh was away, and the pregnancy made her face glow.

She held him tight, and he kissed her forehead.

"I sure missed you," Josh said.

"It's so good to have you back," Sarah said. She looked toward the lake. "So that's him."

"In all his glory." Josh moved to the passenger side and opened the door. "He made us stop to buy you roses. But he forgot about them as soon as he saw the lake."

"Is that Pap-paw?" the girl said.

"Yes," Sarah said. "That's my dad."

"Who's that pretty lady?"

"That's his wife, Charlotte."

"That's your mommy?"

"No. My mother is Nana. Remember?"

The girl nodded but looked confused.

Josh handed his daughter the flowers and asked her to take them inside and put them on the kitchen table. He put an arm around his wife and said, "I have so much to tell you."

CHAPTER 36

LOTTY CAUGHT UP TO GRAY AT THE EDGE OF THE LAKE, taking his hand as they stepped onto the small, wobbly dock. Gray quickly stepped back. "That's not very stable."

"Let's sit on the bench until Josh brings your gear."

"I've been sitting all day." Gray pulled away and wandered down the bank. "I'd rather fish the river. You don't get the movement on a lake you get with a river."

"Look how close we'll be to our new house," Lotty said, pointing. "It's idyllic, don't you think?"

"We're going to live there?"

"Josh and Sarah invited us. They live in the other house, up there. They want us to stay as long as we'd like."

Gray spoke with an edge. "And how long will that be, Lotty?"

"Gray, why are you being this way?"

He tried to push aside the tension he felt. "What way is that?" He reached behind him. "I thought I had my pad."

"You left it in the car."

"I need it now." He turned and started up the hill, and Lotty followed. Halfway to the car, a fellow met them carrying fishing gear, an orange life vest, and Gray's legal pad.

"Wipe that smile off your face and give me that." Gray grabbed it. "What are you doing with it?"

"Gray, Josh was trying to be nice."

"Well, you've got no business with my things. Leave them alone."

Josh set the fishing gear on the ground and held out the vest. "Lake rules. If you're near the water, you need to wear this. It's pretty deep on this side."

"I don't need that. I can swim."

"It's the rule, Gray," Lotty said.

"It's a stupid rule. I'm not a child." But Gray slipped his arms through and let the man snap it tight. Gray tugged at it. "I can't fish in a straitjacket."

"I can loosen it," the man said.

"No, I don't want to wear this."

"We can buy a more comfortable one, Gray," Charlotte said. "But keep this one on for now. It's for your safety."

"I'm not wearing it!" He pulled and pushed, trying to get free. "I want to go back to our house, Lotty. I don't like it here. I need my desk. I need my pad."

She pointed to it in his hand.

"Oh."

"Your writing desk is inside that storage container next to the guest house," she said, pointing. "We're going to move everything in. You'll see."

Gray pulled at his ear. "No, I don't want to be here! Why can't I get you to understand!"

Lotty put a hand on his shoulder. "Gray, it's okay. Change is hard for me too—for all of us. Can I ask you something?"

"Don't make me answer questions, Lotty. I can't answer questions."

"Could you catch a catfish like you did at the river? Pooch said you're poetry in motion. I want to see how you cast again."

"Pooch said that?"

"He did. Come on."

He straightened the life jacket and moved to the edge of the lake, where the fellow helped him tie the fly on the end of his line. "After you fish," the man said, "there's somebody I want you to meet."

"Yeah, okay. First I need to show Lotty what kind of poetry I can make with a fly rod."

As Gray let the line go and tossed the fly on the water, the Black man told him, "I got a call from someone last night. Remember the man under the bridge you gave your mattress to sometime after we passed through Abilene?"

"Doesn't ring a bell."

"Well, trust me, you did. And you had me go back and ask his name or a family member's name. Well, I left a message for the family, and his mother called. She wanted you to know he's in drug rehab now and is doing real well."

"Isn't that wonderful, Gray?" Lotty said.

Gray was fixated on Josh. "Yeah. And you say I had you go back up there and talk to him?"

"I would never have done it. It's because of you."

"How about that?" Gray said. "That's a little good news, isn't it?"

Gray told Lotty to stand back as he began the back-and-forth motion of the rod. The fly landed, then lifted and traversed the path to a spot a little farther out in the water. Gray stood in the shade of a tree, lost in the rhythm and cadence, waiting for something but feeling part of the lake at the same time.

Charlotte interlaced her fingers and put her hands to her lips. She would not have scripted anything that had happened in the last few days, but the scene in front of her was more than she could have hoped for. Gray had gone from snapping at Josh and her to appearing happy and lost in the task—connected with them instead of on his own island and slipping away.

When the rod suddenly bowed, he smiled at her, a glint in his eye, something communicated without words, and she loved that. Days were coming, she knew, when there would be no such connection.

He pulled the fish to the bank and held it up. "How do you like that?"

"It's beautiful, Gray," Charlotte said, and she meant much more than the fish.

He removed the hook, gave the fish to Josh, and was about to cast again when Josh asked him to wait. Josh turned and said, "Come on, honey. Hurry."

Tiny feet in sandals scampered down the hill, a beautiful light-chocolate girl with curly reddish-brown hair. The sun cast golden shafts behind her as she called out with each step, "Pap-paw! Pap-paw! Pap-paw!"

Gray seemed to lock eyes with the girl immediately, and he grinned. "Would you look at that. You have the face of an angel, young lady."

"You caught a fish," she said, pointing.

"I sure did. Want to see him? You can touch him if you want."

The girl edged toward him, a finger in her mouth, eyes wide.

"What's your name?" Gray said.

"Abby."

"That's a real nice name. It fits you like a glove."

Abby giggled and Gray held out the fish, but the girl backed between her father's legs.

"He's not going to hurt you," Gray said.

"I don't want to touch him."

"Then how about you watch him swim?"

Charlotte was amused that Gray had already forgotten his promise of a fish for dinner. But Abby nodded like a bobblehead doll, and Gray carefully climbed onto the floating dock and lay on his stomach, holding the fish in the water. "I have to let him get used to it again before I let him go. See his gills moving? That's how he breathes. Now watch—I'm going to let him go."

The girl squealed as the fish swam away. "Can you do that again?"

Gray laughed. "You're something else, girl. What a cutie."

A silence fell over them as Sarah tentatively made her way down the hill, cradling her belly with both hands.

"Do you know who this is?" Gray said.

"I sure do," Josh said. "It's Abby's mother, Gray, my wife. Remember I told you we were going to have another baby?"

"Yeah. I remember something about that."

"I want you to meet Sarah."

"Sarah," Gray said. "I like that name."

Gray was about to show the little girl how he fished when the woman drew close enough that he could see her face. He dropped the rod and approached her, as if studying some ancient discovery he had waited all his life to see. He felt he ought to drop to his knees and say something profound, but all that came out was, "It's you." The woman from his dreams.

She held out a hand. "I'm Sarah."

"Sarah," he said, trying to catch his breath. "I've been dreaming of meeting you in person. And here you are. I'm Grayson. You can call me Gray."

"I see you've met my daughter," Sarah said.

"She's the cutest thing in the world. Smart, too."

"And my husband, Josh."

"Right, I know him." Gray couldn't stop looking at her. "I just can't get over it. It's really you, isn't it?"

"I can't get over it either."

"Oh, this is my wife, Lotty."

"I know."

"Can I ask you something, Sarah?"

"Go ahead."

"In the dream, you're in a wedding dress on a bridge, and I'm in the river, and then you fall. Was God trying to tell me something? Do you know what it means?"

Sarah pulled an envelope from her pocket and handed it to Gray. "I don't know exactly what your dream means, but I wrote something to you that maybe later you and your wife should read together."

Gray accepted the envelope as if it were a golden ticket. "Thank you. Sarah, right? I don't remember as well as I used to."

Sarah smiled and nodded.

"Gray," the man said, "we'd like to have you and Charlotte up for dinner before you get settled in your new home."

"That sounds fine. Is it okay with you, Lotty?"

That night as Gray got in bed, he wrote down everything he could remember from the day.

"What was the woman's name again?"

"Sarah."

"And the little girl?"

"Abby."

"I wonder if that's for Abigail?"

"I think it is."

He scribbled everything he could think of, then lay back. "This is nice, isn't it?"

Lotty laid a hand on his chest. "So nice. I can't wait to see you out there fishing again. Is morning a good time to fish?"

"The best time. Fish are hungry, just like us."

Lotty propped herself up on one elbow. "Gray, do you know who the people are in the other house?"

"I know I know that Black guy. But you've got so many friends, Lotty, it's not even funny."

"They are my friends, but they're more than that."

"What do you mean?"

"Sarah, the woman who's pregnant?"

"Yeah, she is ready, isn't she? I had a dream about her. A lot of dreams."

"That's your daughter, Gray."

"My daughter?"

"You were married before to a woman named Alice. She still lives in Sycamore. I went to see her."

"What did you do that for?"

"I needed to apologize. I hurt her. You hurt her when you left her. And Sarah was just a child then."

"I didn't know that."

"So the little girl . . ."

"Abby."

"Right. She's your granddaughter, Gray."

"Is that right? She is something, isn't she? Just as brown from the sun as she can be."

"She's not brown from the sun, Gray. She's brown because her father is Josh, the one who went on the trip with you and who drove us here."

"The Black man."

"That's Sarah's husband. Your son-in-law."

"Is he really? I like him. He's a nice fellow."

"He wanted to go on the trip with you. He thought it might help when we came to live here."

"Help what?"

"Sarah gave you an envelope with a letter we're supposed to read."

Gray squinted. "I think I put it . . ."

"It's in your legal pad."

He flipped through and found the envelope toward the back with some pictures. "Lotty, this is her," he said, holding up one. "The woman from my dreams."

"I know, Gray. Let me have the letter."

Gray gazed at the picture of the woman as Charlotte read.

Dear Grayson, Dear Daddy,

I have held on to a lot of anger at you for a lot of years. And I don't want to live this way anymore. When I heard of your illness, I knew it was time, but I didn't think I could ever get past the pain.

Daddy, you won't remember this, but on the biggest, most important day of my life, I wanted you there. I needed you to tell me you loved me and believed in me and would support me. But you walked away again like you did when I was little. And you wouldn't come to my wedding, you said, because of Josh. But I knew it was because of me. You couldn't love me or the man I love.

Through the years, he's proved to be a good husband and a good father. But he's also seen what not having you in my life has done to me. This house and the one you are in were his idea. He wanted you close to us so the children could know their grandfather. And so you could know them.

But mostly, he did this for me because he knew I needed not just to tell you that I forgive you and love you, despite everything in the past. He knew I needed to show it to you.

I forgive you for not being there when I needed you. I forgive you for the choices you made that took you away. I forgive you for the years you never spoke to me, never seemed to care, even if somewhere in your heart you did.

As I write this, I think I feel a little of what you feel when you put words on the page. You can think something, but writing it makes it real.

I used to think that forgiving meant never thinking of the bad things again. But sometimes I can't get past what you did—the betrayal and the abandonment. But each time, I come back to the bigger thing in my heart, which is not anger at you, but love and compassion for you.

Forgiveness is not never thinking of the bad things again. Forgiveness is choosing to move past them. Or maybe better put, allowing the past to move in next door.

I can't wait to see you fish with your grandchildren. I can't wait to get to know Charlotte better. I want to sit on the bench with you, Daddy, and tell you all the things I haven't been able to share. And I want to hear your stories and regrets and dreams.

They tell me you are forgetting everything. But please hang on to this. I love you. And that's enough for today.

Your daughter,
Sarah

Gray took the letter, put it back in the envelope, and slipped it back into his pad with the picture. "That was real nice, wasn't it?" Gray said.

Charlotte nodded and wiped her eyes.

"She's a good writer, too. You can tell. It's from the heart."

Gray sat up, looking around. "Where's Dubose?"

CHAPTER 37

CHARLOTTE WAS THRILLED AND KNEW GRAY would be touched if he could comprehend that Josh and Sarah named the baby Grayson and called him Little Gray. His grandfather was taken with the boy, who appeared to be a fresh revelation to Gray every day.

He looked like Josh and in many ways acted like Grayson—impetuous, a mind of his own. He walked at nine months, and there seemed to be no stopping him from running headlong at life.

Sam brought Charlotte's car from Tucson, then immediately flew home and came back with the van and Dubose. Gray didn't know Sam and seemed uninterested in the van. He made a fuss over the dog, who smothered him with kisses, but Gray kept asking his name.

Sam didn't stay long. Something was different about him, but Charlotte couldn't coax it from him. Six months later, he returned with a friend named Roxane, with whom he had gone through an alcohol recovery program at a church in Sycamore.

Charlotte feared Gray's decline would be like falling off a cliff after the move, and in many ways his memory quickly deteriorated. But whether it was the laughter of children or the love of his family, he seemed to ease into the twilight like slipping into a calm part of a river.

He had his bad days too, when he pulled his ear more or barked at those who loved him, but he seemed to thrive on the legal pads at his desk and looking at the water. Charlotte often found him just taking in the view from the loft window. He would do the same from the bench each day, often dressed in his fishing outfit but simply sitting there.

Abby and Little Gray would run to him, to his obvious delight, and Charlotte noticed Sarah and Josh's misty eyes as they watched. There was so much of life the kids might have otherwise missed.

Alice drove down for Thanksgiving dinner. Gray didn't remember her—not even their confrontation at Pooch's—and that probably made things easier for her. Everyone enjoyed games with the children, and Josh brought a freshly cut pine into the living room. They decorated the tree and the room for Christmas. Gray sat smiling at the children, clearly entranced by the lights and tinsel.

Not long into the new year, the idyllic fell apart. Gray grew paranoid, accusing Charlotte and even the children of taking his things, hiding things from him. Josh and Sarah became "that Black fellow and his wife," whom Gray was convinced were stealing his money and land he had worked so hard for.

Charlotte, as well as Josh and Sarah, knew they weren't really dealing with Gray then, knew in their hearts that they were battling a disease, but all the knowing in the world didn't make it easier. How could someone so loved exhibit such anger and vitriol and then become placid as a lamb?

Charlotte found that even surrounded by family, Gray had become a full-time job. She even visited a couple of care facilities, knowing this was inevitable, while yet clinging to the hope that she could do enough, be enough to keep Gray with her.

A reporter who had grown up in a town like Sycamore heard what had become of Grayson Hayes and asked for an interview. Charlotte initially said no, but the woman's persistence and her desire to write about loving someone well no matter their condition intrigued her. Finally she invited the woman to spend a day with Grayson.

She titled her piece "A Day with Gray," and Charlotte felt the writer captured a glimpse of the bittersweet struggle. She had shot a haunting photo of Grayson on the bench near the lake, a fly rod next to him and Dubose dutifully at his feet. The reporter sent Charlotte a copy, which she placed in the plastic bag at the back of Gray's legal pad.

A man named Kenny Ross saw the story in a newspaper and rolled up to the guest house in a van with his three children. He explained to Charlotte about his chance meeting with Grayson on his front porch and the conversation that seemed both random and yet planned. "He was a gift to me that day," Kenny said. "I can't explain it, but he gave me a little hope, even though I could tell he was a bit mixed up."

He told her of selling his farm and moving back in with his wife, but how things continued to fall apart until their divorce. "But your husband saved my life that day. And taking the kids camping is one of my favorite things to do. I take what good I find with them and let that be enough."

When Josh returned from work, Kenny hugged him, and they traded stories. He and his children camped by the lake that night and roasted marshmallows at the firepit.

Kenny talked to Gray and thanked him, but Gray merely listened, apparently without hearing. It was clear he remembered nothing of Kenny and didn't even seem to notice the children. By now, Gray was on another journey he was taking alone.

CHAPTER 38

DEL SLADE HAD ATTEMPTED, with the help of his sister Annie, to get his life together, stay off alcohol, and "straighten up and fly right," as his father would have said. Sobriety was one thing, but flying right was hard with a broken wing, which was how Del felt.

Reading the story about Grayson and studying the plaintive photo of him on the bench had the opposite effect on Del than it did most people. Instead of giving him feel-good goose bumps, it rekindled his rage. But this time, instead of impetuously spray-painting words on an old van or threatening to kill a dog (which he swore to Annie he never would have done), Del came up with a plan.

After midnight on his late brother's birthday, Del loaded his hunting rifle and set a course for Tennessee. He arrived in Thompson's Station shortly before sunup on an overcast day. He parked his truck on a lonely stretch of road and walked through a wooded area to a knoll overlooking the lake. With a clear sight line to the bench down the hill, he adjusted his scope.

Shortly after eight, a woman with long black hair exited a cottage to his left. Beside her limped a scarecrow of a man with a fishing rod in one hand and something yellow in the other. A dog lumbered beside them, his tail wagging, but the thing looked old. The woman led the man to

244

the bench and, with what appeared to be great effort, dropped him so hard onto the seat that his whole body shook. The woman sat with her arm around him and laid her head against his shoulder.

No way Del could take the shot now. Grayson had to be alone so no one would hear the gunfire and see Del run.

This would not just be revenge for his brother. Del would be doing Gray's wife and everybody else around him a favor. No more struggle, no more changing his diapers or whatever else she had to do for him. No nursing home bills. They would give him a medal if they ever figured it out. But they wouldn't. He'd sink the gun in the Sycamore River back home, and that would be that.

Ten minutes later, the woman stood and leaned to kiss the man on the forehead. She said something to him, patted his shoulder, and walked briskly back to the cottage. The dog watched her, then edged closer to the man's legs.

To Del's right, the garage door opened at the larger house, and a car backed out and sped away.

Gray was alone and Del was alone, and all that was left was to take a single shot. He looked through the scope, comfortable with the distance and the target. No nervous energy like when he saw a buck and had to calm himself to avoid jerking when he shot.

With the safety off and his finger on the trigger, Del whisper-sang "Happy Birthday to You" to his brother. He aligned the crosshairs on Gray's floppy hat with the ties attached and thought that the black-haired woman wouldn't want to put it in a keepsake box if it was soaked with blood.

"This is for you, Alvin."

On the bench by the lake, Gray was aware of only the sparkle of the water. He wore his favorite hat and held the fly rod, but it had no line because Gray no longer fished. He just sat and looked at the water. He still carried his legal pad and had a pen in his pocket, but it had been so long since an idea came, it seemed forever since he had written even a word.

The pretty woman brought him here from the little house where he stayed. Long black hair. Why was she so nice to him?

He hoped she would come again.

Gray scratched the dog's ears. Birds sang. Somewhere an engine fired to life, then was gone.

A breeze chilled him. Where was the pretty woman? She was nice.

A soft sound like an angel's wing brushed past him, like someone walking on a cloud.

The dog stood and wagged his tail. Gray turned his head. A little barefoot boy came running by in nothing but a T-shirt and a diaper.

"Hi, Pap-paw!" the child said, waving.

But he didn't stop. He kept running.

The toddler gained momentum, headed for the deep end of the lake. Gray pulled at his ear.

The child reached the dock, which seesawed as he climbed onto it.

"No!" Gray tried to shout at the child, but he couldn't make his tongue form the word. He tried. God knew he tried, straining for the word with everything in him.

No!

The dog barked and whined, but arthritis or age prevented him from moving.

The child neared the edge of the dock, bending forward, stretching for something. His muffled scream was swallowed by the water.

Gray dropped the rod and the yellow pad and pushed himself up, moving as fast as he could. A few yards down the hill, he fell and the air gushed from him. He pushed himself up and tried to stand but made it only to his knees. He tried to scream the boy's name at the bubbles in the water, but what was it?

Heavy footfalls behind him made Gray turn to see a bowling ball of a man fly past, wheezing as though he was having a heart attack.

"Grayson!" A woman's voice behind him.

The big man barreled down the hill and onto the dock, nearly flipping it. Over the edge he went, in and under.

The woman behind him screamed, and Gray saw it was the lady from his dream.

"What happened?" another woman shouted. The pretty lady with the long black hair.

"He must have got out when Josh left!" the first woman said.

The women rushed down the hill as if they were headed for an empty tomb. "Little Gray!" the younger shrieked.

The big man's head came out of the water, gasping, and he lifted a limp body onto the dock.

The women leapt on together as the big man went under again.

And Gray could do nothing but watch.

And then he heard soft sputtering, like a newborn, and the cry of the child. A hand from the depths reached for the dock, and the pretty woman helped him up. She shouted into her phone.

By the time Gray heard the sirens, the barrel of a man had trudged up and now stood over him, clothes dripping. The man reached out, and Gray took his hand and stood.

"Is that your grandson?" the man said.

Gray stared, unable to respond.

"I think he'll be okay." A pause. "You don't remember me, do you?"

Gray frantically searched his memory.

"Doesn't matter," the man said. With great effort, he turned and slogged up the hill.

By the time paramedics arrived, the man was gone.

Gray flipped open his legal pad and read words he couldn't remember writing. But they rang true.

Your name is Grayson Hayes, and you are not important because of the stories you tell or the mistakes you have made or the successes of your life. You are important because you are loved.

The End

Acknowledgments

I WANT TO THANK THE MANY PEOPLE I've spoken with through the years who have walked the dementia trail with someone they loved. Your courage spurred me to ask, "What does love look like today?" That question was the thread that ran through this story, and I hope it encourages you to keep loving.

I want to mention Dr. Edward Shaw and Deborah Barr for their excellent writing and advice as I began to flesh out Grayson's story. Their books, *The Dementia Care Partner's Workbook* and *Grace for the Unexpected Journey*, are helpful resources for anyone walking this difficult road.

I also want to thank Steve Johnson and Larry Weeden for their direction, vision, and encouragement to tell this story. Thanks also to my longtime mentor and editing pal, Jerry Jenkins, who made this book much shorter and much better. You always tell me to resist the urge to explain, so I will forgo that here and simply thank you for the many hours invested in my words through the years.

Thanks as well to my family, especially my wife, Andrea, for daily encouragement and advice.

About the Author

CHRIS FABRY is an award-winning author of more than eighty books, including *A Piece of the Moon*, which won a 2022 Carol Award. He's the winner of five Christy Awards and was inducted into the Christy Award Hall of Fame in 2018. Chris has also written several series of novels for young adults, nonfiction titles, and film novelizations, which include the Kendrick brothers' *War Room*, *Overcomer*, and *Lifemark*.

Chris is the host of *Chris Fabry Live* on Moody Radio, which received the 2008 Talk Personality of the Year Award from the National Religious Broadcasters. He can also be heard daily on *Love Worth Finding*, featuring the teaching of the late Dr. Adrian Rogers, and weekly on *Building Relationships with Dr. Gary Chapman*.

A native of West Virginia, Chris is a graduate of Marshall University and Moody Bible Institute. In 2020, he was inducted into the W. Page Pitt School of Journalism Hall of Fame at Marshall University. Chris and his wife, Andrea, live in Arizona and are the parents of nine children.

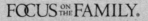

FOCUS ON THE FAMILY.

STRUGGLING WITH SERIOUS ISSUES?

You don't need to do it alone. Talk to someone – at no cost to you.

Find help here
FocusOnTheFamily.com/gethelp